Champagne

Presents

Fairy Tale Lies
Opposites Attract, Book 1

By

DK Marie

Enjoy Tracy

DK Marie

Champagne Book Group
www.champagnebooks.com
Copyright 2019 by DK Marie
ISBN 978-1-947128-98-9
June 2019
Cover Art by Creative Paramita
Produced in the United States of America

Champagne Book Group
2373 NE Evergreen Avenue
Albany OR 97321
USA

Dedication

My first book is dedicated to my best friend, Shanna. For years she told me I needed to put pen to paper. I'm forever thankful I finally listened.

Acknowledgement

There are so many people to thank as this book came to being. First, my family, especially my husband who always supported me and had faith that I'd become a published author. My agent, Dawn, who saw potential in my writing. Champagne Book Group, for picking up my *Opposites Attract* series. My writer friends at GDRWA and also on Twitter. Your advice and support has meant the world to me.

Dear Reader:

Thank you so much for reading this book. This is my first book, however even if it was my tenth or twentieth story, I will appreciate the time you give to my books. I sincerely hope you enjoy reading, as much as I enjoyed writing this story.

DK

Chapter One

Greta Meier dashed down the carpeted hallway of Swift Financial, ignoring the agony of power walking in three-inch heels. That pain was minuscule compared to the dread pooling in her stomach. She'd lost track of time. Again.

Sure, she'd managed to fix the in-house software issue but, meanwhile, had forgotten the new client meeting. Glancing at her tiny gold Rolex, she groaned. Less than five minutes to make it to the other end of the building.

She could picture her boss's disappointed face, made all the more stressful because it was her father. The image had Greta quickening her pace to a near sprint.

Rounding the final corner, she sighed. The large glass doors were propped open. Relief calmed some of her anxiety. She wasn't late.

Inside the conference room, her assistant Rae motioned to the empty seat next to her. Greta nodded and skated alongside the outermost edges of the table, wishing she were smaller, invisible. She hoped no one would notice her near tardy arrival. The last thing she wanted was to come across as the empty-headed daughter of the boss. Someone who'd gotten the internship through nepotism. Therefore, any misstep ate at her confidence like termites to wood.

She took her seat next to Rae and tried to squash her rampant doubts. Running a shaky hand over her chignon, she made sure every hair was in place.

"Where's Allen?" Greta glanced around the table while needlessly straightening the collar of her pale, pink blouse. Realizing she was fidgeting, putting her anxiety on full display, she stilled and met Rae's gaze.

She handed the client folder Greta hadn't had time to open and sighed. "Another virus was detected on Blake's computer. He demanded we fix it, like yesterday. Allen's working on it."

Greta accepted the portfolio, her worry shifting to annoyance. She didn't want to talk about her ex-fiancé, much less be reminded he was in-house counsel. Before their breakup, they hardly ran into each other at work. Now Blake kept inventing problems with his PC and contacting the IT department. Rae and Allen found it hilarious, but Greta despised the drama. It made her and Blake appear unprofessional.

Refusing to meet Rae's playful smile, Greta peered down the table at her father. His back was to a large window with its blinds pulled. The leaves from the giant elm and oak trees swayed in a lazy breeze, helping to block Michigan's hot summer sun from the room. She'd love to be out there, relaxing in the shade, enjoying her summer and free of stress.

Her gaze zeroed back in on her father, and the usual mixture of pride and discontent filled her. She understood he only wanted the best for her, but sometimes his rigidness was stifling. Carrying her father's expectations, and his disappointment of her, was a heavy burden to shoulder.

Thankfully, he hadn't noticed her near-late arrival time. There'd be no displeased glances, no lectures concerning punctuality. He appeared distracted, deep in conversation with a man she assumed was a new client.

She gave an inward sigh of relief, allowing some of her distress to dissolve. Father's career talks turned back the clock, and suddenly she was closer to seven than twenty-seven. Enjoying the reprieve, she relaxed into her seat and studied the client. He sat sideways, elbow propped on the table, large hand covering most of his face as he talked with her father. There was something familiar in the set of the client's broad shoulders and his inky black hair.

Inexplicably, her heart began to race. Watching him filled her with trepidation and an unexpected yearning.

Her father faced the room, pulling her gaze from the stranger to the wall clock. Yup, ten on the dot. A meeting never started late.

She glanced back at the client and choked on an exhale, her heart plummeting. He'd dropped his hand and was facing forward.

It can't be him.

Her heart skipped with joy. Then promptly flooded with dread.

"You okay?" Rae whispered. Her voice sounded far away, wrapped in fog.

Greta couldn't answer because the client's familiar icy-blue gaze had locked on hers. His eyes widened in recognition.

He was clean-shaven, and today his hair was neat and combed back, but there was no mistaking him. *Jacob.* He had one of those striking faces, impossible to forget. The memories of the way those bedroom eyes had heated as he'd taken in her naked body, or how those full lips had ravished her, made him unforgettable.

However, she wished he'd slip from her memory and the conference room. Whatever his reason for being here wouldn't be good for her.

"Good morning. Let me introduce Mr. Jacob Grimm."

Hearing his name, he turned toward her father, allowing her to breathe.

Rae nudged Greta, probably waiting for an answer. Too bad. She was admitting nothing.

"He runs Rework, a business repairing and refurbishing antiques. We're taking it to the next level," continued her father. "He plans on opening a brick-and-mortar shop in Detroit and developing a better online presence."

Business owner? No, no, no.

There had been some mistake. He wasn't supposed to be sitting at her father's conference table. Jacob was a deliveryman. He worked for his uncle. It's what he told her at her mother and stepfather's home. So, why wasn't he lifting heavy things and breaking promises?

Greta flipped through the file Rae had given her. Successful was an understatement. His client base was impressive, as were the big names in the dossier. Stapled to the back of the folder was a copy of Jacob's license.

Foolish woman. Hadn't her father always told her to come to a meeting prepared? Had she even glanced at the file, she'd have recognized Jacob in an instant. Weeks had passed, but that foolish, impulsive afternoon was far from forgotten.

As her father addressed the room, Greta focused on Jacob's picture. She found it safer than facing the actual man.

They'd only spent a couple of hours together, but his wicked full mouth and penetrating gaze had been impossible to forget. Along with his magical ability to destroy all her restraints. Greta still couldn't quite believe how easily her inhibitions had fled in the company of a perfect stranger.

She closed the folder and rubbed her sweaty palms on her pleated linen skirt. She stared at her father and tried to concentrate on his words, though he could've been speaking another language and she wouldn't have noticed.

There was no way she could swallow her embarrassment and work with Jacob. Not even for a day, let alone a week or more.

Her pulse thudded in her ears. What if he bragged about his one-night-stand with the boss's daughter? Father would kill her. Not literally, but professionally. He wouldn't want the family name smeared with tawdry office gossip.

He'd promised, after she graduated with her Master's in Web Development, she'd take over Swift's websites and handle the clients needing web development help. Would the offer still stand if he learned of her history with Jacob?

So much for proving herself with a summer internship. Greta wanted to weep at the disappearance of her imagined stellar portfolio. Swift Financial would have been wonderful on her resume.

Focus. I need to focus and get control of the situation.

Leaning in, she whispered to Rae, "I need to go. Would you and Allen mind handling this account? I'll owe you one."

"What's wrong?" Rae's forehead furrowed in concern.

That question was too big to answer now. Later. "Will you do this for me?"

Rae bit her lip. "I'll try, but you know your father wants you in charge of web designing."

Yes, I know. Hopefully I'll come up with a stellar excuse to wiggle out of the Rework contract.

She'd worry about it later and mouthed a thank you and gathered her papers. When there was a pause in the main conversation, she addressed the room. "I'm sorry. There's been a mistake. Allen Carnaby will handle this account with Mrs. Caitlin." She stood. "I'll find him."

Her father's stern voice stopped her. "No, Ms. Meier, the account is yours and Mrs. Caitlin's. I have another project in mind for Mr. Carnaby." His tone brooked no argument.

Darn it. There went her quick and painless getaway.

She nodded. To argue was pointless and would only anger her father. Returning to her seat, she glanced covertly at Jacob. He'd lost most of his color and looked like he'd been poked with a cattle prod.

Replaying the exchange, she realized she'd been addressed by her last name. Jacob must have caught it, grasped its significance. He appeared rattled.

Good.

Maybe he didn't want to share their secret any more than she did. Thank goodness. It would save her from her father's wrath.

Next challenge—squashing her lingering thrill at seeing Jacob again.

Chapter Two

Her, of all people!

Jacob blinked. Nope, she hadn't disappeared back into his fantasies. Her!

He tried not to stare but found it difficult to accept the rapid-fire shocks. The most nerve-racking item of the day was supposed to be signing his financial dream on the dotted line. Instead, he sat face to face with the woman who haunted an entirely different set of dreams.

He'd strived to banish the memory of their spring afternoon together. He wanted to forget the way her laughter had made him lighter, more alive. He'd tried to forget those soulful hazel eyes and sexy, full lips. Lips made for kissing.

He sure as hell hadn't forgotten the way she'd barely given him time to dress before shoving him out the back door. Confused and insulted, he'd returned to the grand salon, or whatever rich people called those extra useless rooms, to help his uncle finish the job. She'd disappeared, obviously embarrassed by him and what they'd done.

Going by her current reaction, things hadn't changed. She still saw him as a weed in her impeccably manicured life.

Not that he wanted to make their past known. A Meier, not a Silverstone!

The delivery order had clearly stated the items were for a Silverstone residence. Hadn't she made the comment the home was her parents'?

Shit. Was she Charles Meier's niece, daughter, or young wife? Each one of those options landed like a brick in his gut.

Seriously, of all the women in the world, why did it have to be her? Here? Now?

His life revolved around building Rework. His focus so complete, he couldn't remember the last time he'd been on a date or even noticed a pretty woman.

Then two months ago, his uncle Marty called, asking if he'd help deliver and install an antique chandelier. Jacob agreed, expecting nothing

11

more than a little extra cash.

Instead, he'd been knocked on his ass at the mere sight of the woman who answered the door. Her jewel-like amber eyes, accented with those full lips, was captivating. What's more, after they'd left for lunch and talked, her confident reserve and quiet ferocity seduced him. To his surprise, she was as drawn to him as he to her. Watching her struggle between virtue and wickedness, and letting her wild side win, had been the hottest thing he'd ever experienced.

"Mr. Grimm?"

He gave a mental shake and focused on Charles. Freaking Charles *Meier*. "Sorry, what did you say?" Jacob was proud at how calm he sounded.

A Meier, not a Silverstone…

"Would you please accompany Mrs. Caitlin and Ms. Meier to their office," her father or uncle or husband repeated.

Jacob suspected Charles made this request a few times.

"They'll need your insight for the new webpage and additional information to upgrade your accounts."

"Okay. No problem," Jacob replied.

The two men stood and shook hands. Jacob's was trembling, but at least he'd been able to talk past the anxiety trying to claw its way out of his throat.

He followed the two women from the conference room, wondering if he'd jeopardized years of hard work with one impulsive and incredibly hot afternoon. He couldn't lose his contract with Swift Financial. Every bank had turned him down, said his company was 'too niche', this was his last chance.

What was she to Charles Meier? Would she tell him how'd they met and what they'd done?

Sleeping with his wife or daughter might be enough to have the man searching for loopholes in the contract and dumping Rework.

Once in the corridor, Jacob moved next to the women. His focus shifted from the woman who used and dumped him, to the pretty African-American. She was watching him with open curiosity.

He didn't want to have this conversation with an audience. "Greta, can we talk… alone?"

She didn't even bother looking in his direction, answering in an imperious tone and sounding like the princess she thought she was. "No. There's no need, and please address me as Ms. Meier."

The other woman gasped, her gaze jumping between him and Greta. "You two know each other?"

"Yes," Jacob replied.

Greta spoke over him. "Not really."

The hell she didn't. Was she going to pretend they were complete strangers?

"Mr. Grimm," came a man's voice from the conference room.

All three swung around at the unexpected interruption.

The guy stumbled back. Jacob could only imagine the expressions on their faces.

"We forgot to have you sign a couple of things. Will you please come back? I'll show you to the IT office after."

Jacob ran a hand down his face, peering at Greta. From the hard set of her jaw and defensive posture, her talking probably wasn't going to happen. He nodded to the man, moving away from the two women.

Before returning to the conference room, he stopped and faced Greta. "We aren't finished. We have to talk."

The prospect didn't seem to please her but screw it, he needed answers. And to set things straight. There was no way she was going to ruin this for him. After years at a standstill, his business was moving forward.

~ * ~

Before Jacob's large frame had retreated inside the conference room, Rae twisted around and seized Greta's shoulders. "Spill, woman. Please tell me you've had sex with him."

"Rae!" Greta whisper-shouted, checking the hallway. Thankfully, they were alone.

"What?" Rae's tone was pure innocence. Her smile was pure wickedness. "That guy was created for sensual nights."

Or stormy afternoons.

"Geez, Rae. You're married."

Rae's smile widened, and she looped an arm through Greta's, leading them back to their office. "Yes, and happily. But I'm not blind. Now, tell me, how do you know our newest hotter-than-hell client?"

Rae's petite frame and dainty features hid an oversized personality, one that was opinionated and outspoken. She was the complete opposite of Greta. Despite this, or maybe because of it, they'd become fast friends. However, it didn't mean Rae wasn't always shocking Greta.

Like now, with her blunt assessment of Swift's newest client.

"I'd rather not say," she clipped. "Just know this. He's a problem I don't need right now."

"Honey, life's full of problems. At least he appears to be an interesting one. Heck, sometimes problems turn into answers you didn't even know you were searching for."

Greta was in no mood for whimsical notions. "Doubtful. I'm back under my father's roof for the summer, trying to prove my worth as a web developer, while also in the final stretch of my master's program. I have enough stress. I don't need to add man-drama to the mix."

"Me thinks the lady doth protest too much."

"Not so, Shakespeare." Greta laughed lightly, though her smile faded when they reached the IT department, reminding her she'd be stuck here with Jacob for at least a week, maybe more, depending on what he needed. "There has to be a way out. I can't work with him."

Once inside, Rae closed the door then pulled her chair next to Greta's. From her friend's tenacious expression she wouldn't rest until the whole story was told.

She laid a gentle hand on Greta's arm. "Did something bad happen with him?"

Touched by Rae's concern, some of Greta's embarrassment slid away. "No. Nothing like you're imagining."

She had no desire to reveal her sexual escapades. At the same time, she didn't want Rae to think Jacob was some deviant. He might be careless with another's emotions; however, she wouldn't risk the small possibility of sabotaging his career with false gossip.

Time to fess up. "I behaved shamelessly with him, and now I'll be reminded of it daily."

Rae frowned, perhaps in confusion.

Greta sighed. "I'll tell you, if you promise me two things."

"Sure. What do you need?"

"One," Greta ticked off her conditions on the tips of her fingers, "don't judge. Two, could you talk to my father about covering the Rework account?"

"The first one's easy. We've all made mistakes, and, like I've said before, he looks like a fun one." Rae winked. "And I'll do my best with the second."

The woman was incorrigible. Greta couldn't help smiling. "Okay." She took in a deep breath. "Around two months back, my mother and stepfather were out of town, and their housekeeper was on vacation. My mother needed me at their place."

"The estate?" Rae asked.

"Yes. They needed me there to accept a delivery…"

Chapter Three

Two months earlier, midmorning.

Greta twisted her key in the lock of the large oak double door to her mother and stepfather's house and peered over her shoulder at the sky. Wind whipped through the trees and angry clouds gathered, promising a wicked May storm. The air gave off a vibe of rowdy danger.

Trepidation ran down her spine, and goosebumps rose on her arms. Even as an adult, she disliked thunderstorms. The violent beauty and chaos unsettled her. She preferred things calm and safe.

Stepping inside, she dropped her purse and keys on the vestibule's delicate antique table. After heaving the heavy door closed, she disengaged the alarm then headed for the kitchen, passing the circular stairway on the long trek to the back of the house.

Her t-strap sandals clicked along the marble floor and echoed off the walls. The sound was desolate and usually bothered her. Not today. Right now, her sole focus was on getting that first cup of coffee.

Striding through the high-arched entrance of the kitchen, Greta made a beeline for the coffeemaker. After starting it, she leaned against the counter and yawned, wishing she'd stayed the night instead of getting up early to make the drive from her father's place.

Her mother wasn't home, waiting to dissect Greta's life, pointing out the ways she was lacking. Guilt fused with frustration. Her attitude was ungrateful, but her mother's overbearing ways chafed.

She'd hoped after moving away for college, the dynamics between them would change. No such luck. Whenever she visited during school breaks, her mother ran her life like a drill sergeant. Paraded her around to every boring social event in Petite Bois, and making sure everyone knew Greta was dating Blake, the most eligible bachelor.

After the breakup, Mother berated Greta privately for leaving Blake and insisted she give him another chance. If she spent too much time with her mother, she might wear her down. Not because she loved or wanted Blake, more from pure exhaustion. Mother was relentless.

That fear kept visits brief and infrequent.

They'd begun dating her last year of high school. Blake's family was longtime friends with both her mother and father and her family adored, heck still adored, him.

She had too, in the beginning. His confidence and cockiness made her feel sheltered and protected. Though, after a time, his arrogance and vanity ate at her admiration. The final offense was his wandering eye…and body.

Recalling the image of him kissing the curvy blonde, his hands under her skirt was no longer a punch in the gut. Instead, the overwhelming sensation was relief. Marrying Blake would have been a disaster.

It ate at her, all she'd given him. Three years of her life, her virginity, and for a while, her dignity. There was also the colossal mistake she made when they were together. The one in which she suggested he work for Swift. Even hinted to her father that Blake would be a perfect fit and put his resume on the top of the pile. That last blunder was coming back to haunt her this summer.

The coffee machine dinged, bringing Greta to the present. She stifled another yawn and grabbed a mug. The deliverymen were supposed to arrive between ten and one. The way these things worked, they'd probably turn up fifteen minutes after one.

Before the thought was even fully formed, the eerie chime of the doorbell echoed through the silent house, startling her. So much for the theory of late arrivals. The bell rang seconds later. She set her empty cup on the counter and made her way back to the front.

Impatient people. I mean, give me a minute to make it to the door.

"I'm coming," she called pointlessly; the trek from the kitchen to the front of the house wasn't a couple of steps. No one would hear her.

When she reached for the enormous handle, the bell chimed yet again. "Hold your horses," she muttered, yanking open the door.

A reprimand hung from the tip of her tongue, and there it froze.

A tall, hulking man stood before her. She wasn't frightened.

No, she was mesmerized.

A clap of thunder chased a strong gust of wind. It whipped around him as if trying to caress him with greedy, invisible hands, pushing midnight-black hair into his face. He thrust a free hand through the wild wavy locks, revealing stormy blue eyes.

His gaze bored straight into her like he could read every single one of her thoughts. Knew her deepest desires.

Her heart skipped a beat, and she tore her eyes from his. Not knowing where to look, her gaze skittered over his face and shoulders, taking in the light stubble on his strong jaw. Her focus rested briefly on a full, generous mouth before moving to his open collar. There the barest hint of ink from a tattoo showed. She shifted back to his thick disheveled hair and had to resist the urge to run her hands through the unruly locks.

These unwelcome thoughts surprised her. He wasn't anything like the perfectly coiffed men in her life, yet she liked what she saw. Maybe because she'd been thinking of Blake, and this man was clearly his opposite.

The man cleared his throat, his Adam's apple fascinating her for a couple of beats before she made her way back to his stunning eyes.

"Um, I'm Jacob Grimm with Careful Moves."

Jacob. A strong and masculine name. It suited him.

"We're delivering a living room Baroque set and installing a Lobmeyr chandelier." He glanced at the clipboard then back at her. "Is this the Silverstone residence?"

"Oh, yes. Sorry. Come in." Greta stepped aside, hoping he didn't notice the heat creeping up her neck and cheeks. She'd been gawking at him like an idiot. He was probably wondering if she was a mental case. "Let me show you the room."

The hallway was wide enough for them to walk side-by-side, even as they moved past the main double stairs. Silence fell between, not uncomfortable, but it made her aware of his warmth and the unexplainable pull toward him. She studied him surreptitiously, noting his height. She was five ten, yet her chin didn't reach his broad shoulders. He had incredible biceps, muscular with a light dusting of hair. Ink peeked from his shirtsleeve, and she wondered if it was a continuation of the tattoo at his collar.

She gave a mental shake.

Why was he so fascinating? He wasn't her type. At all.

A deliveryman.

She didn't have anything against them. She'd just never noticed before. At least not like this.

Was it the brewing storm or the man himself, giving the air an electric charge?

Stopping at the threshold of the great room, she explained the layout her mother and stepfather wanted for the set. Also pointed to the light fixture they wanted removed and replaced with the antique chandelier Jacob delivered.

The room was enormous, but he told her they'd need to take apart the double doors and possibly the frame. He asked where they were to put the old stuff. Greta tried to remember where her parents wanted the original set stored. She was finding it difficult to concentrate. Jacob stood close, and all she could focus on was how good he smelled. It took every single ounce of her willpower not to lean in and inhale him.

A charged silence filled the room as her gaze drifted from his tantalizing neck to focus on his face. She was startled to find him studying her with more than a hint of polite curiosity.

"Sorry," he muttered hoarsely, breaking eye contact and moving back. "I'm gonna let the other men know we might have to break down the door and frame before they begin unloading." He started down the hallway.

As he moved farther away, she wondered about his apology. Was it for their close proximity or the brief heat she'd seen flicker in his eyes?

Either way, distance between them was a good thing. She breathed through her nose and let it out her mouth, running her fingertips along the V-neck of her sundress. Her minds-eye flashed to his hands taking the place of hers and dipping in past the cotton neckline.

Get yourself together, Greta.

She distanced herself from Jacob, from her unsettling desires. Once in the kitchen, she leaned against the counter, letting relief and disappointment flow through her. She couldn't understand her sudden and visceral reaction toward a complete stranger.

Shoving her agitation aside, she grabbed the mug she'd discarded earlier and poured her much-needed coffee while vowing to stay away from the movers. Particularly the one with sexy, volatile, hunger-filled eyes.

Clutching the cup as if it were a buoy keeping her safe from treacherous waters during an approaching storm, she left the kitchen and kept her gaze locked straight ahead and away from the great room. Needing a quiet sanctuary, she climbed the main stairs to her stepfather's library. Books always had a calming effect on her.

Gripping the railing, she slowed her pace, denying the urge to dash up the final steps like a child trying to outrun messy emotions. Reaching the top, she crossed to her stepfather's overly masculine and stuffy room.

She'd never cared for the leather furniture, dark paneling, or the ostentatious desk. However, the papery smell of books was heaven on her frayed nerves. Running her fingertips along the nearest shelf, she picked a couple different titles and sat on the couch. Settling into the supple leather cushion, she opened the book on the top of her pile and prepared to lose herself inside it.

And failed miserably.

By twelve she quit. She'd enough of reading the same page over and over. Her mind kept wandering from the book to a particular man in the great room.

Restless and hungry, she left in search of food. When she made her way to the stairs, the movers' voices floated to her.

"I parked us under a large tree near the front of the driveway. Let's eat there," came a man's voice she didn't recognize."

"I didn't bring anything but saw a few restaurants within walking distance. I'm going to see what I can find."

Greta recognized the deep timber of Jacob's voice. It sent a shiver of pleasure down her spine. She stopped at the bottom of the stairs as the three men came into view, moving past her and toward the front double doors.

Without thinking too much about her motives, she interrupted them. "Sorry. I didn't mean to eavesdrop. I overheard your lunch dilemma." She inclined her head in Jacob's direction. "There's a great carry-out close by. I was going to walk there. You're welcome to join me."

The three men eyed her in varying stages of surprise. Jacob opened his mouth, but a guy with a gray beard answered first. "Thank you, ma'am. We don't want to be a bother. I'm going to share my lunch with him."

Jacob and a tall, rail-thin guy standing next to him broke into raucous laughter.

"What?" Gray beard asked, sounding offended.

"Marty, you eat like a horse," replied the other worker through his laughter. "I can't picture you sharing an apple, let alone half your lunch."

"Besides," Jacob said, his gaze locking on her. "I'm starving. I want everything."

His words sent a wicked buzz of anticipation zinging through her. She dropped his gaze, afraid her desire was painted on her.

"Jacob…" Disapproval dripped from the older man, the one Jacob had called Marty.

"Sorry. I didn't mean to cause a problem." Greta turned away, embarrassed.

Was her little infatuation with Jacob so obvious his boss felt like he needed to protect his employee from her?

"I'd like to go with you," Jacob called after her, his heavy footfalls coming closer. "Are you leaving now?"

She stopped and faced him, refusing to meet the other men's eyes. "Yes, I'm ready now. Are you?"

His long legs ate up the rest of the space between them, and he stood in front of her. "Like you wouldn't believe."

His words sounded like a whispered promise. A thrill shivered through her, growing and spreading. Her whole body throbbed, keeping in time with her quickening pulse.

Take a breath; he's just a man.

She led him through the living room and to a short hallway to the back patio. They passed the inground pool and cabana, stepping to a tree-covered pathway.

"This is a shortcut. It will take us to the back gate and straight on to the main street," she told him.

His gaze met hers, moving briefly to her mouth before studying the path.

Flowers bloomed everywhere. Roses, lilacs, and other plants she couldn't name. The sight took her back to her childhood when she'd pretended the courtyard was a fairy tale forest. Even now, it hasn't lost its magical appeal. After living in a college town apartment, on and off for the last six years, she'd forgotten its beauty.

Greta ran her fingertips over the different flowers and leaves, very aware of Jacob. He was the type of man any woman would have a hard time overlooking, yet her usual need to fill the silence was absent. Her ease around him was unexpected and wonderful.

Reaching the back gate, he unlatched it and held it open for her, stretching his sea green polo a crossed his muscular chest. She tried not to stare.

Needing a distraction, she asked the first question that popped in her mind. "Is Marty your boss?"

Not real stimulating. Still, it was better than asking some of her other questions. Such as, was he willing to take off his shirt?

Sure, way more interesting, but not appropriate. *At all.*

He nodded. "Yeah, he owns Careful Moves."

She pointed to her left, indicating their direction. "He didn't seem pleased with you leaving. Is he afraid you won't come back?"

"I might not. He's been a real ass. Sorry." Jacob winced before smiling. "But no, he doesn't like his men hanging around the clients. Doesn't want anyone claiming we're unprofessional."

Greta held in a laugh. If his boss knew half of the crazy, improper thoughts she had this afternoon regarding one of his employees, he'd worry more about his client's actions than those of his employees.

"Sounds like my father. He's a real stickler for that kind of stuff."

"Oh, yeah, what's he do?"

"Business owner—" She stopped mid-sentence. A huge gust of wind swirled around them, blowing her unbound hair into her eyes before diving under her dress and lifting it.

She gasped, clutching the cotton material and glancing at Jacob, catching him eyeing her legs.

He averted his gaze to the roiling clouds. "Think the storm will pass?"

"Who knows?" The weather. A nice, safe topic, though another part of her mind was dissecting the hungry way he'd eaten up the sight of her legs. "It's been looming, so far nothing except wind and heavy clouds."

He turned his attention from the sky. "Find anything interesting in your library?"

The sudden topic change threw her, but she rolled with it. "No. I skimmed through *Gatsby* and reread my favorite scenes."

Reading was stretching the truth. What she'd really been doing was staring without comprehension, too busy straining to hear Jacob's voice and footsteps, and wondering why she cared.

"*Great Gatsby*. I love it, even if the ending's depressing as hell."

She cut a sideways glance. Was he serious?

He must've caught her skepticism, because he chuckled. "I know, amazing. I can lift heavy stuff *and* read."

"Not what I was thinking," she lied, knowing the heat flooding her cheeks gave her away.

"Uh-huh, sure. Believe it or not, I can read books without pictures. Just last summer I graduated from Dr. Seuss levels. My family's proud."

"Ha, very funny." Greta was horrified to hear herself giggle. She wasn't a gigglier. "What do you like to read? And please, don't give me the names of children's authors…unless, of course, it's the Grimm brothers."

He groaned, a smile tugging at the corners of his mouth. "God, no. I had enough of those when I was a kid. My mom was obsessed with those stories."

"In what way?"

"Let's see. She read all of their stuff, both in English and German. Married a man with the last name Grimm and named her boys Jacob and Wilhelm…"

"Oh my God. You're a Grimm brother. I love it!"

"Glad you love it." He gave a wry smile. "But if you ever happen to run into my brother, Will, whatever you do, don't call him Wilhelm."

With difficulty, she held in another atrocious giggle. She loved his dry humor. "Duly noted."

They rounded the corner, and her favorite sandwich shop came into view. "There it is, Mattie's Deli. Best lunches in Petite Bois."

"Good thing." He frowned at the darkening sky. "The storm might break open any second."

"Maybe, still this is Michigan. You never know, it might pass us by."

Facts and desires were churning within her violently as the clouds above; she couldn't tell truth from fiction. Only knew she didn't want to rush her time with him.

Jacob was a stranger she wouldn't see after today. It didn't matter; she wasn't quite ready to give him up. She was too sensible to ever act on her attraction. However, it sure was fun standing close to the flame.

They crossed the street, and he held open the door to the deli.

Stepping past, she brushed against him. The slight contact had her insides tightening in keen awareness, and she had to force herself to keep moving.

The heat might be fun, but a single flame could become an inferno and consume everything in its path.

He'd come in close behind her. All she had to do was lean back to press against his delectable chest.

Resisting the urge was difficult, making it nearly impossible to concentrate on the menu posted above the counter. She didn't try and ordered the first thing her eyes focused on: a turkey sandwich with homemade sauce.

Turning, she studied him while he read the menu. The impulse to run the pads of her fingers along his jaw was hard to resist. It made her heart beat a little faster.

"If I order the large fruit salad, will you have some?" he asked, seeming oblivious to her ogling. *Thank God.*

She nodded, and he added it to his order. The teen-aged boy behind the counter handed them a ticket, and they moved off to the side to wait.

Jacob leaned against the wall, crossing his feet at the ankles and shoving his hands into his front pockets. "Thanks for bringing me here. Left to my own devices, I'd probably have spent my lunchbreak wandering around trying to find food. Or worse…sharing lunch with Marty."

She laughed at his dire tone. "I don't mind. I needed to eat, and I like talking with you."

"Yeah, it's been nice." He sounded shocked.

Greta opened her mouth, licking her lips, planning to tease him. His gaze zeroed in on her mouth, making her playfulness evaporate. Uncrossing his feet, he shifted closer.

She didn't step back, and he advanced. Jacob's gaze jumped to her eyes then back to her mouth, teeth capturing his beautiful full bottom lip briefly before letting go.

She wanted to lick the moisture left behind.

Dragging her gaze back to his eyes, she found desire swirling within them. He ran a thumb gently along her lips, before leaning close enough that his breaths mingled with hers.

He was going to kiss her, and she wanted it. Might have even whispered, "please."

For once in her life, she didn't care about rules and consequences. Her only concern was discovering the taste and feel of his mouth on hers.

"Order ready for Greta and Jacob!"

Greta jerked back. The teen behind the counter was holding their two white paper bags.

Jacob exhaled. The warmth of his breath brushed against her neck.

She glanced back at him and caught desire, and perhaps regret, flash across his face.

"I'll get them," he murmured, then left to retrieve their food.

Greta ran a shaky hand through her windblown hair then down her sides. She hoped organizing her outward appearance would slow her racing heart and runaway urges.

To her relief, self-discipline and the respite of space locked up some of her desire. By the time Jacob returned with their lunches, she was more composed.

Without a word, they headed out under the ever-darkening spring sky, neither acknowledging the almost-kiss. Thunder rumbled, and the wind shoved at their backs, pushing them down the sidewalk at a brisk pace. The storm would hit, the only question was when it would strike and how much damage would it leave behind.

The rain held off until they were inside her mother's gardens, then the skies opened. Greta took Jacob's hand and tugged him to the nearby guesthouse. They reached the front door as an earsplitting clap of thunder crashed around them, followed by a bolt of lightning that lit up the murky afternoon.

She flipped open the keypad, typing in the six-digit code. Seconds later it flashed green, and she exhaled with relief. Thank goodness, the password hadn't changed. Twisting the knob, she shoved open the door, pulling Jacob inside with her.

He booted the door shut, not letting go of her hand. He cocked a questioning brow and scanned the house. Greta followed his gaze, taking in the calm, muted tones of the spacious living room. She stopped at the beautiful Alphonse Mucha lithograph hanging above the couch. It was her favorite. She loved its meandering lines and vibrant colors, but what spoke to her was the way the woman appeared serene and confident. Would she ever be like that, or was it unattainable, merely an artistic illusion?

Jacob cleared his throat. "Whose place is this? We're on your property, right?"

She glanced at him and nodded. He was eyeing the hallway. The one leading to the three bedrooms.

Rooms with large beds and soft sheets.

The image of Jacob sprawled naked on one of the beds flashed through her mind. Miles of tawny skin against crisp, white sheets. Delectable.

She shook her head, trying to clear away her sinful visions, and took a deep breath. That was a mistake. The action caused her to inhale his scent of rain, cedar, and man.

She cleared her throat. "Yes. It's the guesthouse. We can eat here and wait out the storm."

"Guesthouse. Of course it is." He let go of her hand and set their bags of food on a small table next to the door before bending to remove his damp boots.

The absence of his hand left her cold. She shoved the crazy reaction aside and followed his lead. Leaning over, she tugged on the clasp of her damp sandals, causing her other wet foot slip to from under her.

She fell into Jacob. *Hard*

He let out a startled grunt and grabbed her waist, losing his own footing and slamming into the wall, stopping them both from landing in a pile on the wet tile floor. They froze for interminable seconds before she noticed her hands were clutching his tantalizing biceps and other parts of her were pressed firmly against him. Firm muscle, mixed with his scent was an erotic fantasy come true.

Nonetheless, she forced herself to shift from his hold. She needed to before she did something embarrassing, say, like licking his exposed neck.

"Sorry. It appears my years of ballet haven't helped much. I'm probably the least graceful person you'll ever meet." She hoped her voice didn't betray how much she liked being against him.

"I don't mind. Fall on me anytime." His tone was light, but his eyes were heavy and full of hunger.

He exuded pure carnal desire, and it didn't help one bit with her restraint. She was starting to suspect they'd need a whole continent between them to remove the rising sexual tension.

She stepped farther away, her body screaming in protest, and tried for nonchalance. "I'm starving. Ready to eat?"

"Yes." He kept his volatile gaze on her, and she had the distinct impression he wasn't talking about food.

Yet, he didn't bring her back into his arms.

Like she wanted.

Grabbing their lunches, she headed to the kitchen. Seconds later, heavy footsteps followed her.

The open floor plan had the granite countertops and barstools separating the living room from the kitchen. Greta pulled out a stool and sat. Jacob took the seat next to her, and she handed him his lunch.

He unwrapped his sandwich, gazing around the room. "Is that a Selmershiem dumbwaiter?"

Following his gaze to the corner of the kitchen, she spotted a small intricate table. She shrugged. "I don't know. Maybe."

"How could you not know?" He scowled, his gaze jumping between her and the table thing.

"For starters, I don't *own* any of it." What, was she supposed to keep track of the odds and ends her mother and stepfather bought? They loved their swank and antiques, but she couldn't care less.

"What do you mean you don't own it?" His expression swung from outrage to confusion. If his tone wasn't edged with hostility, she'd have found it funny.

"This is my parents' house." For diplomacy's sake, she'd long since referred to her mother's husband as a parent, even though Greta had never cared much for Nigel. She preferred her father's unpretentious ways.

"Oh, I didn't realize…"

Pretending not to be defensive, Greta folded back the paper wrapping around her sandwich. "Do I look old enough to have amassed enough money to afford this house, let alone the main house and the surrounding property?" She arched an eyebrow. "Please be gentle with your answer."

"No. Sorry. Of course you don't look old." His grin was disarming, making the rest of his sentence hurt more. "I figured you to be around my age. I assumed you either married rich or bought it with trust fund money. People around here are guaranteed this stuff right outta the womb. Homes, money, trust funds… stuff like that."

People around here?

What a jerk.

She set her sandwich on its butcher paper and scowled at him. "People like me? Did you hear the part about being gentle?"

His forehead creased, and he must've replayed his words in his head because his expression turned to one of chagrin. "Sorry. It was a shitty thing to say."

"Yup. Even worse than insinuating I appear old…"

He leaned back and groaned, running a hand over his face. He dropped it and met her frown head-on. "Shit. I apologize. My only excuse is I've spent too much time working for the uber wealthy. Opulence and privilege made many of them arrogant and insufferable. I was dead wrong to lump you in a category because of your address. I'm sorry."

His apology sounded sincere. Still, his comments had stung. His original assumption of her and her hometown was irritating.

What did it matter? They'd have lunch and go their separate ways.

"Apology accepted." Greta gave a tight smile. "Come on. Let's eat."

Jacob cleared his throat and reached for his sandwich. After a few minutes of awkward silence, they began to talk of innocuous things, and soon their small dispute was forgotten.

He asked about the house and the antiques he'd spotted, surprising her with how much he knew. When she wasn't much help, he switched, asking if she liked living in Petite Bois. After telling him, she was only visiting, and her place was in Lansing, they switched to talk of the state's capital. Greta found talking with Jacob was as enjoyable as ogling at him.

His skewed sense of humor and candid way of speaking was both refreshing and fun. She glanced at her sandwich and was surprised to find most of it gone, along with a majority of the fruit salad they'd been sharing.

"You want the last strawberry?" Without thinking, she popped it whole into her mouth.

She froze before biting down, realizing her faux pas.

Amusement played over his face, and he gave her a wicked smile. "Yes. I do."

He was having way too much fun at her expense. Straightening her spine, she stared him in the eyes and pushed the berry out with the tip of her tongue. She raised her brows with a come-and-get-it look.

Disbelief flickered across his face, giving her a burst of satisfaction. Seconds later a wave of lust replaced it, and his gaze pinned her with a promise of paradise.

"With pleasure." He bent, taking his time, biting off the tip of the berry, brushing his mouth softly across hers.

After swallowing the small piece, he traced his tongue gently along the bottom of her lip, capturing a small bead of juice. He tasted of strawberries, desire, and sin.

The erotic playfulness of his mouth was the hottest thing she'd ever experienced while fully clothed, heck, maybe even naked.

"That was one hell of a sweet strawberry," he hummed, running a thumb along her bottom lip.

She swallowed the fruit and resisted the urge to suck his finger into her mouth. "Maybe it wasn't the berry," she said, with surprising boldness, relishing the way he fixated on her mouth.

"Maybe not." His voice was laden with desire. "I'll need another taste to be sure."

He came near again, pressing his lips tentatively as if waiting for her to pull away. When she didn't, he explored her mouth with a little more heat. His tongue brushed against hers, like the sweep of a match ready to ignite.

She grasped his shoulders then ran a hand to the back of his neck and slid her fingers into his hair. His hand traveled up her thigh, and his mouth ravished hers with delicious expertise; the myriad of sensations was exquisite. The brush of his lips and the scrape of his rough stubble against her sensitive skin sent a coil of need between her legs. He made her simultaneously melt and ignite with need.

His hands snaked around her waist. "Come here," he rumbled.

The desire in his voice matched her own, and it didn't even occur to her to resist. She moved to sit sidelong on his lap.

Maybe later she'd regret her impulsiveness. Right now, all she wanted was to lose herself in the warmth of his muscular body and sensual touch. Her hands returned to his hair, and this time she dug her fingers around the thick locks and tugged him closer. A deep moan escaped him, thrilling her to the core and emboldening her.

Breaking the kiss, she slid off his chair and stood on shaky legs. His fingers gripped her waist, urging her back toward him. As she straddled him, her dress slipped farther up her thighs. He ran his calloused hands around and cupped her lace-covered bottom. She couldn't resist rocking against him.

"Greta…you're killing me," he growled against her mouth.

He gathered the material of her dress in his hands, and they separated long enough for him to pull it off. Tossing it to the floor, he cupped her breasts and drew his tongue over the tops of them, sending shivers of ecstasy throughout her body.

Needing more contact with his skin, she tugged at the hem of his shirt. He took the hint and leaned back, yanking it off. His naked torso was a sight to behold. Even the tattoo covering most of his upper left chest and shoulder was appealing.

She ached to touch every inch of him. She settled on running her fingers lightly along the design of an intricate raven, beak starting at his collarbone and the body moving to his chest.

Tracing along the wings to a broken clock on his bicep, she murmured, "Why a raven?"

He didn't answer, and Greta glanced at his face. His concentration riveted to the trail her fingers were making. Maybe he sensed her gaze because he gave a small shake of his head and peered into her eyes.

"They represent renewal, reflection, heal—" His words cut off when her fingertips circled one of his nipples.

He sucked in a sharp breath before capturing her lips in a kiss hot enough to set her blood on fire. He traced his mouth along her jaw to her neck, not stopping until he reached her breasts.

He nudged aside her white lace bra, placing his mouth on her nipple and breast. Using his lips and tongue, he teased and tasted her, bringing her close to climax. The part of her brain still capable of thinking was amazed. Orgasms were few and far between for her, and to be teetering on the edge of one when he hadn't even touched her below the waist was a miracle.

"Fuck, you taste good. I want to lick and taste you everywhere, not just your breasts but your arms, your stomach, your thighs…between your thighs," he rasped against her flesh, never stopping his heavenly assault.

His explicit talk should shock her, be a turn-off. Instead, she loved it as much as his touch. She tried to slip her hand between them, to his slacks, but was distracted when his mouth trailed to her neck and bit. The pressure was perfect; a little pain and so much pleasure.

"More," she pleaded.

A clap of thunder reverberated through the house, followed by a flash of lightning. The power flickered then went out. Jacob didn't seem to notice, and she wouldn't have cared if a tornado carried them off to Oz.

All that mattered was he didn't stop.

His hands slid under her bottom and picked her up. "Where's the bedroom?"

"Down the hall, last room on the left."

He stood, supporting her with his hands under her bottom. She wrapped her legs around his waist, and he carried her, continuing to ravish her with his lips, tongue, and mouth.

They somehow made it to the bedroom, though she would've let him take her in the hallway. She'd never desired a man like she did him.

He stopped at the side of the massive oak bed, sitting on the edge with her on his lap. She readjusted her legs from around his waist and crouched on her knees, his body inches from hers. Resting her palms flat against his strong shoulders, she pushed until he lay against the scarlet duvet.

The storm made the day dark, leaving just enough light from the window over the bed for her to take in his magnificent body. Her gaze took in his perfect chest and torso, following the enticing trail leading into his gray work slacks. Her eyes widened, taking in the impressive bulge straining to break free.

With shaking hands, she trailed her fingers down his body and stopped at the button of his pants. She bit her bottom lip, hesitating, then ran her palm along his erection.

A gratifying shudder passed through him. "Your touch is a mixture of sweet bliss and torture."

"Torture?"

She glided her fingers up his body, removing his slacks and boxer briefs. Standing, she stared. Stark naked he was even more gorgeous than she imagined.

"Yes, torture," he grated, scooting to the center of the bed. "You're devouring me with your eyes. Come here."

She stopped at the edge of the mattress. Placing shaky hands on his ankles, she slid them up his body. His muscles went taut at her touch, and, by the time her hands reached the junction of his thighs, most of her timidity had evaporated. She kneeled between his legs and took his hot, pulsing erection in her hand.

He arched toward her touch, a guttural growl escaping.

In the face of his sensuality and obvious pleasure, her inhibitions fled. She wanted every inch of this beautiful man. With her hand grasping him, she leaned in and took him in her mouth.

His hand buried into her hair, and her name rasped from between his lips. His words sounded like both a plea and a prayer.

The way his back arched off the bed and the sounds of him rapidly unraveling, and knowing she was the cause, gave her a high she'd never experienced.

"Greta…Greta, you need to stop…have to stop. I'm not ready for this to end."

His short, choppy breaths told her he was close.

Suddenly, he gripped her under her arms and drew her up his body. When she was flush against him, he rolled over and oozed down her, deftly removing her panties. Coming back, he halted at her waist and bit her hip. She bucked at the unexpected pleasure, and he grasped her bottom, covering her sex with his mouth.

Greta tried to bring her knees together. Her ex had disliked the act, and, in turn, she now shied away from its pleasures.

Jacob nudged her legs apart. "Don't you dare."

She hesitated, peering at him through her uncertainty and apprehension. Hunger stared back at her. Desire was etched on the hard plane of his face. He wanted this, wanted her. Her insecurities vanished, and she relaxed her legs.

He conquered her with his mouth. Within minutes, he had her writhing and whimpering with complete abandonment. Then he did something incredible with his tongue, and all coherent thought escaped as she was engulfed in a wave of pleasure. Her legs tightened around him, but he continued to lave her with his mouth, not stopping until her spasms had subsided.

She released the death grip she had on his hair, hoping he wouldn't rebuke her for the loss of control. He made his way up her body, placing soft kisses along the way, with the last one on her neck. She prayed they weren't done. His erection pressing against her thigh suggested they weren't.

Thank God.

Her climax had been pure bliss, yet she wanted more. This new insatiable side was thrilling and scary.

"I don't have any condoms."

"What?" Her lust-fueled brain didn't want to comprehend his

devastating words.

"No condoms. Your touch, your mouth, it drove me crazy. I only remembered two seconds ago."

"Really?" She huffed in consternation. "Aren't guys required to carry them?"

"Believe me, had I known…"

An old memory jolted her. Months ago, her sister, Cindy, had jokingly given Greta condoms as a breakup gift when she left Blake. "I have a couple in my purse, on the kitchen table. Would you—"

Jacob was out the door before she finished her sentence, returning in record time, purse in hand. He was a vision of pure male satisfaction as he strode toward her, without a hint of shyness.

Why would he be? He had the body of a Greek god and a wicked countenance to match, one that promised naughty and delightful times.

"You have any idea how appetizing you are lying there rumpled and sexy?" He slid in next to her.

He bent, kissing right under her ear, moved to her jaw, and last to her mouth. There he stayed. Kissing and nibbling her into a frenzy, all the while removing the condom from its wrapper.

Once it was on, to her surprise, he didn't immediately thrust inside her. Instead, he rested on his forearms and nuzzled her neck.

Did he want her to beg? She would. "Please, Jacob." She rocked her hips, needing everything he had to give.

He stared into her eyes. "Are you sure?"

"God, yes," she breathed. Wrapping her arms around his neck, she brought his mouth back to her lips.

He entered her slowly, desire stamped on every strained muscle and each shallow breath.

She gasped at the pure ecstasy of it.

He immediately stilled. "Are you okay? Want me to stop?"

"Don't you dare."

He exhaled a low, sexy laugh against her neck. "Thank God. It might've killed me."

Driving in deeper, he filled her completely and groaned. He rocked his hips, firm and steady, transporting her to a paradise where only touch and need existed.

She met him thrust for thrust, each one becoming more powerful and urgent than the previous. Rapidly, her body tightened as another powerful orgasm built.

"Greta, you feel incredible," he grated through his clenched jaw, like a man trying to hold back a violent storm, barely able to contain it.

Without warning, another orgasm ripped through her body, and she splintered into a million pieces. She bit his shoulder, hoping it would hold her together; instead, he groaned her name and shuddered with his own release.

Later, rain drummed against the window, tapping on her conscience, reminding Greta she was entwined with a stranger.

She tried to care but couldn't. Her body was too languid and satiated.

Jacob smiled and kissed her temple before leaving the bed to dispose of the condom. As he shut the bathroom door, Greta's phone chimed inside her purse. It was her mother's ring tone.

So much for an afterglow.

Chapter Four

The present…

Rae leaned back and fanned herself. "That's one hell of a first meet. I'm not grasping the problem."

Greta had expected scorn or disappointment, not Rae's captivated endorsement. It threw her off-kilter. Greta wasn't sure how to answer, and silence filled the office.

Rae straightened, no longer playful. "Was he a jerk after?"

"No," Greta hedged. "There wasn't a whole lot of, 'right after.'"

"What do you mean?"

"My phone had been going off, um during…and well, neither of us heard it until after. By the time I checked, there were a dozen missed calls from my mother. I called her back and discovered her and my stepfather, Nigel, had come home early from their trip.

Rae pursed her lips. "Uh-oh."

Greta nodded. "If they'd caught us together, they would have destroyed the moving company Jacob had been working for."

"Are you exaggerating?"

"I wish." Greta shoved back from her desk and turned her chair to face Rae. "Last fall, Nigel purchased a bureau for his office. One of the movers nicked a wall carrying it in. The company had the small imperfection fixed, yet my parents had them blacklisted. What do you think they'd do if they found Jacob and me together, in bed, instead of him doing the job he was hired to do?"

"Doing you, instead of the job," Rae chortled, before saying dryly, "Your mother and stepfather are petty, huh?"

Greta shrugged. What could she say? There was no defending them. They *were* callous toward those they believed beneath them.

"Anyway," she continued on with her shameful story. "I panicked. Mother was on her way to the guesthouse. I told Jacob he had to leave."

Rae made a face. "Did you tell him why?"

"No. We barely had time to exchange numbers before I shoved him out the back door, with only half his buttons done."

Wincing, Rae made a "go on" circle with an index finger. "And?"

Greta straightened. "And...he never called. End of story."

"Ah." Her friend and confidante grinned. "Now you're having a touch of morning-after shame. Two months later." Her smile widened.

"Yes. Something like that." Greta wasn't sure if she was telling the truth. They were both consenting adults, and hands down, she just experienced the best sex she'd ever had. Hard to regret.

No, it wasn't shame. More like embarrassment mixed with fear. The consequences of her reckless actions were going to spill over into her career.

"That's why you were cold with him today? In the hall?" Rae asked.

Wait. What?

"I wasn't cold," Greta scoffed. "I was merely letting him know the past is the past. He's a client and nothing more."

"Why?"

"Because I don't want one careless afternoon to wreak havoc on my career plans." Hugging herself, she whispered, "And I don't want his pity."

Rae cleared her throat, watching. She was clearly waiting for an explanation.

"I gave him my number. He never called. Obviously, he only wanted one thing. I don't want him to now pretend differently because of my last name. It would be better for us both to forget that day."

"Are you certain he only wanted an afternoon delight?"

Greta pursed her lips. "Did you hear the part about him not calling?"

"Have you considered he didn't call because you literally shoved him out the door right after the deed?"

"No. Yes." Greta groaned. "I don't know."

She dropped her head in her hands, talking through her fingers. Recalling her mistakes was mortifying. This wasn't her. She wasn't the type of woman to have reckless one-night stands. "I was embarrassed for the way I'd thrown myself at him. I feared the backlash for me, and for Jacob. I'd reacted without thinking."

"Okay." Rae took a deep breath then exhaled. "I get why you got rid of him, but he doesn't know your reasons. It's understandable he didn't call you. Maybe you should tell him."

"Why?" Where was Rae going with this?

"Are you still interested in him?"

Greta sat straight and shrugged. No way was she going to mention her flush of happiness when she first saw him. The brief flicker of hope. "Even if I was, it wouldn't matter."

"I hate to parrot, but why?"

"If it gets back to my father I had some tawdry fling with a client, he'd be livid. He'd say, that if I'm foolish enough to mess around with a client, I'm not ready for the responsibility of this job."

"He wasn't a client at the time," Rae interjected.

"The timeline doesn't matter. Bad choices aren't allowed in the Meier family."

"You're certain Jacob Grimm is a bad choice?"

"Yes. Flings usually are mistakes. Plus, we have no common ground to build on." Greta sighed, ready to move away from her embarrassing past. "Really, this conjecture is irrelevant. Too much time has passed, and now I have to work with him. Which brings me to my initial request."

Rae tilted her head, clearly waiting for Greta to continue. "I'm going to ask Allen to switch our accounts. I won't have to work directly with Jacob. Will you back me up?"

Rae's face clouded with worry. "I will, though I think it's a bad idea. Your father—our boss—specifically appointed both of us to handle Rework's account. He'll wonder why, after he refused your request, you did it anyway."

Greta's choice came to a couple of excruciating weeks working with Jacob or facing an inquisition with her father. Her career was more important than her discomfiture.

"You're right. When Jacob returns, could you give us a couple minutes?"

"Sure. Talking will probably do you both good."

Greta didn't agree, but what other choice did she have?

She focused on her computer and hoped Jacob would spend at least another half hour away from the IT department. It would give her a chance to gather her wayward emotions before having to speak with him.

Unfortunately, less than ten minutes later there was a light knock on the door. Greta glanced over to find Jacob resting against the frame.

He was mouthwatering in black slacks and a gray button-down. With a clean shave and his hair neatly combed back, no wonder she hadn't recognized him right away. Without the mover's uniform, a scruffy jawline, and rumpled hair, he was almost a different man. Only the unruly gleam in his eyes remained the same.

"Sorry. I hope I'm not interrupting," he said evenly, his expression giving away nothing.

"Not at all." Rae stood. "We were working on other accounts, while waiting for you. Anyway, I'll find another chair and scrounge up drinks and snacks." She gave a quick wave and shot out the door.

Jacob's brows furrowed. "What was that about? Is she trying to get away?"

"Um, I told her I wanted to speak with you alone. She wasn't very smooth, huh?"

"Nope." A spark of humor curved his full lips. It was a gorgeous sight.

"Listen, I apologize. Earlier, I was rude." After talking with Rae, Greta realized she might've overreacted.

"No worries." He shrugged and came inside the office, sitting in Rae's vacated seat. "We were both surprised."

"Yes, but I'm the one who behaved badly."

His grin pulled wider, and she wondered if he was going to tease her. Maybe remind her how indecently she liked to behave around him.

Geez, this is awkward.

There was no teasing. Instead, he asked, "What happened to you being a Silverstone?"

"Never was. It's my stepfather's last name you saw on the delivery forms, that…um, day, not mine. Charles is my father."

"Shit." Jacob cleared his throat. "Well, at least he's not your husband."

She guffawed but didn't comment. There were too many other questions. "So…the moving thing, it's part-time?"

"No. Sometimes I help my uncle Marty; he owns Careful Moves, if he's desperate for an extra pair of hands or needs me to install some antique for a customer of his. You know, like the chandelier your parents had purchased."

Oh.

A heavy silence filled the room. What to say now?

The quiet became oppressive. She gnawed on her bottom lip and fidgeted with her small gold and diamond bracelet. "Can we pretend the afternoon never happened?" she blurted.

Anger flashed over Jacob's features. "Fine," he said flatly. "I'm sure you'd prefer it."

"I don't mean to offend you. I thought it best for us both, given our current situation…"

"Yes. We wouldn't want Daddy learning his precious daughter had been messing around with the help."

Jerk. There he went again, like when they first met, assuming she was some elitist snob.

"Of course, I don't want my father knowing you, and I had some sleazy fling, especially with you disappearing right after. It doesn't paint either of us in a good light."

His expression was ice. "I disappeared because that's what you wanted."

Her guilt brushed against his anger. It appeared Rae had read the situation better than Greta. "I gave you my number."

"That was to quiet your conscience about our "sleazy fling"."

She let out a caustic laugh. "Wow, a business owner, delivery guy, and psychologist. A man of many talents."

Some of his other more carnal skills flashed through her mind, and she roughly buried those memories.

"Oh, please, anyone with half a brain could figure you out. The condom was barely off before you were shoving me through the back door. The rest of the day you avoided me like the plague. I was a fuck to you, nothing more."

She shoved her chair back and away from Jacob. She needed space from his crude words and anger. "My mother was on her way," she snapped.

"Exactly. You didn't want your family to know you'd been slumming it with the deliveryman."

His irritation was surprising. She'd expected discomfort or annoyance, running into a past fling. Instead he appeared more upset with her supposed brush-off, than anything else.

"I was—I was unnerved." She stumbled over her words. "I had never done that...before. Plus, if my mother and stepfather had any inclination of what we'd done, it wouldn't have boded well for your uncle's business. They once blacklisted a moving company merely because they dropped and dented something. Can you imagine the repercussions for your uncle's business if they'd found us together?"

He stared at her, blinking a couple of times, as if rewiring his brain. Then his shoulders slumped, and the anger seemed to drain from him. "I had no idea. Why didn't you tell me, instead of avoiding me?"

"Because I didn't want to take the chance of making my parents suspicious. The guilt would've killed me if your uncle was punished for my recklessness." She stared at her lap, running a palm along her skirt, and decided to tell him everything. "Like I said, I'd never been so reckless. I didn't know how to act around you. Or how'd you treat me after I behaved inappropriately."

The wheels of his chair squeaked, seconds later his fingers rested on her chin, lifting with two fingers. Startled, she faced him. He ran his hand along her jawline.

His touch was comforting.

"Do you think I'm that type of man? To spurn you for something I want just as much?" He gave her a wicked grin, the one she remembered and had adored. "And I'll have you know. I loved your inappropriate ways."

A shiver of want coursed through her. The way he said "inappropriate" made her want to do improper things to him.

Before she could form a response, there was a light knock. Rae lingered at the door. "So...should I leave again?"

Jacob scooted back.

"No. We're good," Greta said.

Because, really, what else did they have to say to each other? They'd had a fling, and it'd been incredible, but nothing would come of it. Even without their incorrect assumptions, they'd probably have suffered through a couple awkward phone conversations before calling it quits. They had nothing in common. Plus, she'd recently left a long, disastrous relationship. The last thing she needed to do was jump into another one.

Not that Jacob had mentioned anything of the sort. For all she knew, flings were his thing. He gave a curt nod and stood, giving Rae back her seat. She offered him another one.

Greta took a deep breath, arranging her expression into one of indifference. "Mr. Grimm, let's go through your business portfolio. I need to get a better grasp on what type of online presence you'd like to have, after which I'd like to show you a couple design ideas..."

~ * ~

Greta's posture relaxed, and her words lost their tight edge once she focused on work. Jacob was jealous.

He, on the other hand, was finding it hard to concentrate on anything except *her*. His fingers burned to touch her again. He kept having to resist the urge to lean forward and run them along her lips and down her neck, where perhaps he'd stop at the couple of open buttons of her respectable blouse.

Her conservative outfit didn't reveal much, but her lush curves were impossible to forget, no matter how well hidden they were under her oh-so-proper clothing. Or forget how good she'd felt in his arms and pinned under his body.

Okay, time to move away from those types of thoughts.

Shifting in his seat, he tried to settle his mind back on web design.

"Time for a break," came a male's voice, two seconds before he strolled in the office. A pretentious-looking man walked through the doorway, carrying four cups of coffee. He handed one to Jacob. "Sorry, Mr. Grimm. I'm not sure how you take your coffee. I left it black and brought cream and sugar."

In tan chinos, loafers, and a light blue button-down, the guy screamed smarmy but had a laidback smile. "Thanks." He grabbed a few creamer and sugar packets. "And Jacob's fine."

The man nodded. "Same here. I'm Allen, Allen Carnaby." He set the coffees on the desk and offered his hand. "I work in the office with these lovely ladies. However, I'm not assigned to your account."

Though Greta did try her damnedest to give it to you.

After handing the women each a coffee, Allen set the last mug in front of what Jacob assumed was his workstation. Leaning forward, Allen checked his reflection on his darkened monitor and fixed his already perfect blond hair.

Yup. Smarmy. Jacob managed to hold in a snort.

After Allen finished primping, he turned to Greta. "I spent the morning in the legal department. Blake says hi."

"Be quiet, Allen." She shifted; the topic appeared to make her uncomfortable. Yet, it piqued Jacob's curiosity. "Don't be petulant because you couldn't spend the morning in HR flirting with Emily and Hannah."

Allen gazed at Greta, all starry-eyed and shit. "I'm offended. I only flirt with you."

Never mind. The guy isn't nice. He's an asshole.

Greta raised an eyebrow and took a sip of coffee. "Uh, huh…maybe if I was the only woman in the room."

Her blatant disinterest went a long way in soothing Jacob's need to punch Allen. Funny, until now, Jacob hadn't known he had a jealous side. Now it lived inside him, a beast trying to claw from his chest.

What the hell is going on with me? I don't even know this woman. Why should I care?

"Anyway," Greta shifted her focus to Jacob. "This coffee break is great, but are you ready to get back to work? I've gathered enough information from you to begin working on your webpage. Rae, you want to discuss financials?"

She motioned Jacob over. He blinked.

Yes, perfect. Maybe the distance would help him focus on what was important. Rework.

All morning his mind had been on her, letting his business take the back burner. She'd talked about his website and other such stuff, and he listened with half an ear. He was more focused on her scent and soft skin than the next stage of Rework. He couldn't remember the last time he'd been this distracted, and it needed to stop. He shook his head, trying to lose his annoyance with Allen, along with his lust toward Greta.

"Yes, I'm ready." Jacob scooted his chair to Rae's desk.

"My first question is more of a curiosity." She tapped a pen on his file. "Your client base and income's impressive. Why'd you wait so long to do this?"

Damn, she dove right in, going straight for the jugular. In any other circumstance, he'd have appreciated her blunt manner. But this was personal. Not that she knew it.

Best to keep it vague. "Nothing to do with Rework. For a while, my money was needed for other things. Personal stuff." Jacob glanced at Greta. She was staring at her computer screen, a little too focused. She was listening. No way was he going to share what those issues were, not with her believing he was some sort of reprobate. "Anyway, everything's been resolved, and I'm able to put my funds and time toward expanding Rework."

"Fair enough." Rae handed Jacob a thick ream of papers. "Let's go over some of the changes you'll need to make."

Chapter Five

The rest of the day and most of the next he'd spent with Rae and the financials of Rework, with Greta asking Jacob periodic questions regarding web design preferences. Allen came and went, not spending much time at his desk. From what Jacob could gather, Allen was in charge of Swift's computers and dealt with installing and fixing inhouse software issues.

Jacob couldn't decide how he felt about Allen. He was laidback and amusing, but his obvious attraction to Greta annoyed the shit out of Jacob. It didn't help the guy was a perfect match to her patrician beauty.

However, the size of the IT office was Jacob's biggest problem. He swore the space shrank smaller and smaller with each passing hour.

Listening to Greta's soft, lilting voice and catching whiffs of her tantalizing scent left him beyond aroused. Concentrating on anything work-related was becoming next to impossible as a battle between trying to focus on Rework and wanting Greta naked and under him raged within him.

Rae nudged his shoulder, waiting expectantly. Shit, had she been talking? "Sorry, what?"

"Are you ready for lunch?"

"Hell yes," he almost shouted.

Jacob was ready to crawl from his skin. He needed more than a break. He needed a cold shower.

The others eyed him like he'd grown a second head. "Sorry. Didn't realize how hungry I was until you mentioned lunch," Jacob lied.

Allen leaned back in his chair, eyeing Jacob. "Okay, maybe you should pick. What are you in the mood for?"

His gaze shifted to Greta. Jacob was in the mood for her. He wanted the same lunch he had those weeks back. He wanted to lick the sweat from her flesh and devour her pleas and moans.

To his surprise, she was watching him. Her gaze dropped from his, but he caught the slow flush creeping along her lovely neck and cheeks. Was she thinking the same thing?

"Seriously, what's going on? Am I missing something?" Allen

threw up his hands. "You two have been shooting furtive glances at each other since yesterday. Now I ask a simple question, and you both look…well, I don't want to say how you both look. What gives?"

"I don't know what you're talking about." Greta's expression spoke of indifference. The slight tremor in her voice told him different. "What would you know, anyway? You've hardly been in the office these last couple days."

"I don't need to be here more than five minutes to notice." Allen's gaze shifted to Rae. "You know anything?"

"Don't ask me." She stared at her nails then began picking at them.

Damn. Jacob hoped those two women never played Poker.

He cleared his throat and almost laughed when Greta threw him a thunderous expression. Did she think he was going to start describing the erotic noises she made in the throes of an orgasm?

He tried for a bored tone. "No story or big scandal. We know each other. Slightly. A few weeks back I was working another job. It landed me at her mother's house. We had lunch. Now it's weird seeing her in a different environment. That's all."

Rae snorted and coughed. "Sorry. Something in my throat."

Jacob eyed her, wondering how much she knew. What had Greta told her?

"Uh-huh, why not mention it until now?" Allen didn't move. Instead, he settled into his chair and crossed his feet at the ankles, as if ready to wait out the afternoon for an answer.

Jacob put on his sunglasses and stood. "Because it's not a big deal, and none of your business." He clapped his hands together, signaling the end of the topic. "Are we going to keep talking about lunch or actually go and eat?"

Allen rose, studying Jacob. "Fine. We'll go, but I have to know. How'd you get Greta to go with you? I've been asking for months, and all I get are refusals. Tell me the secret. I'll be in your debt."

"Fuck your debt," Jacob scoffed, sounding too angry and not caring. Picturing Allen with Greta made the edges of Jacob's vision go red. Though he liked hearing she'd repeatedly rejected the guy.

Allen raised his hands in surrender and smiled impishly. "Nothing going on between you two, huh? Yeah, right. For the last two days, Rae has dug into your business and nothing upset you. I make one comment concerning a date with Greta, and you practically turn homicidal."

Rising, Rae sighed. "Testosterone's getting thick in here. We should leave now, Greta. Next thing you know, they'll be arm wrestling or whipping out their you-know-whats to see whose is bigger."

Jacob and Allen laughed, melting away the tension. Eyeing Rae,

Allen asked, "Does your husband know this side of you?"

"Sure, and it's his favorite. Now, let's go. I'm starving. If we stay much longer I'm going to start gnawing on my chair. Mexican or Cajun?"

~ * ~

La Mejor Cominda's décor wasn't much. Formica tables with small cacti centerpieces and booths with green, red, and white upholstered seating. On the walls hung festive Day of the Dead masks and frames. The furnishings weren't what filled the restaurant to maximum capacity. The exceptional tacos and mojitos brought in the crowds.

Too bad the delicious food was wasted on Greta. She couldn't focus on anything but the man who just vacated the seat across from her. She'd hoped spending long hours at work with Jacob would dull his allure. So far, no such luck. She was drawn to him, maybe even more than when they first met.

She should've learned her lesson with Blake. Apparently, she had a taste for men who were nothing but trouble. Her ex-fiancé looked like the perfect package on the outside; he was rotten on the inside. Jacob had the bad-boy aura that women like her sister, flocked to, not someone Greta usually liked.

Maybe she was attracted to mistakes.

Her mom always said Greta couldn't make a good choice without her guidance. Then again, Mother had picked and still loved Blake, so who knew?

Speaking of women flocking to a bad-boy, Greta wasn't the only one admiring Jacob. He'd excused himself from the table, wanting to wash his hands. As he made his way back from the restroom, several women ogled him with open interest, leaving Greta to wonder how the constant attention affected his character. If dating and sex were easy for him, did it hold any importance? She had to consider he might not have found their time together as liberating and exhilarating. For him, their afternoon together could have been nothing more than ordinary, everyday fun.

Didn't matter. They were temporary work colleagues. Nothing more.

Rae nudged Greta with her elbow. "Was your lunch bad?" Her gaze followed Greta's. "Or is your sour expression from thinking dark thoughts concerning our newest client?"

They watched him stride through the restaurant, scooting between two tables, making his way to them. A woman's hand darted out, wrapping around his wrist, stopping his progress.

Rae scoffed. "Wonder what that's about."

"If I were to guess, I'd say the woman is hitting on him." Greta dragged her gaze from Jacob, watching Allen take his seat from across her and Rae. "Did you have any problems putting the lunch on Swift's account?"

He shook his head.

Rae ignored them both, watching the interaction between Jacob and the woman. "It'd be tough dating a man like him. Women are drawn to him. He's got that appeal, and it's more than his looks."

"Maybe he just knows how to play them," Greta replied tartly, wondering if she'd been a game to him.

"I agree," Allen interjected, making a grab for Rae's lone chimichanga. "Don't get me wrong, I like the guy, but he's, without a doubt, a player."

Watching Jacob incline his head toward the attractive redhead, a gorgeous smile playing on his lips, Greta had to agree.

Rae laughed and swatted Allen's hand away. "Whatever, you're only agreeing because you don't like competition. And you sure have it. Jacob has his sights on our Greta."

Greta's stomach dropped. Rae would never betray her confidences and tell Allen. It was Jacob's possible interest that made her heart beat faster, waking that reckless side she needed to suppress.

Needing to change the direction of the conversation before Rae accidentally let something slip, Greta said, "It doesn't matter. I'm not interested. We're acquaintances and barely know each other. We have nothing in common."

She was protesting too much and needed to stop. Was she trying to convince them, or herself?

"Yeah, Rae. Get with the program. She only wants me." Allen wiggled his eyebrows at Greta.

She laughed, glancing at Jacob, sliding in next to Allen.

"Who wants you?" he asked Allen. "I noticed the blue-haired grandma two tables over eyeing you. Is it her?"

Allen snorted. "Who can blame her? The ladies love me. However, I was referring to Greta."

Anger flared in Jacob's eyes, but his tone was mild. "You wish. You're not what she wants." He gave a cocky grin, saying no more.

Thank God.

"Okay, you two. Let's not start this again. The only thing I'm interested in is getting back to work," Greta said firmly.

Though, to be honest, she found Jacob's reaction extremely gratifying. Did it mean he also felt the pull of temptation, like her?

Chapter Six

"Okay, I'm done." Allen shut down his workstation and stood. "I'll see you both tomorrow."

"What time is it?" Greta peered at the clock over the door. Four was early, and Allen wasn't one to leave prematurely.

"Remember? My mom needs me to drive her to the doctor's."

"Oh, right." Greta stretched, releasing a kink in her back while glancing around the office. "Where's Rae?"

"Left. Maybe an hour ago. She was needed in another department," answered Jacob in a distracted tone, flipping through a stack of papers in front of him.

They'd spent the morning discussing the many options for expanding his online presence. He seemed slightly overwhelmed at the myriad of possibilities.

"Real observant, Greta." Allen grabbed his jacket from the coat rack. "You both have a nice evening." He waved and left, letting the door swing shut behind him.

Alone. With Jacob.

The office shrank and had become a secluded island. Her heartbeat drummed in her ears, making her wonder if Jacob could hear it. She tapped her nails on the tabletop and stared out the window, trying to slow her beating heart.

"Relax, I'm not going to try to seduce you, or anything," he said in a monotone.

She turned from the view outside to Jacob. He was staring at the papers in front of him, his jaw ticking. His eyes were too focused on his work. He was annoyed.

"I didn't think you would."

In truth, she was afraid she'd do the seducing. She understood they were a bad match; however, her body was in no mood to listen to her brain.

He stared at her. There were hard, angry lines around his eyes and jaw. "Yeah, then why are you acting like a rabbit ready to bolt now that we're alone?"

"Jacob, why do you always assume the worst of me?"

He sighed, and his shoulders slumped; the irritation seemed to drain from him. He ran both hands through his hair, returning it to the disheveled state she liked. "Sorry. I'm in a pissy mood. To be honest, working with you is difficult. I still want you."

His bluntness surprised her, and she found herself answering with the same honesty. "It's difficult for me too. I feel the same."

Jacob twitched as if startled by her admission. She must be good at hiding her emotions.

After a moment of loud silence, he said, "Maybe we shouldn't ignore it."

Her heart jumped with eagerness. She promptly locked down the emotion and shook her head no. "Bad idea."

"Why?"

"What we had was a moment, nothing more. Just because we're attracted to each other doesn't mean we're good together. We're not compatible. At all. Plus, now we work together. At least until my internship's over."

"Our working together is temporary. Once the computer stuff is done, I'll only be here occasionally." He paused. "Wait. What do you mean internship? This isn't your full-time job?"

"No. Not yet. I'm interning for the summer. In the fall, I'll be back in Lansing. I have another semester until my masters is completed. After which, if my father approves of my work during this internship, he'll hire me full-time."

Something like disappointment flashed across his features but was quickly replaced with a teasing smile, one that played at the corners of his full, sexy mouth. He leaned forward and took her hand. "How do you know we aren't compatible? We didn't talk a whole hell of a lot the first time we met, did we?"

She dropped her gaze as images of their "first time" flashed through her mind.

"Come on, Greta." He squeezed her hand. "Let's try one real date. Dinner or a movie. No sex. I promise. Only talking."

A strangled choke came from behind. Greta jerked her hand free from Jacob's grasp and found Tim, from the mailroom, standing in the doorway.

Her gaze flew to Jacob, promising torture and dismemberment, before moving back to Tim. "He's joking. What do you need?"

Darn it. This, right here, proved they were a bad match. He was much too forward with his actions and words. By the end of the workday, she'd be the most interesting piece of office gossip. If this got back to her father, she'd never hear the end of it. Social status didn't bother him it did Mother. However, he'd be furious to find his daughter the center of company gossip.

She wasn't positive he'd refuse her the position of web developer over office chatter, but why chance it? The mere thought of losing favor with her father caused anxiety to rear up and wrap around her like a vise.

Jacob wasn't worth the risk.

Her heart might beat wildly whenever he was near; it was an empty desire and nothing more.

It'd pass.

Heck, there was a sliver of time she'd felt the same way about Blake, and it didn't last. Neither would this.

What she needed to do was focus on finishing her masters and on building her portfolio, by working for her father. There wasn't a place in her life for lust and its delights. Or its complications.

Her plan was simple. She'd keep her distance from Jacob and resist her inexplicable and overpowering attraction. Nice and easy.

Yeah, right.

She suspected her self-control was going to be severely tested.

Chapter Seven

"You going to stare at that recorder thing until it magically fixes itself?"

"This is a World War II German Magnetophon, not a recorder." Jacob set his wire cutters aside in defeat. He swiveled his chair to face his brother standing at his door. "And yes, I was hoping it'd fix itself because my mind sure as shit isn't in it."

"Why? Things not good at Swift?" Will came inside Jacob's work/bedroom.

Did he want to get into it with his brother? Guys sucked at this stuff. Still, a sounding board might help sort his shit.

"Yes and no. The business side is fine... Um, you remember the girl I was telling you about? The one from Petite Bois?"

Will collapsed into the seat next to Jacob's workspace, stretching his long legs like he was getting comfortable, preparing to stay awhile. "Yeah, she's the rich lady you slept with some weeks back. Then pined after like a teenager for weeks but wouldn't call her."

Jacob huffed, annoyed. Sounding boards weren't supposed to talk back. "Remind me again, why do I tell you anything?"

"Because I give great advice."

"Nope. Not true. At all."

Will scratched his nose with his middle finger. "Anyway, did you finally man up and call her?"

"No, asshole. I ran into her at Swift Financial. She works there."

Will's eyes widened. "No shit. Small world. Is she anyone important?"

"Her father owns the company."

Will's eyes bugged. Jacob was afraid they might fall from his head.

"Ah man. Damn." Will whistled. "Was she happy to see you or plotting to have you tossed on your ass? Again."

Jacob ignored the dig. "At first she wasn't happy. Now we're okay. I think."

"Where's the problem?"

"We'd never work as a couple, or anything, but…" He shrugged not sure how to finish the sentence.

Will scowled. "You want her? Even after she threw you out like, well, like white trash?"

Jacob stood and began removing one of the Magnetophon's reels. "She had her reasons."

"Such as?"

"Her mother and stepfather are pricks. She was worried they'd do something to damage Marty's business if they caught us together." He gave a grunt of satisfaction and the reel slid loose. He set it down and started on the next one.

"Yeah, I guess catching their patrician daughter in bed with the mover does play like bad porn." Will chuckled, dodging the pair of pliers Jacob threw at him. "What's the problem now?"

He sat on the edge of his desk, trying to separate his obligations from his desires. "Because now I'm working with her father. Mixing business and personal stuff is never a good idea. There's no telling how Charles Meier would react to his daughter dating one of his lowly clients. Or what would happen when it crashed and burned between us."

Hell, he wasn't even sure Greta was interested. Getting a read on her was impossible. He'd never met a woman so apt at hiding her emotions. He'd catch a flicker, a glimpse that made him believe it wasn't one-sided, then boom, she was impassive. A beautiful and cold marble statue.

"What makes you certain everything will turn bad?" Will asked.

"Remember Trisha?"

"I knew you'd mention her," Will groaned. "Just because Greta and her family share the same zip code doesn't mean they're the same."

"I dealt with Greta's mother. Believe me, she's the embodiment of wealthy snob. She disliked me and hadn't even known what I'd been doing with her daughter."

Her condescending attitude irked him. Freaking rich people.

"Plus, Greta told me we're 'too different' to date. I'm assuming the difference is the zip code you mentioned. Our polar opposite upbringings." Jacob needed to move and stood. "And, as I said, there's Charles. He might not give a rat's ass about my social status. Then again, he could. I'm finally able to open an actual brick and mortar shop. I don't want to fuck it up over some woman."

When they were together, she felt like more than "some woman" he had the hots for, but he wasn't going to admit this to his brother. He barely acknowledged it to himself.

He stopped pacing and faced Will, catching his pained expression before he hid it. He still blamed himself for Rework's past financial strains.

Before Jacob could refute Will's guilt, he spoke. "You deserve this opportunity more than anyone I know. If you're worried, back off. Find another pretty woman to mess around with. God knows it won't be a problem for you."

"I don't want to mess around with some other woman. I won't with her either. Greta's right, we're wrong for each other. The draw is probably sexual chemistry, and nothing more, shit though, it's strong."

"TMI dude." Will rose, brushing the front of his jeans before walking toward the door. "You've made a decision. Stick with it and get back to work. Isn't your Micro-something due at the end of the week?"

"Yeah, it is." Jacob sat, returning to his work and contemplations. He didn't hear the door shut.

Chapter Eight

Walking through the halls of Swift Financial, Jacob's steps were as steadfast as his decision. He'd be the embodiment of professionalism with Greta. He'd locked his attraction to her in a metal box and shoved it into a dark, dusty corner of his mind.

Yes, he wanted her and maybe even had a chance, but the odds of it leading anywhere were slim to none. She was right; they were too different. It'd be stupid to risk pissing off her father and gambling with the well-being of Rework.

His staunch resolve lasted all the way to the IT office.

Until he caught sight of Greta, sitting alone and lost in her work. She was so damn beautiful. Her soft auburn hair was in a loose bun, showing off her long, slender neck. The sight beckoned him to run his fingers along the exposed skin.

She turned from her computer, offering a shy smile and a mug of coffee. "Allen told me you'd be in right after lunch. Not sure if you drink it this late in the day, but here." She handed him the cup. "Two creams, one sugar, right?"

He faltered. "You remembered?"

She shrugged. "I've a good memory for details."

He did too. When it came to her.

He could recall basic stuff, like her fondness for American classics and modern-day romance novels, while other recollections were scorched into his memory with a soldering iron. Like the birthmark under her left breast or the incredibly erotic whimper she'd made when her orgasm built.

Shoving those unhelpful memories aside, he silently repeated his professional oath and took the empty chair next to her. "Where are Allen and Rae?"

"They're around. Should be back anytime."

He glanced over in time to catch the wicked glint in her eyes.

"Relax, I'm not going to seduce you," she teased, throwing his words from the other day back at him.

He laughed. "Couldn't resist, could you?"

"No. Sorry." She smiled, appearing quite pleased with herself.

A playful Greta was hot.

"It wouldn't take much. A crook of your finger and an inviting smile. I'm downright easy when it comes to you," he replied, with way too much bluntness. He needed to shut up.

"It appears I have the same problem," she said so softly he almost hadn't caught it.

He *should* pretend he hadn't heard, yet he craved more of her mischievous side. It reminded him she wasn't all straitlaced and coolness. The combination was sexy as hell and got under his skin. He wanted more of it, more of her.

Unable to stop himself, he came closer, his meager resolve crumbling like old parchment paper.

When mere centimeters separated her enticing lips from his mouth, she shifted back. "I–I'm sorry," she stuttered. "I shouldn't have flirted."

Jacob groaned and leaned back. "Stop playing hot and cold with me." He stared straight into her eyes, struggling to smother his frustration and sudden spike of desire.

Is this a game to her?

"I don't mean to." Her tone was clipped, her posture ramrod straight. The cold blueblood was back. "I wasn't lying when I said I'm still attracted to you. However, that doesn't mean I plan on acting on it." In a kinder voice, she added, "You can't deny we're polar opposites. Plus, everything's more complicated because of work."

Jacob ran a palm along his brow, trying to hold back his growing aggravation. Not sure who he was more annoyed at, her or himself.

She'd basically been repeating the reasons he had given Will for staying away from her.

The problem was, when she was close, none of it mattered, and he found himself arguing for the exact opposite. "We don't work together. Your father's company is giving me the means to expand Rework. He owns a small percentage of it. He doesn't run it, and he's not my boss."

Jacob waited for her to meet his gaze. She didn't. "Listen, I'd be lying if I said it didn't bother me your father owns Swift. I'm not stupid. I know he might be less than pleased to have his daughter dating someone like me. He could make my life difficult. Hell, he could cancel my contract."

His heart skipped a few beats. Starting back at the beginning would kill him.

"Father would never do such a thing," she gasped. "You're being ridiculous."

"Come on, Greta. I'm sure he'd much prefer his daughter not dating a middle-class nobody. It'd be an easy way to get rid of me."

"Now you're the one making assumptions without facts." Anger sparked in her hazel eyes. "My father's not that kind of man. He knows how to keep his business and personal life separate. Unlike you."

Jacob ignored the dig and asked the question he was bursting to know. "Would he be upset if we dated?"

"Maybe, though not for the reasons you think."

"What are they?"

"It's quite embarrassing." She sighed and shifted in her seat, as if she'd rather be anywhere than having this conversation with him. It stoked his curiosity.

"My father has his heart set on me getting back with my ex. He probably wouldn't like anyone who got in the way."

Jacob's heart stuttered for a beat.

Shit. Another guy. Probably some asshole named Winston the third who was a member of the yacht club and was friends with the president.

"Do you want to get back with this old boyfriend?"

"No. If I'd wanted him back, we'd be together." She wasn't bragging, merely certain.

Good.

"If you're not pining after or seeing this guy, why not go on a date with me? Is it because your dad's wishes overrule yours?"

"No, of course not."

Her tone said the opposite, yet he persisted. "What do *you* want? Don't overthink it. Believe me, I've done it enough for the both of us."

Her head tilted as if weighing her options.

"A date, Greta, not marriage." Getting her to agree shouldn't rate this high on his list of important accomplishments. He didn't care. All that mattered was getting her to agree to one date. "You've already told me you're moving back to Lansing in the fall. It's not like I'll be following you there. Hell, maybe after spending some time together we'll find the only thing we have in common is sex, and we'll go our separate ways before you even return to college."

He leaned forward, closer, breathing in her tantalizing scent. "Hell, reliving some of our chemistry wouldn't be a terrible, would it?"

Her face reddened. Her gaze didn't waver. "No, it wouldn't."

Those words were the only invitation he needed. Jacob closed the distance between them, slanting his lips over hers. He gave the kiss everything he had, even knowing the consequences of it might be steep.

Repercussions didn't mean much when risk tasted and felt so damn good.

Chapter Nine

Blake had a million things to do, yet here he was delivering paperwork to Greta like some lowly secretary. All to get a couple of minutes with her. It was humiliating. He was a Kingstine, and Kingstine men didn't grovel.

The elevator opened, and Blake stepped into the corridor, catching sight of Allen waiting with a group to get inside.

Allen wasn't a friend or equal, but since Greta had broken things off, the man had become downright insufferable. He was almost smug, and, at times, Blake swore the other man was internally laughing at his efforts at reconciliation with Greta.

Blake paused mid-step, spite tiptoeing along his bones. Was it possible Allen was delusional enough to believe he now had a chance with her? Blake shook his head, clearing away asinine thoughts. Everyone at Swift understood Greta was his.

Allen caught sight of Blake and parted from the group, letting the doors slide shut without him. His smirk was on full display. "Having *another* computer problem, Blake?"

"No," he snapped, trying to tamp down his annoyance. He didn't want the other man to know he was getting under his skin. Humiliating him. "I would have summoned someone from your department and not wasted my time coming here. I have important papers, and I have to make sure," he glanced at the file's tab, "Mr. Grimm receives them."

"I'll be heading back there shortly. I can take them for you." Allen reached for the papers.

Blake held tight to them and shook his head. "No. They're important. I want to hand them over myself."

Allen retracted his hand. "Okay. Don't let me stop you." He pressed the elevator button, his damn smirk back in place.

Mortification ran through Blake's veins. Allen was probably aware the file was nothing more than boiler-plate stuff for the new client. Something any lowly intern could deliver.

He wanted to wipe the damn grin off Allen's face, and he would, soon. When he was back with Greta, and she ran the IT department, he'd convince her to fire Allen.

For now, he pretended not to notice Allen's smugness. Blake nodded a curt goodbye and started for Greta.

Before he could get rid of Allen, he had to win Greta back, and regrettably, that meant lowering himself to a delivery boy. She wasn't taking his calls, and he wanted to invite her to his father's annual education fund-raiser. A perfect place to reconnect.

In the past, she'd go on about the importance of helping others. Personally, Darwinism, survival of the fittest, worked for him. However, if her soft heart got her to accept his invite, he'd take it. After an evening with him, she'd be back with him and planning their wedding.

The Kingstine and Meier family would be a powerful union.

Usually she listened to him. She needed to stop being stubborn. And dramatic. He'd had one too many scotches that night and had gotten carried away.

He couldn't help women wanted him. They liked his looks, his power, his money. He wasn't to blame when they threw themselves at him. It was inevitable he'd slip up once in a while, but Greta was the one he wanted as his wife. Didn't she understand the importance, the difference?

If she didn't know now, she would soon enough. She was reasonable. He could get her to see things his way.

Reaching the IT hallway, Blake paused by an empty conference room and checked his reflection in the door's window. His expensive cut didn't allow for a hair out of place. His tie was tight and straight, and the fit of his jacket was impeccable.

Putting on his most charming smile, he opened the door to Greta's office.

Chapter Ten

Jacob's kiss was even better than Greta remembered. The press of his lips, the way his tongue commanded and teased stroked all her desires.

She was at Swift, for goodness sake! This needed to stop. Her internship might be temporary. Her career goals at her father's company were not.

She didn't date men from work, and she most certainly did not fool around with guys sporting tattoos, dangerous eyes, and perhaps loose sexual morals.

Yet, instead of pushing him away, she wrapped a hand around his neck to deepen the kiss.

"This is a problem," she murmured, pulling back and trying to wrangle in her hormones. Impossible. She wanted more of his lips. *More of him.* What was wrong with her?

"Doesn't feel like a problem to me. Are you overthinking things again?" Jacob shifted back an inch to watch her, his eyes aflame with desire.

She could easily lose herself in his ocean blues.

He didn't understand; overanalyzing, second-guessing, was her way of life. Of course, if he kept kissing her, she was liable to forget her name, let alone her misgivings.

"My mind tells me to be restrained. Then you come near me, and my body screams something else…"

"That's a problem? Remember, no over thinking. Simply enjoy." He brushed his mouth along her neck and nipped lightly under her ear.

Oh. How did this man instinctively know all her sweet spots? The areas that lit her core on fire and made her want to beg.

"Seriously," he whispered. "If you need to take things slow, I'll stop right now. Whatever you want and need. You only have to tell me."

His words brushed hotly against her ear and into her soul. With his body close and the promise of pleasure near, caution was forgotten.

To hell with responsibilities and repercussions. She shifted, fusing his lips with hers.

"What in the hell is going on?"

Greta recognized the voice. Blake's scorn and disbelief carried across the room, landing on her like ice water.

~ * ~

Jacob jolted back. A guy around his age, in an expensive suit, took two furious steps inside.

His hostile gaze fell on Greta. "You do remember this is an investment firm and not a broth—"

Anger stacked inside Jacob like cinder blocks. "Stop talking. *Right now*. Who the hell are you?"

He couldn't be just a coworker, not with the way he spoke to Greta. Another freaking family member? A brother?

The man studied Jacob with distaste. "I'm Mr. Meier's attorney. I need to find a Mr. Grimm." He leveled his contemptuous gaze back on Greta. "However, before I find him, it appears I need to remind employees about workplace decorum."

Jacob glanced at Greta. Her expression was a mixture of anger, embarrassment, and oddly enough, guilt.

He turned back to the douche standing by the door. "I'm Jacob Grimm. Are you Greta's governess, along with the company's lawyer?"

"Hardly. I am her fiancé."

Jacob's stomach plummeted, and he forgot to breathe.

"Ex, Blake. You keep forgetting that one important detail." Greta's tone had a plaintive tinge to it.

Jacob took in a large swallow of air. Ah, this was the ex-boyfriend. This was the guy her father wanted as his future son-in-law? Guess Charles had better business than personal sense.

Blake spared Jacob a cursory glare before returning his focus to Greta. "Is this how you welcome all our new clients? What's the treatment for the higher-level ones?"

Seriously?! No wonder this asshole is an ex.

Greta blinked, clenching her fists in her lap. Jacob was sure she was going to rip into this dickhead. Instead, she avoided them both and said, "I'm going to get more coffee. Need anything?"

Jacob tried not to gape. "No. I'm fine. Thanks." His gaze never left her.

He was so far from fine he wouldn't have been able to identify it in a lineup. Jealousy and bewilderment coursed through him. He wanted to rage at Greta for not defending herself. Even more, he ached to punch the pompous lawyer standing in front of him.

How could Greta date, let alone become engaged, to such a jackass? Jacob wasn't sure which bothered him more, the man's pretentiousness or his shared history with Greta.

Jacob stood, and both men waited in the loud silence until she left.

The door shut, and he faced Blake. "I see why you're an ex."

Blake waved a hand dismissively. "For now. We're working through some issues."

His nonchalant attitude grated on Jacob's nerves, and he couldn't resist taunting the other man. "I'd say from the way she was just kissing me, she might not be interested in fixing those issues."

Anger flashed through the other man's eyes. He immediately masked it with a condescending smirk. "Only shows me she's confused. Make no mistake, Greta will be back. She and I were together for over three years, and, face it, you're not her type." He regarded Jacob and didn't appear impressed. "You may have put on a suit today. It doesn't change the fact you're an inconsequential nobody. She'll learn soon enough."

Jacob laughed, more amused than concerned. It was a wonder both Blake and his ego could fit through the damn door. "Wow, you're an arrogant asshole. Is it one of the issues you need to work on?"

Blake flushed red, and his hand clenched into fists. "A fair warning. If you continue to pursue Greta, it will not end well for you," he hissed.

Jacob snorted and cocked a brow. "Why? You gonna beat me up?"

"A man of my stature doesn't stoop to street brawls. That's for your kind. No, I worry if you continue down this path, your little dream may never become a reality—"

Jacob's adrenaline spiked. "What the fuck are you talking about?"

"Language, Mr. Grimm," Blake tsked. "I'm referring to your pissant company, Rework. Do you think Charles would appreciate someone like you messing around with his daughter? Who knows what lengths he'll go through to keep you away from her?"

He was getting under Jacob's skin, hitting too close to his own fears.

Hiding his doubts, he scoffed, "I believe Mr. Meier's a smart businessman. He knows I'm an excellent investment. Plus, you're his lawyer; you should know we've already signed a contract."

Tired of the man and growing impatient, Jacob thrust out his hand. "Give me the paperwork and head back to your cubicle."

Blake handed over the file. "I'm sure there's a loophole…but really, why bother." He gave another one of those condescending shrugs. "You'll be gone from here soon enough, and Greta will forget you. I honestly cannot believe she even noticed you in the first place. Our little separation must have unsettled her more than I realized."

Jacob plastered on a fake self-assured grin. "You're right. I won't be here long. Guess I better make sure my presence is memorable." He leaned back, tucking his hands in his pockets. "Though I've been here less than a week and have made good progress, don't you agree?"

Blake's calm exterior slipped. He took an aggressive step forward, a man ready to detonate. Jacob slid his hands from his slacks, steeling himself for more scalding words and the possibility of violence. He surreptitiously scanned the room for any possible objects Blake might try to use.

A phone buzzed, piercing the air and the confrontation. Blake cursed, yanking a sleek cell from his pocket. After reading a text, he slipped it back inside and regarded Jacob coldly.

"You're temporary. Sometimes women like to slum it for a bit, see what the other side's like. She'll bore of you soon enough. Now, I have to go. Charles needs me, and I don't have any more time to waste on you."

"Fuck off. I never asked you to stay," Jacob growled.

"More vulgar language from a foul man. I'm not surprised." Blake sniffed. He strolled out, leaving in his wake the stink of expensive cologne and discontent.

Chapter Eleven

Discord wrapped itself around Greta. She pulled at the collar of her blouse, trying to breathe, but the guilt was strangling her. Before the door to the IT office had clicked shut, she'd known leaving Jacob to deal with Blake was a mistake.

Not that it stopped her from running like a frightened rabbit. She despised conflict and needed a couple minutes alone, away from Blake's animosity and Jacob's allure.

So, here she was, hiding in the break room and making the slowest cup of coffee in human existence, loathing her spineless ways. She should have told Blake to give her the papers and leave. The possibility of his anger, and future repercussions chilled her blood.

Stirring her coffee, she heaved a heavy sigh and, since there was nothing she could do about Blake, she shifted her focus to Jacob. There was no doubt she wanted him. She'd never desired Blake, or any other man, the way she did Jacob.

Maybe he's right, and I'm overthinking it.

She'd lived under her parents' oppressive rule, only to move on to Blake's demanding and overpowering ways. Maybe a little reckless fun was what she needed.

Heck, at twenty-seven, there was no hurry to settle down. Why not have fun with Mr. Wrong until Mr. Right came along? With any luck, Jacob would burn away the growing restlessness presently taking root in her. With it extinguished, she'd be able to settle into the proper woman everyone needed her to be.

With her decision made and nothing left to do in the break room, Greta left. She strode the carpeted hallway, mug in hand, eager to see Jacob. Turning the corner, she spotted Blake heading in the opposite direction.

Good.

Plastering on a hopeful smile, she entered the shared office. Jacob was facing the window at the rear outer wall, his back to her.

She set her mug on the nearest desk, Allen's workspace. The ceramic clinked against the wood surface, and Jacob faced her. Anger etched his handsome face. Blake must've thrown his worst, and it had stuck.

The urge to swivel on her heels and leave again was fierce. She locked her legs, unwilling to do it again.

Taking a deep breath, she came closer. "I'm sorry. I didn't know he'd be stopping by. What did he say to make you angry?"

Icy blue eyes pinned her. "Oh, not much. Only that your break is temporary, and if I continue to pursue you, my contract with Swift will be in jeopardy."

"He's such an asshole!" Greta slammed a palm to her thigh, her irritation overflowing.

Jacob's mouth twisted in surprise. "Wow, woman. I didn't even know you knew cuss words."

"Yes, well, sometimes they're the only accurate words to use." She smiled weakly. "Anyway, Blake's lying. He's *not* my fiancé, and he doesn't have the power to end any contracts. Only my father has that authority."

"He tells me it's what your father will do to keep me away from you."

Greta huffed, "Oh please. Blake is full of hot air. As I told you earlier, Father would never end a sound business deal because of personal feelings."

He might, however, hinder her career advancement. Give her fewer accounts, and, in turn, thin her portfolio. Heck, maybe he wouldn't even hire her after graduation. She doubted it. Still, there was enough worry to have her stomach twisted in knots. She shoved her anxiety aside and focused on Jacob.

His expression was full of doubt, but he didn't press the issue of losing his contract. Instead, he switched topics. "Were you and that douchebag really together for over three years?"

"Yes." She rested a tentative hand on his firm chest. "It doesn't matter. He's the past."

Relief seemed to flood his eyes, and Jacob closed the distance between them, kissing her gently. It spoke of new beginnings. Of friendship, intimacy, and passion.

"Good, because I'd like to be your present," he whispered against her lips.

"Only had lunch together? You two are merely acquaintances? Barely know each other, huh?" Allen drawled from somewhere behind Greta.

She shot back from Jacob with a startled yelp, embarrassed and flustered. She tried to hide it with a glare aimed at Allen.

He gave a playful leer. "If this is how you are with near strangers, I want to get to know you less."

Heat flooded her cheeks. She dropped her gaze from Allen's, moving to her chair on shaky legs.

Jacob flopped next to her, appearing more annoyed at the interruption than getting caught. "This office should have a freaking revolving door. It'd make it easier for all the damn traffic."

Allen sat at his workstation and swiveled to face them, his brows almost to his hairline. "I'm not the only one to interrupt your little tête-à-tête?"

Jacob snorted. "I had the privilege of meeting Blake."

"Ah yes, I ran into him by the elevator. He's always willing to become courier boy if the destination's the IT office."

Jacob grimaced. "Thanks for the warning. He's a real nice guy."

"Sorry. Had I known you two were necking like teenagers, I'd have called to warn you. Anyway, Blake isn't nice on his best day, and if he walked in on what I just did…unfortunate…"

"Unfortunate for him, not me." Jacob gave a devil-may-care smile.

Could this be any more embarrassing?

Greta raised her voice over the two men, desperate to change the subject. "Wow, look at the time. Shall we call it a day?"

"Umm, it's only four," Allen said. "But hey, works for me. I've finished the important stuff."

She cleared her throat and sat straighter, trying to appear professional. It was hard when she could still taste Jacob's lips on hers.

"No. Sorry." *Idiot.* "Jacob just got here. I'm sure he'd like to get to work."

"I wouldn't mind…if you agree to leave with me. I rode my motorcycle in today. We could go for a ride, or if you're not a fan of bikes, there's a park down the street we could walk to–"

"You have a bike? What kind?" Allen cut in.

"Triumph Bonneville. Worked on it throughout winter. Got it running last week."

"You drove it wearing a suit and tie?" Greta wondered. Jacob on a motorcycle in a proper suit; hot. The vision was definitely making her warmer.

"Yup. Couldn't resist riding on such a nice day."

"If you don't go, Greta, I'll gladly take your place," Allen said.

"No offense, man." Jacob's gaze bounced between Greta and Allen. "You're not who I want to ride off into the sunset with."

Allen laughed, shaking his head. "Agreed. You're cute and all, but I like to wrap my arms around someone a little smaller…and without male parts. I was thinking more along the lines of you giving me a lesson. I've always wanted to learn."

"Sure, why not?" Jacob agreed.

Greta interjected. "Right now?" Was she losing her impromptu date? "What happened to *us* going for a ride?"

"Oh, I didn't mean I'd teach him right now, especially if you're free." Jacob glanced to Allen. "Another time?"

"Sure, sure…pretty face comes along, and friends are forgotten."

"Yeah, you called it." Jacob chuckled, turning back to Greta. "You sure you want to go for a ride? If you're afraid we could do something else."

"Sure. Sounds like fun." Butterflies tumbled around in her chest, slamming into her nerves. Flying down the road at high speed without the metal confines of a car was a terrifying image.

She didn't want to wimp out, so she focused on a vision of wrapping her arms tightly around Jacob, her face resting against his strong back, and inhaling his tantalizing scent.

The image helped. It gave her the courage to stand, wave bye to Allen, and follow Jacob to his bike.

Chapter Twelve

The motorcycle was beautiful, matte black with a long, tan seat. The sight sent a tremor through Greta; half fear, half anticipation. She pictured James Dean cruising the open highway on it. Of course, she'd rather not end up like Dean.

Though, he'd died in a car crash. Right?

Either way, she was asking Jacob to skip the highway.

He grabbed a helmet from the handlebars. Twisting around, he placed it gently on her head. "This might be a little big on you. Here, let me adjust the straps."

His fingers grazed along her jaw while he worked the fastenings. This close his light stubble enticed her and his aftershave tickled her senses. It was nice. *Really* nice.

She closed her eyes, savoring his touch and scent.

"All set," he said, less than a minute later. "You okay?"

Opening her eyes, she focused on his face. His brows were knitted, his gaze searching hers.

"I'm fine. Just nervous." She'd closed her eyes to calm her heart from desire, not fear.

Her gaze shifted from his bottomless blues to the top of his head. "Where's your helmet?"

"I only brought the one." He shrugged. "There's no helmet law in Michigan. I won't get a ticket."

"A ticket doesn't worry me. I care about your head."

"I have an extremely hard one." He knocked lightly on the side of his head. "I'll be fine... You're not chickening out on me, are you?"

He was impossible to refuse when his gorgeous, playful grin made an appearance. "No, though, would you mind if maybe we skipped the highway?"

His smile widened. "You're adorable when you're nervous, but you'll see, it's easy, nothing to fear." He lightly kissed the tip of her nose, then leaned back, watching her, wordlessly asking if she was okay.

She wanted to throw herself into his arms, but resisted, in case anyone was watching from the expansive windows running along Swift. She was already taking a risk getting on the back of a client's bike. She didn't need to be caught making out with him as well.

His expression went blank. She couldn't tell if the separation bothered him.

"There are a couple things you need to do." He raised two fingers. "Lean with me into the turns and be careful getting off the bike, the pipes will be hot."

"Understood. And you're okay with no highways, right?"

"No highways. I promise. Unless you change your mind." He shucked off his suit jacket and stored it in a canvas bag strapped to the bike. He swung a long leg over the seat. After righting it and releasing the kickstand, he peered at her. "Ready?"

Nope.

She nodded, running her sweaty palms on her slacks and trying to swallow her heart back into her chest, where it belonged, instead of her throat. She'd look like a fool, suggesting it and then reneging. Ignoring her protesting, tingling limbs, she got on the back of the bike, sliding impossibly close to Jacob. She gripped him vice-like with her thighs and arms, realizing much too late, a motorcycle was sexy in theory, terrifying in reality.

"You won't fall off. I promise." He rubbed her hands, but she couldn't make her fingers loosen her death grip. He twisted around, his gaze meeting hers. The corners of his mouth twitched, and his eyes shone with humor. "But, I might pass out if you keep squeezing so tight."

"Sorry." He probably thought she was behaving like a foolish little girl. She used what dignity remained to ease her hold.

Jacob chuckled and shifted. Seconds later the bike roared to life. Greta's heart ran back in her throat trying to escape the terrifying ride. Abandoning dignity, she returned her death grip.

He let out an "oof" but was smart enough not to laugh. The gears clicked, and they were off. So slow and gentle, the start was almost anticlimactic.

He took them through residential neighborhoods and onto the main road, keeping under the speed limit. Her heart found its proper place, and she even felt silly for her fear.

It wasn't terrible, was even nice.

She loved the way the powerful bike rumbled under her and *adored* having an excuse to wrap herself around Jacob's muscular back and thighs. Every time they turned, his muscles slid against her, steadily heating her.

She rested the side of her face against his solid back and lost herself in the joy of a summer ride with a handsome man.

"Um, Greta," he said sometime later. His deep voice stirred her from a relaxed trance.

"Hmm?"

"You're killing me here…"

Her grip was loose and relaxed. In fact, her hands weren't even wrapped around his waist. They were–

Oh. She was strumming his abs. His lower abs.

Mortification flooded her. "'Sorry. I didn't realize…"

"Don't apologize." He moved. "It's only my slacks are becoming uncomfortable."

Warmth bloomed throughout her, and this time it had nothing to do with embarrassment. It also woke her dormant wicked side. Before sanity could return, her hands lowered farther.

The bike swerved, and she screeched.

"Shit. Sorry. Took me by surprise," he said hoarsely, after straightening the bike. "Won't happen again."

"Yeah, well, to be safe, I'll keep my hands above board." She slid her hands to his shoulders, both frightened and thrilled at his reaction.

"Damn it," he muttered loud enough to be heard over the engine.

She laughed at his sullenness, scooting back and taking in the surroundings. They were on an old white bridge, crossing a vast expanse of water. She recognized the place. Belle Isle.

"I haven't been here since I was a little girl." She was delighted. "I came here once on a field trip, shortly before the zoo closed."

"Bits and pieces of the zoo remain, but it's fenced off. The aquarium and gardens are open on the weekends." He tilted his head toward a pretty glass conservatory and a lovely old brick building with a green metal roof. "Anyway, I know the perfect place to park. From the western end of the island, we'll be able to see both Windsor and Detroit."

"Sounds wonderful." She snuggled closer.

After he parked, they walked along the cracked and pitted path, then onto the grass, making their way to an old retaining wall. Sitting, they talked of nothing and everything.

He made it easy to relax and enjoy the flawless summer day. He was comfortable in his skin. She found it soothed her normally anxious disposition.

In all honesty, she hadn't wanted to come home for the summer. Her degree required an internship, and her father insisted his place was perfect for her to get on-the-job experience. As usual, he was right. However, dealing with Blake and Mother wasn't easy. The only bright spot had been her new friendship with Rae.

And now Jacob.

Greta raised her face toward the sky and closed her eyes. The sun sparkling off the Detroit River and the warmth of Jacob next to her was delightful, and contentment oozed into every pore of her body. "Do you come here often?"

"Not much now. As a kid, I was here all the time. We came here with my parents, and there was the annual family reunion with my mom's side."

Greta had a pang of wistfulness. "I'm jealous. It sounds like fun. Most of my family's get-togethers were either related to Father's business or some boring social event hosted by my mother."

"My father was a cop and my mother a librarian." He grinned. "We weren't invited to many black-tie events."

He didn't sound regretful or disappointed, simply matter-of-fact. His life was different from hers.

She wanted to know more. "Will you tell me about your family? Do you only have the one brother? Wilhelm."

"Oh, hell. Please, if you ever meet him, don't call him Wilhelm."

"Sorry, Will." She peeked one eye open to glance at Jacob. She'd remembered him telling her this. She'd hoped teasing him would gift her with another one of his sexy smiles. It had worked.

"Yeah, he's my only sibling. And there's nothing to tell. My life's boring. Let's talk about you. I'm sure it's much more interesting."

"Doubt that. Come on." She nudged his shoulder. "Are you afraid you'll let spill an awful secret? Do you have a wife in Canada and throngs of nameless children running around?"

Jacob burst out laughing. "No, I don't have a wife or any kids. Thank God. Where do you come up with this stuff?" He sounded both amused and appalled.

"Sorry. I have an overactive imagination. It tends to head straight to worst-case scenarios." She smiled and squinted at him through silted lids. "Guess you'd better tell me. Who knows what I'll think up."

"No kidding." His turn to bump her lightly on the shoulder. "Seriously, what don't you already know? You've read my business files."

"That's your professional life. I want to know you, not Rework."

"Like I said, I'm boring. My life is my family and work. I have a couple of close friends I hang out with from time to time. Mostly I work."

"I know your work life. I want to know you."

"Ah, my family." He stared at the Detroit River, picking at the loose concrete along the wall. "I love them, but well, we're a mess."

"Families are messy."

"Sure, life is messy, but we're a mess. There's a difference. A big one." All the humor leaked from him.

Not wanting to upset him further, she said, "I'm not sure I agree. Anyway, if you want to talk about something else, I understand."

"No, you don't." He studied her, his smile returning. It warmed her more than the sun breaking through dreary, gray clouds. "You've been raised to be polite and not pry. Though, God knows what's going through your head. You've probably conjured a life where my parents are secretly part of the mob, and my brother's their hired killer."

"No, of course not." She laughed, and after a pause, smirked. "Maybe drug smugglers, running between here and Canada. Oh! Or perhaps a family of gypsy thieves."

"Hardly." He chuckled. "We're a boring working-class family. Like I said before, my mother was a librarian, and my dad was a cop. He was on the force almost twenty years. Will's my only brother. He's three years older than me and not a thief or smuggler. In fact, he lives with me and has recently graduated from culinary school."

Brief and concise. She suspected much was left out, but didn't want to pick at sore spots. "Wow, you two must be close. I love my sister, Cindy. However, if we still lived together, I'd have strangled her a long time ago."

"Oh, I get the urge quite often with Will. We've always been close, but we live together more out of necessity than anything else."

Curiosity ate at her. She wanted to know more but, remembered this was a light, summer fling. His problems weren't hers, and from his body language, he'd rather not share.

Instead, she asked if his parents were retired. The way he'd mentioned their careers sounded as if they were in the past.

He gazed at the water, slumping as if Atlas had dumped the weight of the world on his shoulders. There went not upsetting him. What had she said?

Again, she didn't press and let the silence wash over them. She faced the peaceful waves on the Detroit River. She was going to ask if he wanted to leave when Jacob spoke.

"I live with both my brother and father. Like I said, we're helping each other. My father was laid off, and Will had to move back home to get his life in order. He'd spent too many years partying and made a real mess of his life. Thankfully, he's straightened himself out, turned his life around. Finished his culinary degree in the spring."

Jacob's expression was both defiant and proud, as if daring her to speak against his family. Probably wondering if she was going to criticize his them.

In truth, she was touched. She'd love to have a close-knit family that worked together and helped without judging. She loved her parents and they'd always provided for her, but she wasn't close to them. There were too many expectations and rules, especially from her mother and stepfather.

Forgetting her family problems, she scooted closer and leaned against Jacob. He placed an arm loosely around her waist.

"I'm glad your brother is doing better, for his sake, and your family's."

She felt him nod in agreement. Not wanting to pry into his brother's personal struggles, she changed the subject yet again. "Ever since my local librarian directed me to *The Lion, the Witch, and the Wardrobe*, they became my favorite people. Where did or does your mother work?"

He shifted away, dropping his arm from around her, rubbing both hands over his face. "Damn, Greta. You're hitting all the sore spots today."

Her heart hitched. Was there tragedy where his mother was concerned too? Greta hoped she was wrong.

She tried to lighten the mood. "Am I? Seriously, we can change the subject. Tell me, what's your favorite summer activities? Mine is bike riding, though, after today, I may have to switch to motorcycling."

He smiled a sad smile. "Glad to hear it. And it's okay. Your questions are innocuous enough. It's not your fault my life's fucked up. Good thing we're keeping things simple, huh? You wouldn't want to get snared in my mess. Anyway, my mom used to work at Detroit Public Library, the main branch. She died seven years back. Ovarian cancer."

His words were blunt, with a deep sadness behind them. Her heart broke for him. She might not be close to her mother, yet even the thought of losing her made Greta want to weep.

"Jacob, I'm sorry." She took his hand and rested her head on his shoulder. "What was she like?"

"Amazing. She was kind, with a killer sense of humor. She was the glue holding our family together." He sighed deeply and continued in a more pragmatic tone. "Anyway, my childhood was a normal middle-class upbringing. My dad worked a lot, and my mom was part-time. Both parents loved us and we knew it... even if my brother and I were always in trouble."

"Sounds wonderful." She meant it. A carefree childhood, one with love given freely, not based on met expectations, would've been heaven.

"It ended my senior year in high school. My mom was sick all the time and always tired. The doctors found cancer. Everywhere. Throughout her body. My mom tried to fight it. Watching her suffer and fade fast... It sort of put an end to my old way of life. Much of what I did before her illness had become silly and inconsequential. Her death shifted my priorities."

Jacob seemed to droop as if his sorrows were sucking him dry. Maybe they were. She kept quiet, hoping he'd continue. She was willing to listen and hopefully lighten his burden.

"After her death, things fell apart. Fast. Will, already a big partier, had no one to hold him back. He spiraled out of control. My dad was no help. He was too busy drowning in his own problems. He wasn't able to cope with losing my mom and sank his pain in whiskey. He became more distant and was constantly late for work. When his department needed to lay off officers, my dad was given the pink slip. For a while, he did nothing besides mourning my mom and drinking."

"I'm sorry." She was at a loss for words.

He gave a self-deprecating smile. "Sorry you asked?"

She kissed him lightly on the lips. "No. I'm sorry you've had to endure those difficult years."

"Yes, well, it's life, and I cannot complain." He lifted one shoulder then let it drop. "Yeah, losing my mom hurts, it always will. But I have a lot to be grateful for. Will's been clean for almost two years, and my father's stopped drinking. When Will moved back home, Dad didn't want alcohol around the house tempting Will. They're both working on a second chance...it's not something everyone is given."

"True, but it doesn't minimize the pain"

"No. Only time does that." Jacob exhaled heavily. "It was also an unpleasant wake-up call."

"How so?"

"Throughout my childhood and teenage years, I'd wanted a marriage like my parents. My mom adored my dad, and he thought she hung the moon. When she died, my dad became a ghost. Now I'm not sure I want to risk losing a part of me, like he has. It scares me shitless."

Greta empathized, though feared love for other reasons. For her, love meant losing herself to another. Her mother demanded Greta be the perfect socialite. Her father, the business tycoon. Blake, his Trophy Wife.

What would a man like Jacob demand she become for his love?

He gave a deep sigh and chuckled. "Sorry. I sound like fucking Eeyore. Anyway, I don't know anything about love and marriage. I've never been in love or had the urge to shackle myself to someone in wedded bliss."

"Wow, you make marriage sound wonderful." She laughed. "More like a prison sentence than a happily ever after."

"With some of the women I've dated, marriage would be a prison sentence. Besides, happily ever after is only in fairy tales, not for people like me. Not for the real world."

His outlook stung, though it shouldn't. They had nothing more than a summer together. She should be thrilled; she'd never have to worry about giving him her heart and him devouring it.

He didn't want it.

It made things between them simple.

So why was the day suddenly less sunny, even though there wasn't a cloud in the sky? Why was there a slight ache in her chest? She kept her smile in place, wanting to keep the moment light. "Maybe you need to rework your version of the fairy tale, Mr. Grimm."

Jacob scrutinized her, giving a playful leer. "I don't know. Maybe you're right. Fairy tales are interesting. I always did find Gretel very appealing." He wiggled his eyebrows. "I can most definitely understand why the witch wanted to eat Gretel."

She flushed at his overt innuendo and couldn't resist sparring with him. "Yes. Do remember how it ended for the witch when she displeased Gretel."

He flashed a grin, overflowing with amusement. "Noted. I'll do my damnedest to make sure Gretel's never displeased."

Chapter Thirteen

Greta sat with her sister at an elegant glass table, listening to her complain. They were at their favorite French restaurant, Fourier. Usually, Greta found the stylish patio with its large embroidered umbrellas and wrought iron fencing soothing. Today, however, the relaxing atmosphere was lost on her.

Cindy was in one of her moods. "Come on, you have to go with me. And don't tell me you already have plans. If you do, cancel them. We've barely seen each other since you've returned home."

"Go where? I'm here with you now," Greta replied calmly before ordering her favorite white wine. "Don't lay the blame on me. You're the one always working. Perhaps we'd see more of each other if you'd stop traveling every time you had a couple days to 'visit' some distant relative on the East Coast."

They both understood "visit" meant traveling with friends or meeting with some distant relative who liked to party.

She shrugged one delicate shoulder "It's like what Mother says. My looks won't last forever. I need to take all the good modeling jobs. I can't help a lucky by-product is lots of travel." She paused, ordering her wine, picking right up where they left off. "And don't get stuffy with me. Remember when you finally relaxed and took a year off from college to travel with me? You had a riot."

"Yes, okay, I did enjoy myself," Greta admitted.

Cindy huffed. "It was more than enjoyable."

She was right. Their year traveling Europe had been incredible. No, great was being in her late twenties and still working on her master's. Something not unheard of, or even uncommon, but it bothered her. Had she not taken time off, she'd be done with school and on to the next chapter of her adult life. One where she had independence and the respect of her parents. Hopefully.

"Yes, but vacations and good times can't last forever. I'm not like you, taking a class here and there, not worrying about the future."

"How would I know what I want from life when my only

experiences are from my high school and university? I have to experience life first before I know what I want to do with it."

Greta cocked an eyebrow, her skepticism on full display. "Traveling and partying gives you insight? Funny, I never needed either to know what I want from my life and career."

Her sister shrugged. "Guess we'll keep on viewing life through a different set of lenses."

Greta couldn't argue and nodded.

Cindy lifted a brow. "Now back to my original complaint."

Darn it.

Her sister pinned Greta with disapproving eyes. "I want more than lunch. And if you weren't constantly sneaking off with *that* guy, you'd be spending more time with me. After your internship, I won't see you until Christmas."

Greta glared at her sister. Not only was Cindy gliding over the fact she was never home, but the way she said Jacob's name held way too much haughtiness.

Cindy had the same light blonde hair, high cheekbones, and haughty expression as their mother. It appeared she also had the same attitude when it came to men.

She didn't approve of Jacob. Neither would their mother.

When Greta had confessed her steamy afternoon with Jacob to Cindy, she'd been thrilled. Congratulating her on finally having some fun. Apparently, he was good for sex, but not the "type" of man to date.

Snob.

"That guy has a name. Jacob. And I haven't been sneaking off," Greta grumbled.

Cindy quirked one perfect eyebrow and leaned back in her chair. "You've been with *Jacob* for what, almost a month? Yet, I'm the only who knows you two are dating."

"A month isn't much time. Why would I mention him? It's not like we're getting ready to pick engagement rings."

"You're telling me since you've come home, Mother hasn't mentioned a thing concerning your dating life?"

Cindy's disbelief wasn't unwarranted. Their mother was notoriously nosey and vocal about who her daughters could and could not date. She'd deem Jacob unfavorable. Her scorn was the real reason he hadn't come up in conversation. Greta wanted to enjoy Jacob until she had to return to university without having to deal with her mother's games.

"Plus, you're staying with Father. How could he not know? Do you sneak your guy in and out the back door?"

Greta's cheeks heated. Guilt overrode her annoyance. Cindy's scenario was a little too similar to her spring storm fling with Jacob.

"We don't go to each other's houses. We meet someplace between." Greta broke eye contact, peering at the menu. "And Father isn't nearly as inquisitive as Mother. Anyway, what's the point of mentioning Jacob? We aren't serious, and I no longer need my parent's approval to go on a date."

The waiter approached, setting their wine on the table and asking if they were ready to order. Greta did so happily, hoping the interruption would end the topic of conversation.

After he left, she took a sip from her wineglass, closing her eyes and savoring the taste. The sauvignon blanc was a perfect blend of savory herbs. She focused on the taste, instead of Cindy's snooty attitude, and some of her ire slipped away.

"It's a good thing you're not waiting around or needing their approval because you'd never get it with Father. And definitely not Mother. You're right," her sister continued, breaking Greta's repose. "Why mention him and upset the family? You two won't last past the summer."

Greta opened her eyes to glare at her sister. "What makes you say that?"

She kept telling herself the same thing, yet it hurt to hear it confirmed by someone else.

Cindy smoothed her perfect, blonde locks then gazed at her manicured nails. "What you two have is lust, nothing more. I get it." She met Greta's eyes and smiled sympathetically. "If I spent years with a man like Blake, I'd also want some dirty fun. Jacob isn't a long-term man for you. He doesn't fit in our world, or you in his. What will you do once the thrill of sex wears off?"

"Don't be such a snob. Just because he doesn't look like my type doesn't mean he isn't." Greta reached for her wine, changed her mind and set it back down. She'd need her wits to deal with her sister. "It's not any of your business, but for your information, we've only, you know, had the one time."

Why am I telling her this? I need to stop arguing with her. And myself.

Cindy's eyebrows were almost to her hairline. "Why not? I thought you're with him because he's a good lay."

"Be quiet," Greta hissed, glancing at the elderly couple at the next table who were now watching them. "I'm with him because I like his company. And, like I've said, we're meeting in public places, not each other's homes. What are we supposed to do, be intimate in a dark parking lot or alley?"

If she were honest, the situation bothered her. *A lot.* This was supposed to be carefree fun, playing around with their crackling chemistry the more time she spent with him, the more she dreaded her return to Lansing.

And they hadn't even done a thing to quell the crushing attraction, which sat front and center in her mind, driving her crazy. She never had him alone. And, darn it, she wanted him alone and naked.

This side of her was shameful but undeniable. The need to be in his arms again was almost compulsive. She wanted the pleasure, the comfort. He allowed her wild side to shine and didn't shame her for it. The freedom to feel without restraint was freeing. Lately, she craved it like the sun or fresh air.

Greta caught sight of their waiter approaching and prayed Cindy wouldn't answer her rhetorical question about where she and Jacob should have sex. She placed her napkin on her lap and tipped her head pointedly at the waiter, hoping her sister would get the point.

Thankfully, Cindy remembered her manners and dropped the conversation when their waiter set their plates in front of them and refilled their wineglasses. He asked if they needed anything else, and, after they said no and thanked him, he left.

Once their server was out of earshot, Cindy made a shooing gesture at Greta. "Enough of this chatter. Fret about your boy toy on your own time. Let's get back to my original complaint. *Again*. I want time with you. I miss you."

Greta swallowed her annoyance. "I miss you too, but I'm not interested in clubbing."

"I wasn't going to suggest it."

"Uh-huh."

Her sister lived for nightclubs.

"Honest." Cindy turned her palms up in an 'I'm-not-hiding-anything gesture'. "I want you to go with me to Jane Glengarry's midsummer party. I bet some of your old friends will be there...when was the last time you saw them? Don't you miss them? If not for me, do it for yourself?" She finished with saccharine sweetness, like a woman who knew she was getting her way.

With a sigh of defeat, Greta reached for her fork. "Forget modeling. You'd make a great lawyer or politician. You have the gift of persuasion."

"Does this mean you'll go with me?" Cindy smile was broad and triumphant.

Greta sighed. She was such a push-over. "Of course."

Chapter Fourteen

Greta followed Cindy through the sliding door and onto the stone patio. Standing under its two tiers, Greta scanned the backyard. Jane's party was a success. People milled all over the expansive yard and appeared in high spirits, laughing, dancing, and drinking.

They moved past the double balconies, and Greta took in the night's gorgeous summer stars and the many fairy lights tangled in the branches of almost every tree. Her gaze shifted from the sky back to the yard. Candles floated serenely in a lagoon-style pool, and farther in a band was playing old school hits to the delight of those letting loose on a large wooden dance floor.

"Meier, is that you?"

Greta recognized the voice and twisted around to find her old high school friend, Lily, standing a few feet away. Her smile widened, matching Greta's. They hugged, squealing in delight. Lily's chestnut brown hair and clothing style were more subdued than in past years, but she still had the same mischievous smile.

"I knew it was you," Lily said. She leaned back, checking Greta out. "It's great to see you, though surprising. Aren't you supposed to be taking classes through the summer? What are you doing back home?"

"Sorry I haven't called. I've been staying with my father while interning at his company. It takes up most of my time." Greta's gaze flickered away at the slight lie.

Cindy gave a sarcastic snort. "Work. Yeah, that's it."

Lily tilted her head, clearly waiting for an explanation. To Greta's relief, her sister's attention shifted to a man standing by the pool. She said something about needing to talk to Owen and left.

Greta nodded, though her sister missed it. She was already down the two stairs and moving toward the pool.

"Want to get a drink?" Greta asked Lily.

She agreed, and they walked to the bar built into one side of the balcony's frame. Two bartenders were hard at work, mixing, pouring, and chatting.

They scooted between bodies at the packed bar, and Lily asked, "Did you come here with your sister or Blake?"

Greta's blood froze; her buoyant mood turned sour in a single heartbeat. "He's here?"

Lily raised her hand, getting the attention of a bartender. After they gave their orders, she faced Greta. "Yeah... and by your expression, I'd say you didn't come here with Blake?"

"No. We broke up—"

Lily's eyes widened.

Messy dread bloomed in Greta's chest, like a field of poisonous, revolting flowers. *He's behind me.*

An armed snaked around her waist, pulling her against him. Blake smelled of booze and too much cologne. "I was hoping you'd be here," he slurred in her ear.

After she stepped to the side and away from his unwanted arms, her relief was immediate, but also short and dismal. His hand returned to the small of her back.

She wanted to slap it away; however, in Blake's obviously inebriated state, he'd probably cause a scene. She swallowed her annoyance and accepted her Manhattan, thanking the bartender.

She spotted her old neighbor Elizabeth and recalled reading in the local paper that she married a guy who owns some type of eco-friendly company.

Greta waved at Elizabeth, making her way from the bar and Blake. He was busy talking with a guy from his old lacrosse team and didn't notice her inching away.

Lily smirked, seeming to understand what Greta was doing, and stood between her and Blake, asking him a question and allowing Greta to sneak away. Gratitude flooded her. She owed Lily, big time.

Greta reached Elizabeth and congratulated her, asking about her husband. They talked, and Greta continued to put more distance between herself and Blake.

Lucas, Elizabeth's husband, sounded like a wonderful man, and Greta was delighted for her friend's happiness. Their talk also had her thoughts circling back to her ex. She tried to figure if she'd ever glowed when talking about Blake like Elizabeth did with her husband.

If she did, Greta didn't remember it.

In the beginning, before she noticed the heavy drinking and his wandering eye, she found him handsome and well-suited to her and was happy to have a man her parents liked; however, she was never enamored.

Studying him now, she didn't find him attractive. He was too perfect. Boring.

Jacob's messy, carefree good looks outshined Blake's aristocratic perfection.

A man who could have been a young Gregory Peck joined their group, introducing himself as Lucas. Greta forced her thoughts from her ex and Jacob, asking Elizabeth and her husband how they met.

Heavy drums and bass sang through the night air, as a band played the opening chorus of an old 90s song. The booming melody gave Greta an idea for another escape plan.

She set her drink on a nearby table and turned to a man on her right. "Would you like to dance? I love this song." She gave her friendliest help-me smile.

In truth, she'd never cared for the tune, but that wasn't the point. At this stage, she'd dance the Macarena with a garden gnome if it got her away from Blake.

The man offered her a smile and his hand. She practically dragged him to the dance floor, wanting to create space between her and her ex before he tried to stop her from leaving.

The relief washing over her was tantamount to a tsunami. She didn't even care she was running like a frightened child. It gave her what she needed, a way to avoid Blake without creating a scene. She'd hide in the crowd of the dance floor for one song then find Cindy and leave.

However, as she swayed under the summer stars, her steadfast decision to leave flew away on the light breeze. Lily, along with other old friends, joined Greta on the dance floor, and Blake slipped from her mind. She hadn't danced like this in ages and had forgotten the magic of music.

Her thoughts drifted to Jacob. Next time they spoke, she'd ask if he liked dancing. Picturing his arms wrapped around her, moving to the rhythm, warmed her more than the summer humidity.

A pair of male hands rested on her waist, and Greta jerked away, certain Blake had found her. It was her original dance partner. He appeared confused at her reaction. She offered an apologetic smile before telling him she was leaving.

The reminder of her ex-boyfriend had brought back her anxiety. He probably had a good buzz and was more than ready to spill his displeasure on her. The idea was like a lead balloon to her buoyant mood.

The exhilaration of dancing evaporated.

She bid everyone a quick goodbye, making promises to meet soon. Leaving the dance floor, she tried calling then texting Cindy.

Both went unanswered.

No more waiting. She'd find her sister.

Moving through the backyard, she soon discovered seeking and finding were two very different things. She made her way to the house, her aggravation increasing. She desperately hoped searching the three levels wouldn't be necessary.

As it turned out, luck, along with her sister, had deserted her.

Greta climbed the stairs to the second floor. With one hand running along the banister, she typed another message to Cindy. At the top step, she hit send and scanned the hallway.

Deserted, except for the one person she'd been trying to avoid all night.

Blake.

He caught sight of her, and his expression became one of drunken lust and reckoning.

Her evening was about to take a nose dive.

Drunken Blake was never fun. Mixed with his righteous indignation and disbelief she'd left him and was refusing to come back, would make him a monster.

Dread pooled in her stomach and her feet became bricks, making it impossible to beat a hasty retreat.

"What are you doing? Trying to find me?" Blake slurred, coming closer. He encircled her waist, standing way too close. The overpowering reek of whiskey made her gag.

She jerked back and tried to wrench free of his grasp. "No. I'm trying to find my sister."

He gave a drunken snort. "Knowing Cindy, you've come to the right place. She's probably in one of the bedrooms."

"Screw you, Blake." Greta tried to go around him.

He shoved her against the nearest wall. "I'd be more than happy to screw you." He leaned close enough she could taste his liquor fumes.

Panic flooded through her, and again she tried to shove him away, but he held tight. "Let go of me! If you want to get laid, find someone else. We. Are. Over."

"I want you." To her dismay, he kissed her rough and possessively. *No!*

"Get off of me!" She yanked her head to the side, trying to escape his wet lips.

His hot, suffocating mouth found her neck. "Come on, Greta. Stop fighting me. Quit wasting your time with that reprobate. You belong with me." Blake groaned, grinding his pelvis against her and sliding a hand under her dress."

"Enough!" Panic and fury gave her the strength to escape his drunken hold. Taking advantage of her hard-won freedom, she ran down the stairs and straight to the crowded patio.

Once she was far enough away from Blake, her racing heart

calmed. She tried calling and texting her sister.

Again, no answer.

Greta sat wearily in the nearest chaise lounge, ready to simultaneously cry and throw her useless phone into the pool. Until she noticed a recent missed call from Jacob. He must've tried to reach her when she was fleeing from Blake.

She needed to focus on finding Cindy, but the reassurance of Jacob's calm voice was too much to resist. She hit redial.

"Hello?" His deep voice reverberated through the phone, sounding both distracted and tired.

"Am I calling at a bad time?" She sincerely hoped not. Hearing his voice eased her emotions.

Which itself worried her. Had she broken up with Blake only to become dependent on her summer fling?

"No, not at all. I was hoping you'd notice I'd called. I miss you and could use a break from this pain-in-the-ass piece I'm working on."

She laughed, forgetting her worries. "I miss you too."

They weren't supposed to miss each other. Right now she didn't care.

"Are you still at the party? You have a lot of background noise."

"Yes. Unfortunately," she grumpily replied, playing with the folds of her dress. "I'm leaving right after I find my sister."

"You lost your sister?" He sounded both amused and worried.

"Yes, it's what I get for hanging out with Cinderella past midnight. Maybe I need to start searching for a glass slipper."

His laughter carried through the line, warming more than her heart. "Maybe you should. Besides losing your sister, are you having fun?"

"For the most part…"

"Why? What's wrong?" The humor had slipped from his voice.

Jacob's instant protective mode was lovely. Especially after the scare in the house, but since there wasn't much he could do, she decided to play down the incident. "Nothing serious. Blake was also invited."

"Shit. Is he bothering you?" There was a definite edge to his voice.

She should end the call. "Nothing I can't handle." Because, darn it, she needed to learn to manage some things on her own. "I have to go. I need to call my sister."

"Not fucking likely. What's the address?" Jacob barked.

Disbelief rolled through her. *Is he angry with me?*

He was acting like a darn caveman. She couldn't stomach his anger, along with Blake's near assault. "I'm sorry I upset you. I'll talk to you tomorrow."

Before she could hang up, she caught his words. "I'm not upset at you. I'm pissed at your sister. How could she ditch you with that asshole around?"

Greta raised the phone back to her ear. "She doesn't know he's here. We'd split off. I was visiting with old friends from high school."

"Doesn't matter. You can't find your sister now. Give me the address. I'm not going to let my girlfriend get pestered by some—" He inhaled deeply. When Jacob spoke again, his tone was softer. "Please don't make me drive all over your city trying to find this party. I will if you don't give me directions."

Girlfriend.

He'd never called her his before. She liked it. Okay, he could be her caveman.

Smiling, she gave him the address. Disconnecting, she hugged the phone to her chest, thrilled her *boyfriend* was coming to her aid.

"Who was that? Your guttersnipe boy toy?"

Greta stood, whirling to face Blake.

She idly wondered how he was able to track her like a bloodhound, yet she found it impossible to find Cindy. Maybe she should ask Blake for help. He seemed to have a knack for finding people. Even those who preferred to be invisible.

Chapter Fifteen

Striding up the long brick pathway, Jacob no longer wondered why Greta couldn't find her sister. In fact, he worried he might have the same problem with Greta. The Glengarry house and property were enormous. A small city could've fit comfortably inside its perimeters, and tonight there was enough people to fill said city.

At the front door, he walked in without knocking, figuring no one would hear it over the pounding music. He stopped and took in the massive foyer and staircase to his right. To his left was a set of open double doors leading into what appeared to be a small cinema, and straight ahead was a huge living room. People were everywhere. Some glanced at him with curiosity but didn't approach, and none of them were Greta.

How in the hell am I going to find her?

Jacob had no idea where to start, and decided to go straight. He pulled his cell from his front pocket and tried to call her, though he doubted she'd hear it. Music was pounding from speakers in a room he walked by, and it sounded like a concert was taking place in the backyard.

He was right and hung up when it went to her voicemail. Going farther into the house, he passed a curving staircase, and a woman stopped him.

No surprise. He didn't exactly fit in with the high-end crowd. Most of the men were dressed in oxford shorts and polos. His jeans, faded blue T-shirt, and motorcycle boots didn't quite fit the scene.

He glanced at the woman's hand resting on his arm. Her middle finger sported a huge emerald ring. His gaze moved to her face. She didn't appear angry, merely curious.

"Hi, handsome. You lost?" She was watching him like he was a foreign animal she wanted to possess.

He wasn't interested. "You know where I can find Greta Meier?"

A small smile played at the corners of her mouth. "I'm Lily. What's your name?"

"Jacob. Do you know Greta?"

She nodded. "Yes, I know her. Better question, *why* don't I know you? I know everyone around here, yet I don't recall ever meeting you. I'd remember."

Jacob tried to swallow his annoyance. The way she was ogling him, he didn't have to worry she'd kick him out as a gatecrasher. However, she was more interested in flirting than helping.

"I'm not from around here," he hedged.

"I figured as much. What are you to Greta?"

The woman's lack of help was rubbing on the edge of his already frayed nerves. It had taken almost an hour to get to Petite Bois, and the entire time he pictured Blake's hands on Greta. "Dammit, lady, she's— I'm dating her." He almost said girlfriend but remembered Greta's heavy pause when he said it earlier on the phone. He kept forgetting they were supposed to be a fling, nothing more. "Do you know where she is or not?"

Seemingly oblivious to his rudeness, she grinned. "Really? You and Greta. Huh. You don't look her type."

"Yeah, yeah." Like he hadn't heard that before or thought it himself. "Listen, you know where I can find her or not? It's fucking important."

Giving up on this woman being any help, he stepped around her. He didn't have time to play silly games. Greta had sounded anxious when they talked, and this woman was wasting precious minutes.

"Lower your hackles, handsome. Follow me. I'll show you where I last saw her."

About damn time.

She led him through a house that was more castle than home. "Now I understand why Greta's been giving Blake the cold shoulder this evening." She glanced at him, giving him another suggestive smile.

Man, this lady's flirting is subtle as a hammer to the head.

"She gives him the cold shoulder because he's a dickhead." Jacob wished she'd walk faster.

"Please tell me how you really feel." She laughed, opening a set of French doors that led to a huge terrace. "She was here, oh, twenty minutes ago. She's wearing a powder blue dress."

Lily turned back toward the house. "Good luck."

"Thanks," he replied absently, scanning the crowd and immediately spotting Greta.

She looked good, *damn* good.

Damn, her dress was made to worship her body. It stopped a couple of inches above her knees, flaring in soft folds, showcasing her mile-long, slim legs. The top was mouthwatering, with its fitted lace and a deep plunging neckline.

Less captivating and more infuriating was Blake. He was in Greta's personal space.

Fucker.

Jacob pounded toward them, stopping next to Greta. He kissed her neck, positioning his back to Blake, facing Greta and pretending the other man was invisible.

He slid his hand in hers, entwining their fingers. "Ready to leave?"

Blake shoved Jacob's shoulder. "Who the hell let you in? This isn't some ghetto party. You won't find anyone around here carrying forties in a paper bag."

The guy sounded and smelled like a wino but had the balls to call him trash.

Jacob faced Blake, moving Greta behind him, using his body as a wall. He examined the other man and laughed. If it weren't for the fancy clothes and haircut, Blake could be any drunk on 8 Mile.

"What is funny, reprobate?" he growled, his hands curling into fists.

"You, dickhead. I've never met anyone so far up their own ass." Dismissing Blake, Jacob asked Greta, "Do you want to leave?"

Before she could answer, Blake reached for Greta. "Why are you lowering yourself to him?"

She moved from his hold. Jacob still had to resist the urge to not bash in Blake's perfect teeth.

Instead, Jacob tightened his hold on Greta, willing himself to keep calm. "Come on. Let's go."

Blake blocked their exit, sputtering, "My father is one of the top attorneys in Metro Detroit, hell in all of Michigan. My grandfather and his father were business tycoons. The Kingstine name is synonymous with wealth and power. What does he and his family name have to offer? A discount at the local bowling alley."

Is this guy for real?

Jacob gave Blake a cocky smile. "Well, the men in my family are known for their great sense of humor…and their big dicks. That might be of importance."

Blake's face turned molten red, and a strangled choke escaped. This guy was too easy. It almost wasn't fun. *Almost.*

"If she's been debased by you," Blake grated, "she's nothing more than a cheap whore."

Jacob's humor fled. "You best shut your mouth, or you'll leave here broken and bleeding."

"I'll say as I please, and as I see it, she's a—"

The rest of his words were cut off when Jacob's fist connected with Blake's jaw. He stumbled back and fell on his ass.

Damn. That felt good.

It took all of his self-control not to kick the bastard while he was down. Instead, Jacob hunkered and whispered in the other man's ear, "You want to know if she has lowered herself to the likes of me? She has. But don't worry, I made sure she enjoyed every minute of it. Multiple times."

Blake mumbled a garbled response. Jacob ignored it and stood.

Disregarding the gathering crowd, he walked to Greta and offered his hand. "Shall we?"

She took his hand, appearing a little stunned. "What did you say to him? His expression was homicidal."

"You don't want to—"

Something heavy slammed into him and agony exploded along his back, forcing him to his knees. He tried to get up, was hit again. The blow knocked him forward, palms slamming on the cement.

A deep ache spread, making it difficult to breathe. Fast footfalls and Greta's distant shriek had self-preservation taking over. Pushing past the pain, he rolled to his side as a foot swung past his head.

Blake's shout of rage echoed through the yard and he swung back for another kick. This time Jacob was ready. He grabbed Blake's ankle and twisted. Bellowing in pain, he dropped like a marionette with its strings cut.

Ignoring the agony radiating from his back, Jacob rose to his knees and popped two rapid punches to the other man's face. He jumped up and planted a hard kick into Blake's side and another to his thigh.

As he swung back, Greta's voice broke through his anger and pain. He lowered his foot and turned to her.

Her hazel eyes were desperate, full of tears threatening to fall. "Jacob, please stop."

She pulled his rage in check. He glanced at Blake. He was no longer a threat.

Straightening, Jacob took a lung full of air and released it through his nose. It helped expel the rest of his rage. "Do you want to find your sister before we leave?"

"No. Let's go. I want to leave."

He wrapped an arm around her waist, and the crowd parted as they exited. The music started again, and they made their way through the house, loud enough to cut off the possibility of conversation. Also, Greta's tight-lipped expression radiated, don't-talk- to me vibes.

He held his tongue until they were away from the monstrous house. With each step, the silence became too much. "I didn't mean to lose my temper..." he hedged.

The prick deserved everything he got.

"I know. I understand." She offered a shaky smile. "I can't believe he hit you with that wooden board."

"That's what it was?"

No wonder it hurt.

"Yes, some floating table for the pool." She rubbed his back, and he tried not to flinch. Damn, he was going to have one hell of a bruise come morning.

She must've caught his cringe because her hand fell away, and she muttered an apology. "Anyway, I'm not upset with you. The fallout from the fight worries me."

He was confused. "From your friend? The one having the party? Why, because of a small fight? Nothing was even broken, well, besides the table thingy, and maybe Blake's nose."

Jacob couldn't help smirking at the last part. She didn't return his smile, instead anxiety pulled at the corners of her mouth, as if a million worries were stacking up in her crowded, beautiful mind. She was such an anxious woman. Why?

"He's who I'm worried about, not Jane. Blake's vindictive. His ego won't be able to handle what happened. My rejection and him losing a fight, and with an audience. He'll want retribution."

Jacob waved this off. He'd dealt with his fair share of arrogant pricks; Blake's hatred wasn't a concern. What the asshole might've done to Greta was what ate away at Jacob's stomach lining. "Was he harassing you all night? Why didn't you call me sooner?"

"Because I had it under control" Greta squeezed his hand, probably trying to reassure him. "I'd avoided him most of the night. He was only a problem right before I called you. When I went into the house to find Cindy."

Jacob froze mid-step. "Wait. Did he touch you? If he hurt you in any way—"

He whirled around, heading back in the direction of the house. Forget a broken nose; he was going to break Blake's legs.

Hell, I'm going to castrate the sonofabitch.

"Hey, no. It's fine. Nothing serious." Greta hooked a hand around his elbow. "He got a little pushy. He gets like that when he's had too much to drink. I've learned to deal with it. I know how to handle him."

Jacob stopped, stunned. "Greta. Why the fuck would you have to *deal with it*? He's in the wrong."

"He doesn't know what he's doing when he drinks."

"Are you defending him?" What had her ex done to her confidence?

"No." She cupped the sides of his cheeks with her hands. "Blake ruined my evening. Please don't let him spoil the rest of the night."

She stood on her toes, kissing him. The touch of her lips and soft hands soothed him, but her argument niggled, refusing to leave altogether.

"Fine," he exhaled and pointed. "I'm parked there."

Greta followed the direction and whooped. "You brought the motorcycle. This night *is* looking up."

"I see how it is," he teased, his bad mood lifting. "Spending time with me for my bike. I feel used."

He peered at her outfit. He was an asshole. "Too bad I hadn't considered you might wear a dress. I was in a hurry, and Will's car was blocking in my truck."

"Don't worry." She kissed him lightly on the cheek. "I'll tuck it under me."

Wrapping his arms around her, he pulled her flush against him. "You're definitely my kind of woman. Sexy, smart, and resourceful."

His hands ran from the dip in her back to her neck, before burying in her silky locks. He kissed her. She eagerly accepted his lips and pressed her body firmly against his.

Every part of him hardened with desire. He wanted to kiss her until she was panting and pliant to his touch.

He needed to stop before he couldn't and stepped to the bike. Grabbing his extra helmet from his backpack, he handed it to Greta. He stored the bag in the bike's side compartment. As she fiddled with the straps, he wanted to move back in, to kiss her. Have her body against his.

He swung a leg over the bike and sat, reaching for his helmet and adjusting its fit. Seconds later, there was a slight dip, and Greta settled in behind him. Her arms snaked around, and she slid against his back, her intoxicating scent of lilac and woman filled him.

The ride was going to be sweet agony.

"Where am I taking you?" He sincerely hoped she wouldn't say home.

"Would you mind if we rode around for a bit? We're supposed stay at my mother's tonight, but I don't want to arrive without Cindy."

Two grown-ass women fearing their mother's disapproval was ridiculous, and he figured any trouble Cindy landed in was her own damn fault.

At least her disregard for Greta's well-being had resulted in him having more time with her, so he kept his opinions to himself. "Do you have your helmet strapped and ready?"

When she answered she was, he maneuvered the bike onto the quiet street.

After riding around for a while, he worried her thin summer dress was no match against the chilly night air. "Are you cold or hungry? We could stop at a diner," he asked when they were on a side road, and he could be heard above the engine.

"I'm fine against you. You give off heat like a furnace."

"Now I'm kinda wishing the weather was colder, forcing you to snuggle in more."

Laughing, she somehow managed to move in closer. "Let's ride around a bit longer. Maybe Cindy will call soon."

"Okay. I should feel the phone go off. I put it in my back pocket." Earlier, he'd taken it before setting her purse in one of the saddlebags.

"Hmm, another reason to press in closer. Your body against mine and my vibrating phone…would be exquisite," she murmured huskily, her breath tickling the back of his neck.

This woman was going to be the death of him. "Keep talking, and this is going to be a hazardous ride indeed."

"You can handle it." She ran her hands under his shirt.

"Jesus…Greta." Weeks of tentative kisses and touches had left him in a constant state of arousal.

Now, with her hands dipping along the waist of his jeans, he wondered if it was possible to combust from lust spontaneously.

Chapter Sixteen

Greta had always regarded herself as more of a wine and roses kind of woman. Not someone aroused by motorcycles and leather. However, this particular man, and his bike, was an aphrodisiac.

She strummed her fingertips along his abs, reveling in the tightening of his muscles under her touch. She traveled lower, along the zipper of his jeans. He said her name, and it sounded like a prayer.

Around Jacob, her inhibitions fell away, and she didn't have the strength of character to care.

They stopped at a traffic light, and Jacob twisted around. "If you don't stop, I'm going to pull off at the nearest dark parking lot and take you over this bike."

"Promise?" She traced her tongue along the shell of his ear, relishing the way he shivered and groaned.

Her behavior was scandalizing, but she couldn't seem to stop. Jacob heated her like no other man ever had. He woke her desires, made her pulse pound and her lust bloom.

"Something I can help you with?" he snarled.

Greta jerked back, his sharp voice whipping her from her lust-induced haze. She was mortified to find a car filled with teenage boys idling next to them, ogling her and grinning.

So much for assuming the road would be empty this time of night.

"Keep your eyes on the fucking road." Jacob's menacing tone had the boys whipping their heads around, staring straight ahead, their smirks dropping.

The light turned green, and they sped away. Her humiliation deepened as the tail lights vanished into the horizon. Here she was, sitting on a motorcycle with her dress hiked almost to her panties, practically fondling a man.

In public.

What happened to her ingrained respectability? What was it about Jacob that made her forget it?

The continuation of the ride was PG and silent. Greta wondered if he was angry with her behavior.

Blake would have been furious at the public embarrassment. Would Jacob behave the same, lambast her with a sharp tongue, cutting with cruel words?

Her gut clenched at the idea. She didn't want things between them to sour already. Why did she have to go and screw everything up? She wanted this summer with him. Now it might be ending before it even had begun.

They hit an uneven road, and the jostling shook Greta. She swallowed back the lump forming in her throat and took in the new surroundings. They'd left the main road and were now on a gravel driveway, heading toward a squat building. It appeared deserted.

"What's this place?" She was proud her voice sounded steady, unlike her whirling, worried mind.

"An old veteran's lodge. The building's nothing special. The treat is the park behind the building. It is incredible. Thought we could wait for your sister there." His answer was mild enough, but she caught an underlying tightness.

Anger?

She cleared her throat. "Isn't it closed?"

"What? Did you use your daily dose of recklessness on the ride here?" He drove them around to the back of the building. "Don't worry. The guard never comes outside. I used to sneak back here all the time with my buddies to party."

Curiosity ebbed away a breath of her anxiety, and she asked, "How do you know it's the same security guy? Maybe there's a new one and he actually does his job."

"It's him." Jacob motioned with his head, nodding to a lone rusted four-door in the parking lot. "Same car."

He maneuvered them past the lot and onto a sidewalk. Once they were past the old squat building, the park came into view.

Jacob hadn't been kidding. The place was enchanting. The full moon reflected the water off Lake St. Clair, and dewy grass gave the place an almost dreamlike quality, both romantic and eerie. Even with her anxiety swirling in her gut, this patch of summer serenity calmed some of her worry.

He parked and shut off the bike. Greta scooted off, careful of the hot pipes and his eyes. She wasn't ready to face his disappointment.

Fidgeting with the hem of her dress, she tried to smooth the wrinkles and her agitation. "I'm sorry about the way I acted. I was inappropriate," she mumbled in the direction of her feet.

When he didn't say anything, she peeked at him. Her breath caught.

There was no anger, only hunger.

"Hell, Greta, you can be inappropriate with me anytime you want...though there are consequences."

"Consequences?" Her heart skipped a beat.

"Yes, consequences." He took a quick step forward. In an instant, his lips were on hers, hot and insistent.

Greta's knees went weak. He explored her mouth, and only the incredible sensation of his lips and caresses existed. She was adrift in ecstasy and didn't register his hands under her skirt until he'd slid her panties halfway down her thighs.

She broke the kiss, but didn't move away. "What are you doing?" Panic and excitement ran through her. "What if someone sees us?"

"Too far from the road. Frankly, it's difficult to care right now." He nuzzled her neck but had stilled his hands. "Do you want me to stop?"

She shook her head no, terrified and more than a tad aroused.

He dropped to his knees, taking her panties with him. Grasping her thighs, he shoved her dress to her waist and took her into his mouth.

Whatever anxiety remained, fled. Her head fell back, and she buried her hands in his hair, pleading incoherently.

He laughed against her heated skin. "You want me to stop?"

The vibration, along with his tongue was magical. "No."

The rapidity and the voracity of her climax was so intense she would've collapsed to the ground if not for Jacob's strong arms holding her. Even as her spasms rocked through her, he continued working her with his mouth and tongue until every shock wave receded and began to build again.

Though, before she could go over the edge again, he shifted, kissing a trail from the inside of her thigh to her waist. He straightened and rearranged her dress back in place. Leaning forward, he whispered in her ear, "I've wanted, no needed, to taste you again since our first time."

He smelled of lust, sex, and man. The urge to purr and rub herself against him was fierce.

"Then why stop?" The demand fell from her lips without embarrassment or shame.

"Because," he growled. "I've fantasized about doing this since our first motorcycle ride."

He turned her, placing her hands on the still-warm leather seat. The position had her bent, with his front against her back. He trailed his hands along her arms, down her sides to her thighs. Once there, he slowly bundled her skirt in his fists.

He leaned back. His groan of appreciation and his big hands caressing her naked bottom, further inflamed her lust.

There was the rasp of his zipper then the tear of a condom wrapper.

"Are you okay with this?" he asked.

"Yes...please, now." She shifted back and rubbed against him, leaving no question as to how bad she wanted him.

He pushed roughly inside her, burying himself deep and groaning in obvious satisfaction. "Are...are you okay?"

"Better than okay." He filled her in a way that sent ripples of pleasure to her toes and all the way to the tips of her ears.

His thrusts were deep and perfect. "Fuck, Greta, you feel good. I'm not going to last." His breathing had become shallow.

"Neither will I...please...hard." She needed more than gentleness but found it difficult to articulate her need.

He seemed to understand, slamming deep inside her with a force that reverberated throughout her body, taking her where she needed to go.

Her climax built rapidly, and when he slid a hand from her waist to massage between her legs, she shattered into a million pieces.

He groaned against her neck and stiffened, his orgasm meeting hers. He shouted her name into the night, and it was music to her body and soul.

Chapter Seventeen

Time passed, and nothing existed for Jacob but Greta's body and a crushing urge to never let her go. Still, his heavy weight couldn't be comfortable for her. He reluctantly pulled away. He kissed along her spine, over the smooth material of her clothing. Yanked and fastened his jeans before readjusting her dress and covering her glorious body.

He disposed of the condom and returned, enveloping her in his arms. "You are the sexiest woman alive."

"More like indecent," she whispered, peeking at him through lashes, her cheeks flushing a charming red.

He ran his thumb across her cheek then kissed it softly. "I find you incredibly sexy when you're indecent. Hell, you're sexy when you're decent." He took her hand and they walked to the gazebo near the lake.

It was true. Everything Greta did was seductive.

From the way she chewed her bottom lip when concentrating, to the sexy sounds she made when turned on.

Hell, he could live just off her smile for the rest of his life.

His heart skipped a beat in panic, picturing his father's haunted eyes and broken spirit after Mom's death. It made Jacob want to run from anything too deep.

Greta squeezed his hand. "Are you okay? You tensed."

He nodded, swallowing his nerves and going to the picnic table inside the gazebo. He scooted to the center of the table and motioned for her to sit between his legs. "I'm sorry our first time together again was like this. My plan was more along the lines of candles and a soft bed. Not to take you roughly over the back of my Triumph."

Smiling, she climbed up to sit with him. "Yet, you had a condom." She rested her back against his chest. "As I recall, last time you weren't prepared."

"Sure, I had my plan, but that doesn't mean I haven't dreamt about getting you alone for a while," he murmured into her hair. It smelled like night and flowers. "I learned my lesson. I now follow the Boy Scout motto: Be prepared."

She laughed, cuddling into him. "I don't think condoms and sex are what the Scouts had in mind with their motto." Twisting around, she asked. "Out of curiosity, how long have you been waiting and hoping?"

"Hmm." He squinted, pretending to consider. "When I first saw you in Swift's conference room wearing a sexy, prim suit. No wait that isn't true. I've wanted you since leaving your mother's guest house."

"That long, huh?" She twisted around and kissed him. "You certainly know how to make a girl feel desired."

"You're definitely desired." He kissed her again, deepening it. They'd made love moments ago, yet he wanted her again.

Greta stared at his chest. "Do you, um, happen to have my panties? I'm feeling a bit exposed."

Damn. She remembered.

He bumped his ass up and pulled them from his back pocket. "I was hoping you would forget them. I wanted to keep them. A memento for when I'm dreaming of this later tonight."

Even in the near dark, he could see her face redden. He ran his nose and lips gently along her cheek, enjoying the warmth and softness. "You have the most erotic blush."

"I don't know about erotic," she paused, "although, around you, I can't suppress my lascivious side. I honestly don't know what's happened to me. I have been with only one other man. I enjoyed the sex, but I didn't lose myself. Nothing was this intense."

Blake was her first and only other lover. Poor woman. "Greta, it's us—together."

Her eyes widened. "Really? It's the same for you?"

"Yes. Why are you surprised?"

"I figured you've had many women... and well, I'm inexperienced..."

"I haven't had *that* many. Besides, it's not experience. It's chemistry. And us, together, is explosive."

He'd never craved any of his past girlfriends like he did Greta. And not just sexually, he wanted her around all the time, to talk and laugh with, along with making love.

She rested her head against his chest. He enfolded her in his arms, wishing he could wrap her up and take her everywhere with him. "Are you cold?"

"A little."

"Could you scoot off me? I'll be right back."

When she shifted to the side, he shuffled off the table and ran to his bike. He removed a hoodie from one of the saddlebags and came back.

Greta was shimmying into her panties. The sight made him

stumble. Watching the silk slide up her long smooth legs and the moon's light kiss her soft curves was almost enough to make his knees buckle.

She offered a shy smile, and damn, he did go weak in the knees. Shit. He had it bad for this woman.

He swallowed his chaotic emotions, returning to her and offering her the sweater. "Here. Put this on." He climbed back, opening his arms and motioning to her. "I'll keep you warm."

She slid her arms into his hoodie and clambered to him, leaning back into his chest and snuggling between his thighs. He loved her body against his, and the way her scent filled him. He breathed her in, sighing deeply.

The inky night, along with the waves lapping against the shore of Lake St. Clair, was mesmerizing. He was content, at peace, something he hadn't felt in years, and it had nothing to do with the beautiful night.

It was Greta, in his arms and in his life. His rapidly deepening feelings alarmed him, but nevertheless, he wanted the night to last forever.

"Sleep, it's late," he whispered. "I'll wake you when your sister calls. Rest. I'll watch over you."

~ * ~

"A secluded park in the middle of the night. Really? Is it even safe here? Why didn't you take her to your place?"

Cindy's accusatory rapid-fire questions, mixed with her blatant disdain, managed to muddle through Greta's dozing mind. She reluctantly rose and twisted around to take Jacob's measure. Anger radiated off him in waves so thick she could almost touch it.

"She's a helluva lot safer with me at a secluded park than with you at a crowded party," he shot back.

She needed to end this before it exploded; however before Greta could speak, Cindy raised a hand to them. "Yeah. Maybe you're right. I do feel awful about not hearing my phone."

Greta was shocked her; her sister even sounded contrite. It didn't happen often.

Jacob sounded less impressed. "You should." His tone was cold as the icy waters of Lake St. Clair. "You're the reason we're here. She didn't want to go home without you. We've been waiting around for you to finally notice your hundred missed calls."

"Yes, I know." Cindy glanced away, biting on her bottom lip.

"After everything she went through, her primary concern was you. And now you show up with your judgments. Your contempt," Jacob scoffed, his tone harsh and biting.

Greta rested a hand on his bicep, hoping to calm him. She didn't want Cindy to treat Jacob rudely. At the same time, her sister didn't need to feel guilty for tonight's earlier disaster. "Let it go, Jacob. Please."

"Let me guess, Cindy not answering her phone is your fault. Just like Blake isn't accountable for his actions because he decided to drink."

Greta swallowed her anger. He wasn't being fair, but she didn't want to fight. Not after the incredible night they'd shared.

Instead, she studied her sister and regretted Jacob's harsh words. Cindy was staring at her feet, toeing an exposed nail on the wooden floor of the gazebo. No doubt, Jacob's accusations had wounded her.

She caught Greta's gaze. Nope. She'd read the situation wrong. Of course Cindy didn't care what opinion Jacob had of her. She rarely cared what others thought of her. Greta envied this about her sister. Mischief overflowed in Cindy's eyes, and her frown had become a broad, troublemaking smile.

Oh, great.

"Yes. I heard. A couple of the partygoers mentioned there was an altercation between you and Blake…"

Jacob shrugged. "Yeah. So?"

"I saw Blake. You did a number on him. Watching him walk with a limp and two black eyes was *extremely* gratifying." Cindy paused, studying Jacob. "He's a spiteful man. He will try to get you back."

Cindy was full of surprises. First, an actual apology, and now, concern for Jacob.

Greta glanced to the sky. *Yup. Full moon.* Twisting around, she faced Jacob. "I told you…"

Another unconcerned shrug. He wasn't grasping the seriousness of the situation. "Whatever. Blake can come after me, and I'll kick his ass again."

"Oh, he won't use his fists," Cindy interjected. "He'll fight in a way he knows how to win. The rumor's he's talking about pressing charges."

"He was sporting for a fight." Greta scooted off the table, her gut twisting in knots.

She never should've let Jacob pick her up from the party. Heck, probably never should have agreed to start dating him in the first place, knowing Blake would start trouble.

She was making their lives more complicated. And for what? A summer fling?

Eyeing Jacob, she recalled their night together and the laughter filled weeks with him. Maybe he was worth it.

He turned, resting his feet on the bottom bench, all nonchalance. However, when he stretched she caught him trying to conceal a wince.

She scooted closer and placed a hand on his knee. "You should have told me your back's bothering you."

"I'm fine. It only hurts when I move." His eyes gleamed with humor, but it did nothing to alleviate Greta's concern.

"Anyway," Cindy dragged out the word, turning their attention back to her. "He's telling people you crashed the party and attacked him for no reason."

Greta couldn't help rolling her eyes. "Anyone who witnessed the fight will say different, and Jane won't care that Jacob was there once I tell her he was with me."

"I know. I'm only letting you know what Blake's been saying. He's furious and wants revenge. He's found people willing to say Jacob threw the first punch." Cindy faced Jacob. "Did you?"

"Yes. The prick had it coming. I swear, the way he was talking about Greta…"

She held up her hands. "I have no doubt he deserved it. However, if I were you, I'd stay away from him."

"Easier said than done. I'm still working through legal stuff at Swift. I'm not worried. I've dealt with assholes before."

Dread bloomed in Greta's stomach like a deadly disease. Jacob may have dealt with rude people before. However, Blake's vindictiveness was the stuff of legends.

Everything was getting more complicated by the minute. Sorting her overwhelming emotions toward Jacob was enough. Now added to the mix was the growing trouble with Blake.

She needed to focus on one crisis at a time. Right now, getting home at this late hour and avoiding her mother's questions was at the top. Staying with her parents, she'd regressed into a fifteen-year-old. It was humiliating.

Sighing, she stood. "It's late. We better get home. We'll worry about this tomorrow."

She slid an arm around Jacob's waist, and the three of them left the gazebo, walking toward the parking lot and Cindy's BMW. Jacob's motorcycle was parked on the grass and away from the harsh lights.

Looking at it brought back what they'd done against that bike. Greta was a little appalled at her behavior. Mostly she wanted to do it again.

Jacob squeezed her waist, glancing from the bike and back to her, wiggling his eyebrows suggestively. Her cheeks heated, while other parts warmed. The man was incorrigible.

He kissed her. A quick peck before focusing on Cindy, a teasing smirk playing over his handsome features. "Yeah, you'd better get Cinderella home; it's past midnight. We don't want your riches to turn into rags. You might end up living my life."

Cindy laughed, eyeing Jacob's Triumph. "In this fairy tale, do I get to keep the motorcycle?"

"Sure. The bike's yours. But so is the rest of my life. All of it. You'll be expected to clean your own house. Cook your own meals." He gasped in mock-horror.

Cindy's eyes widened, matching Jacob's feigned panic. "Okay, never mind." She grabbed Greta's hand, tugging her. "We need to get home! Pronto!"

Greta laughed at their antics. "Don't worry. You won't have to cook. His brother does most of the cooking, and I've heard it's excellent."

"This is true," Jacob admitted. "But you'll have to wash the dishes."

Cindy shook her head. "Nope. I don't like the sound of that either. My nails are too pretty to be marred by dishwater." She stopped. "Wait. How old is this brother of yours? Is he cute?"

"Oh, yes. He's hot, the pretty one," Jacob deadpanned.

Both women laughed, but Greta had to disagree. "No. I can't believe he's sexier than you."

Jacob smiled and kissed her solid on the lips. "I like your answer."

Greta had to hold back from skipping the rest of the way to the car. Her mood was buoyant as a helium balloon. She'd had spectacular outdoor sex, and her sister's aversion toward Jacob was fading.

All and all, a good night.

Except for Blake, whispered her damn anxiety, always ready to rain on her sunshine.

Jacob kissed her again, scattering the rolling clouds in her mind. "I have to go to the west side of the state tomorrow for work. I'll be stuck there a few days. I should be back no later than Wednesday. Want to meet for dinner?"

"Yes." She missed him already.

Though, knowing he wasn't going to stop at her work the next couple of days was a relief. She hoped keeping Jacob and Blake away from each other would help them cool off.

She wasn't sure if Blake would take the fight to Swift and prayed he wouldn't. There was enough talk surrounding her and Jacob. This would be the gasoline for the metaphorical smoldering fire.

Her father hadn't mentioned the gossip. It wouldn't last, not if Blake made a fuss. Then what? Would she stop seeing Jacob if her father demanded it?

The mere thought made her want to weep and crawl into Jacob's arms. She had the summer with him, and, darn it, she wanted every second of it.

She willed away her worries. Why keep picking and fretting with it until it bled? She'd never actually do anything. Her MO was to ignore a problem until it could no longer be avoided.

At Cindy's car, Jacob opened the passenger door for Greta. She kissed him lightly on the lips before scooting into the seat.

He sauntered to his bike. She couldn't help ogling his fine behind when he bent to put the key in the ignition. He straightened and waved at them before swinging a leg over the motorcycle. After adjusting his helmet, he righted the bike and roared from the lot.

After watching him disappear into the night, Greta turned to her sister, wondering why she hadn't started the car. Cindy was studying her as intently as Greta had been with Jacob moments ago.

Uh oh.

Now, having Greta's full attention, Cindy batted her lashes. "A secluded park, huh? In the middle of the night. I only have one question."

Here she was dreading Monday and a possible confrontation with her father or Blake. She should've been fearing the drive home with her sister.

"Go ahead, ask away." Greta groaned, knowing the question would be one she wouldn't want to answer.

Cindy gave a wicked smile. "The fight wasn't the only thing I learned this evening. Is it true, you know…about his family heritage?"

Chapter Eighteen

Blake walked into Charles Meier's office, trying to mask his dark mood. The last two days of healing hadn't improved his face, nor his disposition. Both eyes were an ugly mixture of purples and yellows, his nose was swollen and taped, and a big gash ran along his lower lip.

The cuts and bruises were a surface problem and would heal with time. What he needed to get a handle on was the rage eating him from the inside. There was no way that gutter punk was going to win.

Charles took in Blake, and his eyes widened. "Good God, what the hell happened to your face? Were you run over by a damn truck?"

"Looks worse than it feels." Not true, but he sure the hell wasn't going to admit it. He cut straight to the matter, having no desire to discuss the unfair fight. Had he been sober, things would have ended very differently. "Do you recall Mr. Grimm?"

"Yes. He's a hard man to forget. I don't have many clients his age with such a large customer base already established. Why?"

Blake choked down his resentment at the praise. Maybe Charles knew Grimm was fucking his daughter and needed to talk up the thug. Either way, time to get rid of him.

Blake wanted Jacob gone, preferably in a demeaning way. "A strong client base isn't everything. The man's a ticking time bomb. I'm afraid when he goes off, some of the blowback will land on Swift."

Charles clicked his pen a couple of times and exhaled. "Go ahead. Tell me why."

"My first worry is his sketchy background." Blake had spent most of his weekend examining Jacob's past. He'd discovered a great deal.

Charles cocked an eyebrow. "Your other worry?"

His lack of concern with Jacob's unsavory history surprised Blake. Deciding to move past it, for now, he tried another tactic. "I've been debating if I should mention this. Earlier, I visited the IT department. Grimm wasn't behaving in a professional manner with your daughter."

Sure, earlier was stretching things, since he'd caught them necking weeks ago. Not to mention, Greta hadn't seemed to mind. Those inconsequential details didn't matter. He needed to focus on the desired outcome—getting Grimm's dirty hands off *his* woman.

Six months they'd been apart, and what had she done? Without his guidance, she started running around with the dogs. Charles should be begging him to take his daughter back.

Instead, he asked mildly, "I've heard talk… Are you telling me he's harassing Greta?"

"Well…" He sighed, hoping he sounded regretful. "I didn't want to bring unwanted attention to Greta."

Charles's brows furrowed, causing a deep line between his eyes. "She would not mind. Especially if this man was mistreating her."

"I'm not sure how Greta felt," Blake hedged.

"What do you mean?" Annoyance was beginning to edge into Charles's voice.

Damn it.

"I don't know if she did or did not welcome his advances." Blake sat in the empty seat directly in front of Charles and leaned forward. "Does it matter? The incident took place here. Such levels of unprofessionalism, mixed with his background, should be enough to release him from his contract, don't you agree?"

Annoyance flashed across Charles's features, and Blake wondered was it for him or Jacob. "Listen, Blake, I'm displeased with the gossip surrounding my daughter and Grimm, but I do not understand what this has to do with Swift or me personally. Grim hasn't damaged the reputation of my business, and, from what I understand, Greta doesn't mind his attention. While I frown on office romances, and my daughter's actions surprise me, I don't forbid them in any hiring contracts."

"He was pawing at her, right there at her desk," Blake spat, his annoyance pouring out.

Charles cocked his head and lowered his voice. "Are you sure your grievances aren't for yourself and not Swift?"

Blake didn't like the pity in the other man's voice and was unable to keep his growing irritation in check. "Of course not. My worry is for this company and your daughter. She was my fiancée, and I want what's best for her. Grimm isn't it. And, Charles, he *won't* be one of your success stories. He's a no-rate from a screwed-up family. For God sakes, he even has a criminal record. Is this the type of person you want the company to represent? Or your daughter to be seen with?"

Charles's gazed narrowed. "Are you questioning *my* judgment, for *my* company? You're an excellent attorney, and I consider your family good friends, so I'll let your highly offensive attitude slide." He leaned forward, resting his arms on his desk. "Listen, Blake, it's best if you contend with legal matters and let me deal with selecting clients."

Blake was aghast at how bad this was going. He needed to switch strategies.

Now.

"I'm sorry. That came out wrong. I didn't mean to insinuate you don't know your business. I'm merely worried. I believe Grimm's using Greta because she's your daughter. Plus, I'm afraid his criminal past will hurt Swift. What if he has not left it behind? It wouldn't look good for the company, having such unsavory clients. I only want to protect it."

"Blake, you keep hinting to Grimm's past. Rest assured, I'm aware of it. I check potential clients' backgrounds. I'd be a fool not to. Hell, I probably know more about Jacob Grimm than his father."

Blake was astounded. "None of it bothers you? His past or the fact he's dating your daughter?"

"First he was assaulting her, and now they're dating." Charles massaged his temples. He lowered his hands and seemed to study Blake. "Listen, I hoped you and Greta would marry. I like you, and your family; however, who Greta dates isn't my choice. She's a grown woman and will make her own decisions."

"Even when her choice is a lowlife with a record?"

"Greta's a smart woman, and if she's dating him, then I trust he's a decent man. And no, his past doesn't bother me. What matters to me is how a person decides to fix their mistakes. From what I've gathered, Mr. Grimm's doing an outstanding job."

Charles turned back to the file on his desk. "Now, do you mind if we return to work and out of my daughter's personal life?"

"Yes, sir," Blake stood to leave, managing to hide his contempt.

He conceded outwardly, but the topic was far from finished. One way or another, he was getting rid of that white-trash thug.

Chapter Nineteen

"I don't know what time I'll be home," Jacob said into his truck's Bluetooth, while also scanning the parking lot at Swift. Finding an empty spot, he pulled in. "Listen, Will, I'm not by the house and have a couple stops to make. I have no idea what time I'll be home."

"You're not stopping by first? You've been gone all week. Why not drop off your crap and have something to eat?"

Jacob sighed and turned off the ignition, grabbing his cellphone on the passenger seat. He spoke into it, stepping from his black Ford F-150. "No. My drive back took me by Swift. I'm meeting Greta for lunch." After a slight pause, "Okay, Mommy?"

Will laughed. "Kiss my ass, little brother."

Jacob spotted Greta across the parking lot. She was sitting with another woman at a picnic table under a large oak tree.

He wondered again how he'd gotten so damn lucky.

They'd spent a fair amount of time together in the last month, yet he couldn't get enough of her. She was becoming close to a damn addiction, especially after Friday night.

He wanted her body, her laughter, her smile. All of her. He was beginning to understand why people took a risk on love.

"Grimm, you listening to me?" His brother squawked through the phone.

"Sorry. Yeah, I was listening," Jacob lied, readjusting the phone to his other ear.

He strode across the parking lot, to the picnic area. When he reached the two women, he noticed the lady with Greta was familiar but couldn't place her. He'd met too many new faces at Swift to recall everyone.

He nodded a hello in her direction and leaned in to give Greta a chaste kiss before returning to the phone call. "Will, I have to go."

"Are you with Greta now?"

"Yes, Mommy. You monitoring my love life too?" He peered down and caught Greta's curious gaze. "My brother," he whispered.

"No, asshole," Will continued. "I don't want to monitor your love life, except maybe to discover why any woman would want to date your sorry ass."

Jacob sat, straddling the bench, half listening to his brother. "Uh-huh, says the single guy. Anyway, I gotta go."

He slid his phone from his ear, but his brother kept talking. Putting it back he said, "What? I didn't plan on spending my lunch chatting with you. I'm hanging up."

"I did have a point asking if you were with Greta."

"Yeah. Are you going to get to it?" Jacob asked wearily, aware Greta was probably able to hear both sides of the conversation.

"Dad and I are thinking of having a barbeque on the Fourth of July. Inviting over some family and friends. You should ask Greta."

Jacob glanced at her. The way she was watching him, she'd heard the question. "Um, kinda last minute. I'm not sure if she has plans."

He wanted to give Greta an out in case she wasn't interested in getting to know his family and friends. Meeting them made things more serious, and she might not be interested. She said she wanted carefree and simple.

Hell, they had less than a month before she went home to Lansing. A three-hour drive was a lot of road between them.

"I'm free on the fourth," Greta said, cutting into Jacob's musings. He didn't detect any uncertainty in her reply.

"Did you hear?" he asked Will, pleasure and worry holding court in his head.

"Yes. Great! I can't wait to finally meet your mysterious girlfriend." Will disconnected without even a goodbye.

Jacob set his phone on the table, inwardly wincing. He was thrilled she was invested enough in him to want to spend a holiday together, along with those close to him.

He was worried meeting them would magnify their differences. He suspected barbeques in affluent Petite Bois were vastly different than those in Woodbridge Detroit.

"You okay with this? I don't want you to feel obligated to meet my family. You wanted to keep this simple." He pointed between them. "No pressure."

"Meeting your family wouldn't be an obligation. I'd love to."

He didn't know whether to be relieved or upset. Greta's answer didn't tell him where they stood. Did meeting his family and friends mean they were more or did she consider it simply a fun summer outing?

What he needed to do was to stop obsessing. In the end, it didn't matter. When summer was over, so were they. She'd head back to school, and he'd bury himself in work and try to forget her.

"Okay." Jacob rubbed his palms down the thighs of his slacks. "I hope they aren't too much for you."

"Don't be silly. I'm sure we'll get along great." She spoke with way more confidence than he felt.

She motioned a hand toward the vaguely familiar woman sitting opposite. "This is Anna. Anna Kincade."

He leaned across the table and shook Anna's hand, trying to remember where they'd met. She was maybe fifteen years his senior, attractive with short stylish dark hair and stunning sharp facial features.

"Hi, I'm Jacob. We've met, haven't we?"

"Yes. About a week back. You dropped off paperwork for Mr. Kingstine."

"Sorry. I recognized you but couldn't place where we met. I didn't linger at his office. Everyone was a blur." He chuckled.

"I'd wondered. Blake was in such a foul mood after receiving your papers. Now, I understand. Next time you plan on stopping by, could you warn me? I'll take the day off," Anna finished with a dramatic sigh.

"Sure thing," Jacob promised, amused.

He turned back to Greta and peered at the brown paper bag next to her. He sincerely hoped there was a sandwich in it for him. Breakfast hadn't happened today. He needed food.

Following his gaze, she pulled out a sandwich wrapped in butcher's paper. Thanking her, he ripped it open and took a huge bite of his Reuben. After chewing and swallowing, he asked the question that had worried him all weekend. "Any problems because of Friday?"

Her lips folded into a thin line. "I was called into my father's office and given a lecture regarding unprofessionalism in the workplace."

This caught him off guard. What did a fight at a party have to do with work?

Before Jacob could ask, Anna cut in. "What happened Friday?" She rubbed her hands together and waggled her brows. "Do you have good office gossip?"

"Have you seen Kingstine's face recently?" Jacob tried to hold back his smirk. He failed.

"No. I'm working with Mr. Meier this week…"

"Jacob and Blake had a small altercation. Not at work, on Friday," Greta began.

A slight glint of annoyance bubbled in his chest. The most important detail was the fight didn't take place at work. Really? Not the harassment, or the underhanded way Blake attacked from behind. Sometimes her priorities baffled him.

"Anyway," she continued, "now Blake's furious and making trouble."

"Like a whiny little bitch," Jacob muttered.

"Anyway," Greta said loudly, over his grousing and Anna's laughter. "I don't want to talk about him." She crumpled her sandwich papers and reached for her purse. "Jacob, would you do me a huge favor?"

"Sure, what do you need?"

"My stepfather's birthday is around the corner, and I was wondering if you could fix his Rolex? The watch was his grandfather's. Nigel loves the thing." She dug around in an oversized leather bag. "For some reason, it stopped working last year. He'd taken it to a local jewelry store. They weren't able to fix it."

"What your stepfather needs is a specialist, a horologist. I'll take a look at it, though, no promises. Watches aren't my specialty. I typically work on bigger items."

"I won't be disappointed. You're one of the smartest men I know. I'm sure you can fix anything."

"Flattery will get you everywhere." He grinned. Her concrete belief in him made him light as air. He leaned in to kiss her cheek. "When can I have it? You said his birthday is near so the sooner the better."

"Funny you should say that…" She smiled sheepishly, pulling a watch from her purse.

"Oh hell," he choked in disbelief, taking the Rolex. "This is a Zerographe. Did you seriously toss a three hundred-thousand-dollar watch into your purse?"

"It's too big for my wrist," she replied defensively.

Rich people!

"That's your excuse?" Holding in his scowl at her glibness was difficult.

"If you're worried, put the thing on." She grabbed his wrist, rolling the sleeve of his button-down, and sliding on the Rolex. She leaned back and examined him. "Fits perfect, even better than on Nigel. I always thought the thing was too big for his slender wrist."

"Thing," Jacob scoffed, trying to get over the fact she'd thrown the Zerographe into her purse like a cheap Timex. "It's nice. You think your step-father will want it back?" he joked.

She laughed. "No. Go ahead, keep it."

"Any other riches in there for me?" Anna pretended to peer into Greta's purse.

"Only if you consider breath mints or Christian Louboutin lipstick treasures."

"What color's the lipstick?"

"Petal Rose."

"Tempting." Anna smiled, wrapping the remains of her lunch. "I'd better get back. Swanson's two-week notice expired on Friday, and your father hasn't found a replacement. I've been drafted as his assistant until a new one is hired." She stood.

"Who's covering for you in the legal department?" Greta asked.

"One of the paralegals is taking care of the simpler work and sending me the important stuff. Needless to say, I'm swamped."

"I bet. Let me know if there's anything I can do to help."

"Thanks. I appreciate it. Nice meeting you officially, Jacob."

"Same here." He rose and shook her hand again.

After Anna left, he sat and asked the question he couldn't earlier. "What'd your father say? Why would he give two shits about Friday night?"

Greta squirmed. "He didn't. His problem was more with me dating a client."

Cement gargoyles sat on Jacob's chest. "He had no idea we're seeing each other?" He'd told his brother and father almost immediately.

"Well…no."

"You're staying with him, right?"

She gave a hesitant nod.

What the hell?

Trying to swallow back his anger and hurt, he said, "I get we've only been dating a short while, but we've spent a shit ton of time together. How could he not know?"

Fidgeting and not meeting his gaze, she sighed. "I don't know. We don't talk much."

Fuck this! "Are you embarrassed of me?"

He liked Greta. A lot. However, she wasn't going to make him feel like shit because of his zip code.

Her gaze finally met his; the corners of her mouth pulled down in a frown. "No. I'm not. I avoided the topic of us dating because Father doesn't approve of work flings. It's easier not to mention us."

There it was again. That word. *Fling.*

It wounded him to know his growing feelings were one-sided. The hurt stoked his irritability. "I'm nothing more than an itch you needed to scratch before going back to men born with silver spoons up their asses?"

"Didn't you tell me you wanted to keep things simple?" She sounded both annoyed and apologetic. "My father knowing would be the opposite of simple."

She was right. And he was being an asshole.

He ran a thumb along a split in the picnic table's bench, working to release his anger. Once under control, he focused on her. "I'm sorry. I'm being a shit."

He had no right to blame her because he was starting to feel more than lust, and she clearly didn't. It stung, but he had to accept it.

Greta nodded, seeming to accept his apology. She scooted forward, pressing her soft lips against his. The sensation sent a buzz through his blood and burned away most of his frustration.

"I've missed you," she said between kisses.

Her taste made him forget he was hungry. His body shifted to another sort of craving. "Mmm, this is what I wanted for lunch." He deepened the kiss.

His stomach growled, sounding like a trapped bear.

Greta laughed and scooted back. "Your lips might be hungry for me. Your stomach would rather have a sandwich."

"You taste better."

She touched her pink cheeks with her palms. "You love making me blush, don't you?"

"Yes."

He took her hand, placing her fingertips in his mouth and biting gently. He ran his tongue along the tops of them. She stilled, sucking in a quick gasp of air and studied his lips. He reluctantly let go.

He loved heating her up. The Catch-22 was her arousal stoked his own and made his control slip. His arms itched to pull her onto his lap, have her flush against him and ply her with kisses and caresses. Even thinking about it made him hard, but Greta wanted to keep work and play separate.

"One of these days I'm going to find what makes you blush and use it without mercy," she said.

"Good luck. Without a sense of modesty, what could make me blush?" he asked with complete confidence.

"Everyone has something. I'll find it." Her smile was full of challenge.

He loved this side of her.

Hell, what didn't he like when it came to her?

He wolfed down the rest of his sandwich in a couple of bites. After wiping his mouth, he drew her closer, glancing at the office windows. The blinds were closed.

Good.

He nipped her ear. "Are you busy after work?"

To his delight, she trembled against his touch and leaned in for more. "Yes. I made plans to meet Lily for dinner. You free tomorrow?" She twisted her neck, giving him her lips instead of her ear.

He took full advantage, slanting his mouth on hers and groaning when she slid her tongue along his bottom lip.

"Damn, Greta, way to keep it professional." Blake's voice rang out, killing the moment.

Again.

Jacob cursed. Blake was an annoying gnat that kept returning. Circling, refusing to leave.

"Do you even have an actual job, or do you only hang around here to stalk Greta?" Jacob grated between clenched teeth.

Blake's focus was solely on Greta. "Let me know when you're done rolling around in the muck." He sniffed, as if smelling something rotten. "Though, at this point, who knows if his filth will ever wash off you."

"Do you enjoy me kicking your ass?" Jacob peered up, placing a hand over his brow to block the sun, more annoyed at the interruption than the insults directed at him. Blake was an ass, and Jacob was used to shit spewing from him. "You should at least wait until the bruises heal before trying for more."

Was this the retribution that had worried Greta? *Pathetic.*

"Would you both stop." She stood, gathering the lunch trash. "I don't need this at work."

"You're the one who brought it here," Blake snapped.

"No." Jacob got to his feet. He didn't like Blake literally looking down on him. "You're the pussy who ran his fucking mouth to her father."

"Wow. Real nice talk." Blake's gaze swung from Jacob to Greta. "Do you like when he kisses you with that filthy mouth?"

Swallowing his growing anger, Jacob flicked his wrist, wishing he could shoo away the other man like an annoying bug. "Why don't you piss off, asshole?"

"Whatever. Have your fun with the spoiled, rich girl. Well, until she gets bored of your lowbrow ways. Or you tire of her frigidness."

Jacob laughed, loud and hard. "Frigid, are you kidding me? Are we talking about the same woman? I guess 'good breeding' and an Ivy League education doesn't guarantee everything. Like how to properly warm a woman." He tilted his head and gave a condescending frown. "How sad."

"I am superior to you in every way," Blake spluttered. Then he stilled, squinting at Jacob's wrist, and, without another word, turned and left.

"What the hell?"

Greta shrugged. "I have no idea, but it cannot be good."

Chapter Twenty

The Fourth of July had finally arrived, and, for Greta, it couldn't have come fast enough. The previous week had dragged on, each minute slower than the next, as doubts and worries ate at her.

First, there was Jacob's reaction when he learned she hadn't told her father they were dating. His hurt and disappointment cut like a knife.

She used the excuse they were only a summer romance. Her heart was whispering a different story. She was falling for him and didn't know what to do.

Then there was Father. Their talk had been uncomfortable, but she'd been honest. Told him she liked Jacob and wanted to continue dating him. Her father didn't fight it. In fact, he took it better than expected. However, now at work and home, he was more withdrawn than usual. She didn't know if he was upset with her job performance, Blake, or Jacob, and she was too afraid to ask.

To top it off, Jacob was hired for a rush job in West Michigan, and she hadn't seen him since their slightly disastrous lunch at Swift. She missed him terribly.

How would she survive leaving him? There wasn't much time until she had to return to university. Losing him ate at her heart.

Turning onto his street, Greta let her doubts and worries fall away. She'd celebrate America's independence with her guy and not worry about the future. It could wait. Today was the first time they'd spend the whole day together.

Hours together. July Fourth might be her new favorite holiday.

Pulling into the driveway, she double checked the address. A flutter of nerves danced in her belly. She'd also be meeting his father and brother, along with many of his friends.

Dear God, what have I gotten myself into?

What if they disliked her? What if they had nothing in common and the afternoon was full of awkward silences?

She took a deep, calming breath and studied Jacob's house, instead of her doubts. Like the drive through Detroit, his place was an unexpected pleasure. The quaint two-story Tudor was made from pretty rust-colored bricks and had cream trim. It reminded her of a long-ago summer her parents let her go with her best friend for a week to their family cottage in the Irish Hills. Jacob's house even had a similar style wrap-around porch. Greta could almost hear the creak of the rocking chairs and her old friend's giggles.

A soft breeze fluttered the petals of the crimson roses running along the front of the house and crawling up the porch pillars. The delicate fragrance wafted through her car window, caressing and soothing her nerves. Shutting off the engine, she ran her gaze over the house again, piquing her curiosity. How did an out-of-work police officer afford such a home? With one son rebuilding his life and the other opening a shop, neither could be helping much with bills.

Maybe the house was paid off. Didn't matter. Not her business.

Greta went around to the passenger side to retrieve the potato salad and blueberry dessert she bought at her favorite artisan shop. Before opening the door, she caught sight of Jacob emerging from the backyard.

His gaze landed on her, and he broke into a smile bright and warm as the sun caressing her skin. Thoughts of the house and neighborhood scattered from her mind, and she concentrated on remembering to breathe.

The man was downright edible in a faded concert T-shirt and old jeans. It wasn't fair. When she tried casual, she came off as scruffy and in complete disarray.

He quickened his pace, and when he reached her, she stood on tiptoes and kissed him. He returned it before stepping back. His heated gaze ran the entire length of her body, from her cream skirt to her pretty teal, sleeveless blouse.

His admiration was her foreplay.

"You are hot. Even today's perfect summer day can't compete." His intense expression told her he meant it.

Recalling his one-line from their lunch, she wrapped an arm around his waist. "Flattery will get you everywhere," Her words sounded more breathless than playful. Jacob stole her air, along with her restraint.

He was becoming an addiction.

"I hope so." He pulled her closer, leaving no space between their bodies. "Was your drive okay? Did you get lost?"

"Nope. Your directions were perfect. How's the barbeque going?" She could hear rock music and raucous laughter filtering from the backyard.

"Good. Everyone's pretty much here." He glanced away then back, not quite meeting hers. "Including Marty, my uncle... remember him?"

Embarrassment flooded her. "Oh no, how could I forget? He probably thinks I'm such a tramp."

"No he doesn't. And, hey, if it makes you feel better, it's awkward for me too."

"How?" Her curiosity overrode her mortification.

"He reminds me of our afternoon together. My mind wanders to the memories, and it kinda turns me on—then I remember I'm staring at my uncle…" Jacob finished with a mock shudder.

She burst out laughing. "Okay, that is disconcerting. Weirdo."

His hands ran up her sides, tickling her. "Geez, thanks."

She pressed against him, suppressing the urge to wiggle away from his fingers, and gave her best sultry smile. "Maybe there's something I can do to help you."

He stilled. "Yeah? Go on."

"Replace the memory with a new one. Maybe sneak back into the guest house…"

"Yeah?" he murmured, his voice dripping with desire.

She nodded, thrilling at his eagerness.

"Mmm... that's a fantastic idea." He slanted his mouth over hers for one of his signature sizzling kisses. Her body melted into his.

"Hey, Jacob, did we lose you?"

Jacob groaned, breaking the kiss. Greta eyed the lone man on the front porch. Even though they were a couple car lengths away, she could see he was incredibly handsome, and he was Jacob's brother. They had the same broad shoulders, sharp jawline, and thick, straight eyebrows.

"If I knew you were going to hunt me down, Mom, I'd have hidden better." Jacob faced Greta and pointed to the man. "My brother, Will."

"Ha, ha asshole." Will snorted, walking toward them. "I don't care about you. I was hoping you'd lead me to your mysterious woman."

Will's gaze met hers, a playful smile quirked at the corners of his mouth. Yup, there was plenty of difference between the two men, but there was no denying they were brothers. Will's eyes were a warm brown, almost the exact shade of his tawny hair. He also wore it in a neater style than his brother, shaved on the sides and slightly longer on top.

"I'm mysterious?" Greta smiled and offered her hand. "You make me sound more interesting than I am."

"Please, no handshakes." Will opened his arms for a hug. "Not when I finally get to meet the woman who's made my little brother happy."

Greta hugged Will, loving his exuberant personality and friendliness. Around him, her nervousness in the face of meeting so many new people faded.

"Jesus, Will. Can you please not freak her out before we even get into the backyard?" Jacob sounded strangled.

Greta glanced in his direction and was shocked to find his cheeks were slightly pink. She clapped. "Are you blushing? Finally!"

"Isn't it nice having someone around who knows his weaknesses?" Will chuckled.

"Yes. My weakness is having a goofball for a brother." Jacob turned to Greta. "Hell, now you've met him, you're probably terrified to meet everyone else."

"Not at all." Will had set her at ease. If Jacob's family and friends were like his brother, she was in for a fun day.

She stepped around the two men and opened the passenger door of her car, leaned in and grabbed the food. She handed the potato salad to Jacob and kept the pie. With her free hand, she grasped his, ready to party.

~ * ~

From across the yard, Jacob saw his usually reclusive father deep in conversation with Greta. The sight pulled at his heart in ways he was only beginning to understand.

She threw back her head, laughing with abandon at something his dad said. The sunlight kissed her face, and Jacob was jealous. He wanted to be the one caressing her.

Damn. He was lost.

Or was it found?

Her laughter grew, and she wiped at the corners of her eyes. Disquiet stroked along his spine, and he started to worry, wondering what his father was telling Greta. The Grimm family loved to tease and embarrass each other.

That got him moving.

He made his way across the yard to the two wooden lawn chairs his girlfriend and father were occupying.

"…and I walk into the shed to find Will hogtied, and livid," Roger Grimm finished, as Jacob sat in the empty seat next to Greta.

He heaved a heavy sigh. "Ah, Dad, are you telling her the ransom story?"

His father winked. "Hey. I only wanted this lovely lady to know what she's getting into, dating you."

"Did you really try to ransom your own brother to your parents?" Greta was clearly amused.

Jacob grinned and shrugged. "Hey, I was only ten…and I wanted a new bike. I needed the money."

"All I'm hearing is you've been wicked since childhood." Her stern façade fell away when she started giggling.

"Hmm, yup pretty much," Jacob agreed. "What're you doing with such a thug?"

"Good question." She wiped the moisture from her bottom lashes.

"If it helps, I tried to have Cindy arrested."

She told her story, and Jacob couldn't stop laughing. He could easily picture a pissed-off six-year-old Greta trying to have her sister hauled off in handcuffs for taking Greta's beloved doll. He was both amused and a little alarmed by the way she'd patiently bided her time, waiting for her revenge. She'd sprung it two days later when they had a family outing. She'd found a police officer, brought him to her sister, and demanded he arrest Cindy on a litany of charges, ranging from theft to kidnapping.

"They, of course, wouldn't," Greta grinned. "They did speak to her about taking items not her own. It scared her senseless, and she refused to speak to me for almost a week. I, on the other hand, had a serious case of hero worship. For years, I'd wanted nothing more than to be a police officer."

"A police officer? Yet you're dating my extortionist son." His father laughed, clearly smitten with Greta.

He couldn't blame his father.

"Your son's a reformed extortionist, and I never became an officer, so we're okay."

Jacob rose from his seat, taking Greta's hand. "On that note, it's time to get you away from here." Peering at his dad, he smiled good-naturedly. "And get her away from you, before any more damaging stories are told."

"Oh, there are many. I could tell her about the summer you were four and we bought a kiddy pool. Couldn't keep clothes on the boy, the neighbors called him—"

Jacob covered Greta's ears, laughing. His father chuckled, standing when someone called to him. Jacob lowered his hands and guided Greta farther back into the yard.

After a couple of steps, she leaned in close. "What were you called?"

He sighed, but there was suppressed laughter. "The Little Nudist. Most of those neighbors are still here, and the nickname has stuck. At least they've stopped with the 'little' part."

She stopped walking, a smile pulling at the corners of her mouth. She glanced from the zipper of his jeans and back to his face. "How would they know to drop it? You haven't stopped streaking through the neighborhood?"

"No!" He shrugged. "Well, there was this time when I was fourteen…"

Her brows almost reached her hairline, and she crossed her arms over her chest, an amused expression firmly in place. "Fourteen?"

He rubbed the back of his neck. He'd been such a dumb teenager.

"Yeah, um, a group of us, including a guy I want to introduce you to, stole some of our parent's liquor. We got drunk and played a game of dare. The more we drank the crazier the challenge. I had to run down the street. Naked. At six in the evening. My mom and dad locked the liquor after that incident."

Greta's eyes widened before she went into a fit of laughter, leaning with hands on knees. Jacob waited, rubbing her back, not minding in the least his teenage idiocy amused her.

Her melodic laughter was balm to his soul.

When she could stand straight again, he led her toward the garage at the back of the property. His friend Tanner and his band were setting up. Greta glanced at the equipment and turned to Jacob, smirking. "Are you hoping the music will drown out all the people willing to tell me your wonderful stories?"

Damn, this playful side of her was hot. He leaned in and planted a kiss on the corner of her mouth. "Yes, partly. I also want to dance with you. The guy with the guitar is Tanner. He used to be my neighbor."

"Did he take part in the drinking and daring?"

Jacob snorted. "Yes. He had to climb to the roof and piss off it, or something equally idiotic."

She shook her head. "Boys."

"Yup." No sense arguing. As kids and teens, they'd done some incredibly stupid things. "Anyway, his band, ThreePence, has an important show coming up and wanted to try a couple of new songs. Get everyone's input on what works and what doesn't."

Greta took in the band, her gaze traveling over each member. "Wow. Tanner is the epitome of a rocker."

"What? No. You're looking at Jayce. Tanner's the one with the acoustic guitar. Has the short brown hair."

As if sensing eyes on him, Tanner glanced their way and waved. Jacob raised a hand in greeting then pointed to each band member, telling her about them. "Maggie's the singer and creator of the band. The drummer's name is Lincoln. He's a good guy. Jayce plays bass. He's a jerk, and, for reasons I cannot grasp, Maggie used to date him."

"Did she dump him for Tanner?"

Jacob studied his friend. He was leaning in close to Maggie and laughing. To be honest, a time or two, he'd wondered if something was going on between the two of them. "No. What makes you think that?" He was curious how Greta had come to the same conclusion in such a short time.

"Mostly the way they watch each other. Now I know what Allen meant when he referred to our furtive glances during your days at Swift."

Jacob smiled, remembering. The torture, the longing. The fear. "Yeah, I couldn't stop staring. I couldn't believe you were there."

He'd thought his midnight fantasies had somehow creeped into the light of day.

"Same here. Excitement and horrification almost overtook me."

Ouch.

"Damn. You know how to stroke a man's ego," he drawled.

She rested a hand on his bicep, sliding her palm under the sleeve of his T-shirt. "Seeing you excited me. Recalling my reactions horrified me."

He understood, had a similar reaction, but couldn't resist teasing her. "You're not making it better."

Worry clouded her gentle hazel eyes, and he was instantly remorseful. He'd learned Greta was an anxious woman filled with self-doubt. He hated being a cause of her disquiet.

Cupping her face in his hands, he brushed his lips against hers. "I'm kidding. I know what you meant." Taking her hand, he steered from the driveway and to the left, under an old maple tree.

ThreePence had finished setting up and began playing their first song. Jacob wrapped his arms around Greta, and they swayed to the music.

She rested her head on his chest. "I'm no good with words. Let me try again. I was horrified because I didn't know how I'd control myself around you. When we first met, you were a stranger, yet I couldn't stay away. When we met again at Swift, your touch was burned into my memories and I craved it, yet was certain I had to stay away. I was afraid I wouldn't be able to, and I'd make a fool of myself. "

Warmth spread through him like a shot of good whiskey. Knowing the pull was strong for her as it was for him, well, she burrowed deeper into his heart.

He gently grasped Greta's chin and lifted it, kissing her. "Your words sound pretty damn good to me."

They might appear an odd couple yet fit like two puzzle pieces.

Jacob held her tight, having no idea if the songs were fast or slow. All he noticed was her soft body and her heady scent. The combination made him want to bury his nose in the crook of her neck and nibble.

"You should audition as a backup singer," Greta murmured into his chest.

Jacob opened his eyes and leaned back to peer at her. ThreePence switched to an old Tom Petty classic, and he'd been singing along. "You haven't heard me trying to hit the high notes. Picture yowling cats."

"Well, I think it'd be sexy to see you on a stage."

"Yeah, until crowds ran away, holding their hands over their ears." He grinned and, after a pause, tilted his head to the side. "You have a thing for musicians? Do I need to keep you away from Tanner?"

"Nope. No plans on becoming a groupie. You're the only one I want."

"Good to know." He dipped her low, running his lips along her neck.

She trembled in his arms and sighed. "I swear, Jacob, your touch…"

Drawing her flush against him again, he whispered, "Let's go inside where I can touch you properly."

She peered into his eyes, her gaze full of the same desire coursing through his veins. "Won't people notice our absence?"

"Na. Everyone's busy dancing or drinking." In truth, he didn't care if anyone noticed them sneaking off. His need for her overruled everything. Their last time alone was the night at the park, and he craved her like an addiction.

Her heated gaze never left his, and her lips formed a smile sexy enough to melt ice in January. "Why don't you give me a tour of the house?"

Chapter Twenty-One

"Mrs. Silverstone, Mr. Kingstine is here to see you." The maid told Greta's mother.

"Please show him in," Sophia replied, her voice carrying down the cavernous hallway and back to Blake.

The housekeeper returned and escorted him to the living room. Sophia studied Blake as he entered, taking in the faded bruises. Over a week had passed since the fight. The fading yellowing and purple splotches weren't pretty.

Thankfully, her good manners forbade her from asking prying questions. She motioned for him to sit. "It has been a while. I hope you are well." She arched a perfectly shaped blonde eyebrow, indicating her doubt.

"It's always a pleasure visiting you, Mrs. Silverstone, though I have to admit I've been better."

"Please, Blake, you know to call me Sophia. What's wrong? Greta isn't here." She glanced past him as if expecting her daughter to walk through the door.

"She's probably with that reprobate." Blake sniffed.

"What? I'm confused."

"The guy she has been seeing." He couldn't bring himself to say dating.

Sophia's eyes widened, in either alarm or confusion. "What? Greta hasn't mentioned dating anyone."

Oh, Grimm is her dirty secret. Figures.

"I'm not surprised." He put on his most regretful mask. "The guy she's with is trouble of the worst sort. He's not a man you would want your daughter associating with."

"What's his name? Do I know his family?" Sophia's voice was becoming shrill which meant she was close to losing her composure.

"No, you wouldn't know them. His name is Jacob Grimm, and he's from a blue-collar family from Detroit. He lives with his unemployed father and drug-addict brother."

Sophia's lips pulled into a thin line. "You're joking, right?"

"I wish I were. You should see this guy. Disheveled, tattoos..." Blake paused, savoring his last bit of information. "He's even been arrested."

"Oh my God!" Sophia shot to her feet and paced the length of the couch, then sat again, pinning him with panicked eyes. "For what?"

Holding back his triumphant smile was difficult. This visit was better than he'd hoped. Blake took a deep breath, pretending to need a minute. Like he regretted delivering such dreadful news.

In reality, he was working to make sure he sounded grave, instead of pleased. "Something to do with drug dealing."

Her already pale complexion turned ashen. "Are you kidding me? What is Greta thinking?" Sophia took a couple of deep breaths. "How do you know of him?"

"He's one of Mr. Meier's business investments."

"Of course. Charles would take anyone he deemed having an eye for business, never mind their background." She clicked her long nails on a side table. "He never understood certain people are trouble."

"Grimm is definitely trouble for you, and not only because he's managed to hook your daughter."

"What do you mean?" Sophia fidgeted with the collar of her blouse, anxiety in her every move.

He leaned forward, placing both elbows on his knees and hoping his glee wasn't apparent. "From what I've discovered, Grimm hasn't left his bad habits behind. He may have even added thievery to his list of misdeeds. Which is why I stopped by."

Sophia nodded for him to continue.

Coming here was a gamble, but not much of one. The hardest part had been waiting a week to visit Sophia. One of his secretaries had mentioned the asshole was out of town. Blake wanted to make sure if anything happened, it would take place locally so he got all the gritty details from his friends working within Wayne County's bureaucracy.

"I ran into Grimm last week at Swift and couldn't help noticing he was wearing a Rolex. It was unique and familiar. I couldn't place it. Today, it came to me. It looks exactly like Nigel's. The one from his grandfather. Is it missing?"

"Not that I'm aware of. I will check." She paged someone named Whitehill then asked, "I do wonder how this Jacob Grimm would get his hands on it?"

Blake shrugged. He'd wondered the same thing but was positive the watch on Grimm's wrist was Nigel's. No way would Nigel part with his Rolex.

The freaking guttersnipe had probably been there with Greta one time when no one was home and had stolen it. Greta was foolish enough not to notice.

As if reading his mind, Sophia said, "Greta hadn't mentioned stopping by when we weren't home. However, she has a key and the codes to the house."

Blake decided to test another possibility. Again, what could it hurt? "Have you hired anyone of late to repair an antique in the home? He has a little company called Rework."

Sophia shook her head. "No. The name is unfamiliar. Though, we did hire a moving company back in the spring. I believe they were called Careful Moves. They delivered a baroque set and an antique chandelier. One of their employees rewired it."

Whitehill entered the living room, and Sophia requested she check Nigel's jewelry for the watch and also retrieve the paperwork on the moving company.

She returned in less than five minutes, handing Sophia a folder and informing her there was no Rolex in Nigel's jewelry case.

Sophia dismissed the woman and shuffled through the papers. She gasped. "Jacob Grimm is listed here. He's the specialist who repaired the chandelier."

Bingo!

Her expression was ice. "Would you accompany me to Nigel's office? I'll check his safe before calling the police."

Sophia walked briskly from the room, seeming to miss the satisfaction Blake was sure was stamped on his face. He couldn't believe his luck; this was shaping out to be the best Fourth of July.

Chapter Twenty-Two

"Hey! Jacob! Where ya going?" Will called loudly from his position behind the grill.

"Seriously?" he growled under his breath, dropping his hand from the patio's sliding door. He faced in the general direction of his brother and shouted, "I'm going to show Greta the house."

Will's smile was huge. Greta could spot his two dimples from across the yard. "Later," he said. "Food's almost done. I need your help."

Greta smothered a grin. Will knew exactly what he was doing.

"Are you freakin' kidding me?" Jacob muttered.

She couldn't have agreed more. The urge to yank Jacob inside and find someplace secluded was fierce. Guilt stopped her. Will had done most of the cooking, and this was the first time he asked for help.

Turning, she tugged Jacob's hand and they walked to Will. Well, she walked, Jacob practically dragged his feet.

"What can we do?" Greta hoped her features were pleasant.

Less worried, Jacob barked, "Yeah. What do you want?"

"I need you to finish the grilling." Will handed his spatula to Jacob and met Greta's gaze. "I've got a couple things I need to finish in the house. Will you help me?"

She nodded as Jacob muttered creative curses and began flipping the burgers rather roughly.

Will winked, and she couldn't stop a bubble of laughter from escaping between her lips. She hastily covered her mouth, but not before Jacob heard it. His glare shifted from Will to her.

With a wicked glint in his eye, Jacob bent close to her ear. "Go ahead and laugh now. In the near future, I'll have you at my mercy. Writhing and pleading. We'll see who's laughing."

Greta swallowed a groan and tried to appear innocent, smiling sweetly. "Oh, honey, if I am writhing around you, I can guarantee you won't be laughing."

"Ahhh, woman, you're killing me," Jacob growled, kissing her quick and hard before turning back to the grill.

After getting over the disappointment of skipping the "house tour," Greta found she and Will made a great team. They put the finishing touches on the food he'd prepped earlier. With help from some of the other guests, in a short time, they had the many tables overflowing with food.

She proceed to stuff herself silly with the most delicious food. Five-star restaurants had nothing on Will. The man created magic in the kitchen.

When dinner finished, ThreePence gave another impromptu concert, and before the first song ended, Jacob had her in his arms. Much to her delight, Greta discovered he liked to dance, and they did so until the sun dipped below the horizon and the band quit.

After which, the party took on a mellower tone. Many people mingled throughout the backyard. Most gathered around a large brick fire pit built in the far corner of the yard.

Greta leaned on Jacob, enjoying his warmth and the fires. He had an arm around her and was absently running his fingers down her side.

The night was darn near perfect.

She lazily stared at the sparks crackling and rising into the dark sky before glancing at Will on her opposite side, then to his father sitting next to him. They were relaxed and enjoyed each other's company. She couldn't help being envious of Jacob's family. They accepted each other as they were, not as they wished them to be. For all their past problems, they appeared to be a solid family.

She loved and respected her father deeply, but she wouldn't call them close. They could discuss work and politics for hours. However, it never veered to personal matters. She had no idea if her father had dated anyone seriously since her parents divorced. Heck, the only time they'd talked about *her* private life was the extremely brief and uncomfortable conversation after Blake tried to have Jacob's contract canceled.

Mother and Nigel were much worse. They were critical and were obsessed with prestige. Drove Greta crazy. During her infrequent visits, they spent more time disagreeing than talking. Keeping them at arm's length was easier.

The only person she was close to in her family was her sister. Greta cherished their relationship. Cindy could be snobbish and self-centered. However, she was also compassionate, wickedly funny, and honest to a fault.

"Earth to Greta. You in a food coma?" Will nudged her shoulder.

She dragged her lethargic gaze from the flames to Will. "Entirely possible. The food was delicious, and I couldn't stop eating." She leaned back and patted her stomach. "I have to say. You are an excellent cook."

"I'd cook for you anytime, darling." Will cast a teasing leer in her direction.

Jacob snorted, tightening his arm around Greta. "Keep your darlings to yourself."

"Are you worried, little brother?" Will waggled his eyebrows. "You should be. I'm a great catch, handsome, and an excellent cook."

"Uh-huh. I'm the pretty one," Jacob drawled, smirking. "And I can cook. I just like it better when you do it."

In Greta's humble opinion, they were both very handsome. She imagined they must've driven the local girls wild. Heck, maybe still did.

"I knew it!" Will waved a finger in his brother's direction. "You burn stuff on purpose, don't you? Geez, if Mom could hear you now, you'd be in big trouble." His feigned outrage was met with laughter from around the fire.

Jacob shrugged, not the least bit repentant. "I do help with cleanup…"

"Yeah, the easy part," Will grumbled.

Jacob scanned the backyard. Greta followed his gaze. The yard was obscured in the late-night darkness. What could be seen by the fire and patio lights was a disaster. Cups and plates littered the tables.

"Not easy tonight," he said, dropping his arm from around Greta's shoulder and patting her knee before standing. "I should probably get started."

She stood. "Let me help."

Both brothers appeared stunned. Clearly shocked the spoiled socialite would lower herself to clean. She huffed, ignoring them both, gathering the dirty dishes.

Soon, everyone was pitching in, and in no time the backyard was spotless, and guests were saying their goodbyes. To Greta's surprise, Uncle Marty gave her a parting hug and invited her and Jacob to his place for dinner.

Before heading inside the house, she and Jacob stopped by the garage. ThreePence was breaking down their equipment and loading their van. Tanner came over, and, after catching up and telling a couple more funny neighborhood stories, he asked Jacob to take a look at a malfunctioning guitar.

Tanner had mentioned earlier the band was due to play in Chicago the following night and they planned on making most of the drive after leaving Jacob's. Greta didn't want to be in the way, and she wandered into the house, figuring she'd head back to her dad's after Jacob finished helping his friend. She didn't want to leave him, but it was getting late, and she didn't want to overstay her welcome.

Sliding open the back door, she stepped into a small utility room and spotted Will in the kitchen. He was at the sink, hand washing the items too big for the dishwasher. She stood beside him, grabbing a dish towel from the stove's handle. "Let me help."

Will handed her a large frying pan. "Thanks, though it's not necessary. Where's Jacob?"

"Trying to fix something with Tanner's guitar." She dried the pan and set it on the rack taking the grilling tongs from Will. "And I want to help. You cooked all the fantastic food. This is the least I can do."

"Many people brought a dish to pass, and I had help," he replied modestly.

"What? Jacob flipping a couple of burgers?" Greta scoffed. She cut a side glance at Will, smiling. "*And* he was very gracious about it."

A sharp bark of laughter escaped Will. "I can't imagine why—"

Greta shook her head. "Uh, no. I'm not buying what you're selling. Your oh-so-innocent expression reminds me of my sister when she's being mischievous."

"Oh yeah? Do you have only the one sister or a bunch, but is one particularly good at needling you?"

"One sister, and she has an incredible talent for goading me." Greta accepted a dripping platter and began drying it. "I'm older, by three years. We are opposite in appearance and temperament yet, despite this, or maybe because of it, we're close."

"I know what you mean. Jacob and I couldn't be more different. Yet, he's the one I trust above anyone." Will's gaze shifted to the dishwater. "To be honest, I couldn't have survived without him."

She wondered if Will was referring to his troubled past, but didn't want to overstep by asking. "You Grimm men seem pretty tight-knit."

"True. My family's close. Again. Yet it's nothing compared to when my mom was alive." A sad smile flickered across Will's lips.

He surprised her. Will was more open with his past than Jacob.

Greta stopped drying and leaned against the counter to peer at Will. "Sounds wonderful."

He nodded "Too bad I didn't appreciate it at the time. Anyway, we're surviving, now, even thriving. It also helps I like cooking. It's like a part of her is still here with me."

"Your mother taught you?"

"As kids, she said we had to eat, and therefore we had to learn to cook. She considered it her job to teach us since Dad can barely make an edible sandwich. She taught both Jacob and me the basics. Jacob tolerated the lessons. I, on the other hand, wanted to know everything. Like Mom, I enjoy creating something everyone needs and also brings people together. I'd even started taking culinary classes after high school...only to drop out. I was too busy ruining my life. Wasted too many years." Will pulled the plug in the sink and kept his gaze on the water running down the drain before turning to face Greta. "Tell me, do you like to cook? Your mom or dad teach you any good recipes you're willing to share?"

He clearly wanted to shift the topic, and Greta let him. Even if the subject embarrassed her a bit. "I honestly don't know. Never tried."

"Never tried? Not even eggs or rice? Your parents never left you to fend for yourself?" Will's eyes were wide as the saucer plates he'd just washed.

"Oh, they were gone a lot of the time…um…we had a cook. When my sister and I were younger, the cook never wanted us under foot, bothering her. Eventually, we lost interest and stopped asking her to teach us."

"Your own cook, huh?" Will leaned back and eyed her. "That's right. Your father owns Swift. I forgot you come from money. You don't act like it."

She bristled a little. His words were factual. The way he said them was rude. He sounded like Jacob when they first met, and he'd insulted her upbringing. "Why, what does it matter? You act like I told you I was raised in a brothel by a madam."

"Jacob might like that." Will chuckled, moving from the counter to the worn, well-made kitchen table. Before he sat, he offered a chair to Greta. She accepted, albeit with some irritation.

Will held up his hands. "I didn't mean to offend you. Let me explain. A while back he dated a woman from a super wealthy family. I'm almost positive she lives in the same city as you. Petite Bois, right?"

Greta nodded, wondering if she was friends with the woman. "I don't live there now. I was raised there."

"Anyway, it ended badly. Ever since, he's warned me to stay away from rich bitch—um, ladies. He says they're vapid and empty-headed."

It explained Jacob's attitude when they'd first met.

She found it a bit harsh and unfair to judge a whole social class because of one snob. However, she understood why he had. Blake had left her with plenty of invisible emotional scars.

"Jacob doesn't think you're this way. He's crazy about you," Will finished.

His last words halted Greta's growing annoyance.

She quirked an eyebrow. "You sure, or are you saying this because you hope it'll help remove the taste of foot from your mouth?"

He smacked his lips together. "Nope. I can still taste it. Though, in all seriousness, Jacob's enamored. I cannot remember the last time he brought a lady home. I worried the responsibility thrown on his shoulders after our mom died destroyed his softer side. It's nice seeing him happy."

Greta recalled the sad conversation she had with Jacob at Belle Isle. His father's drinking and Will's partying. "I can't imagine the pain you and your family had to bear after the death of your mother. How it changed each of you. I'm sorry."

"So am I. My dad and I didn't handle it well. We left Jacob to clean our messes."

"What do you mean?"

When it came to his past, Jacob was closed-mouthed. She sensed Will wanted to tell his story.

He ran a finger along a gouge, keeping his gaze trained on his fingers. "Without him, we wouldn't have this house, hell, I might not have my life. Or not much of one. I had no insurance or money, only loads of trouble and a taste for drugs. When I finally understood the mess I'd made of my life, Jacob was there to help. He paid for my long-term treatment, and after, he gave me a place to live."

The dam holding back her curiosity broke, and a tidal wave of questions flew at her. She grabbed at the first few. "What do you mean, you would have lost this house? Is it not your father's?"

Will shook his head. "Not anymore. Mom got sick, and they had to remortgage the house to cover her medical bills. After my dad lost his job, he couldn't pay the loan agreement. The house went into foreclosure. Jacob took care of it. He paid off the mortgage debt, and took over the rest of the payments." Will gave a sad chuckle. "He tells me he did it because he's lazy and didn't want to pack his stuff to move."

Greta was speechless. She went from a million questions to her brain going into lockdown. Her mind raced, and pieces of conversations at work fell in place. Jacob's evasiveness when asked why he waited to expand his business became evident. He hadn't been lazy or afraid to take the next step with Rework; he'd been busy taking care of his family. Helping them survive.

Laughter drifted down the hall, and, seconds later, a door slammed shut. The rumbling timber of Jacob's voice carried to her as he stopped, somewhere nearby, talking with his father.

He didn't stay. Almost immediately his footfalls grew louder, and seconds later, his tall frame shadowed the arched entrance.

He pulled up short. "Damn. Why so serious?" He was smiling, but a small worry line formed between his brows.

Greta wanted to kiss it away.

Will stood, stretching. "Us? More like tired. Were you able to fix Tanner's guitar?"

Jacob seemed to relax. "Yeah, I was. Getting the main panel off was a bitch. The rest was easy enough." He came inside and offered Greta his hand. "Sorry it took longer than expected. I hope Will didn't work you too hard." He looked from her to his brother, the worry line back. "Or talk your ear off."

She accepted his hand, and he brought her into his arms. "Neither. I had a lovely time." Catching his gaze, she winked. "Though I'm waiting on my tour of the house."

The corner of his mouth twitched. "How rude of me. We better get started."

Chapter Twenty-Three

The tour was brief.

Jacob guided Greta from the kitchen and past a small formal dining room. She caught a glimpse of a pretty Cherrywood table, chair rail molding, and two-tone walls before he was moving them on to the living room.

Roger gave a distracted smile from his spot on a comfortable-looking leather sectional, one eye on a soccer game playing on a flat screen mounted above the brick fireplace. The room was homey and cozy, with dark Berber carpet and taupe walls.

Jacob asked his father something about the game. While they talked she went to the bay window facing the front yard. At knee level sat a squat antique shelf that was stuffed with every type of book imaginable. Squatting, she glanced over the many family snapshots sitting atop, wanting to examine them and the books, but, after exchanging a few words with his father, Jacob was beside her, asking if she was ready to see the rest of the tour.

He pointed to two bedrooms and a bathroom down a short hallway, located next to the stairs. He told her one room was his father's, the other Will's.

She recalled this side of the house had the spacious porch running along it, with a corner swing. Earlier, she and Jacob had swung leisurely in it. They'd held hands and talked, a gentle breeze blowing through the red climbing rose bushes entangled along the porch, perfuming the balmy air. It had been like something right out of a romance novel.

Jacob had told her his father built the swing and his mother had planted the stunning flowers. Even before knowing the history, Greta pronounced it her favorite spot.

She reached for his hand, about to suggest they return there, but Jacob was starting for the stairs. She followed him. Watching his behind as he made his way up the steps was more enjoyable than any old swing.

At the top, he opened the only door and went inside. Before following him in, she glanced around the narrow landing, with its wrought iron railing and banisters running along its length. The only furniture in the tiny space was a small circular table and two matching chairs. Like the rest of the home, comfortable and lived-in. She wondered if this was where he met with clients.

"You coming in," Jacob called.

She followed him inside. The room was a mix of workstation and bedroom. The space screamed Jacob.

On the wall facing the front of the house, under a window where the roof slanted, sat a semi-made bed. The rest of the room had what must be Jacob's work projects scattered across every space. A squat dresser sat along the same wall as the bed and was piled high with tools and papers. The opposite side, facing the backyard, had long horizontal windows with a custom-made work table under it. Dismantled items, in different stages of repair, were strewn across it. The place wasn't messy, merely productive and creative chaos.

It was all Jacob.

At the far end of the room, a door was slightly ajar, inside was a small pedestal sink and a half-open shower curtain. She squinted, eyeing what appeared to be large chains strewn over the door's frame. No wonder it couldn't close. There were at least five of those hefty cables. They reminded her of ones found on a hoist or some other type of large machinery. How the door didn't buckle was beyond her.

A room like this would never be found at her parent's homes or her friends. Most of them would consider it a sin not to have everything decorated to the nines and spotless. Perfect and ready for a *Good Housekeeping* photoshoot.

This room was like him: unruly, intense, and ambitious. She loved it.

Jacob must have been following her perusal of the room because he walked to the chain-things and pulled them from the door, muttering he needed to buy more hooks. They must've been unwieldy as they appeared. His triceps and back muscles bunched under his T-shirt in the most delicious way.

She could watch him lift heavy things all day.

Geez, when had she become so licentious?

He carried the chains to an empty spot on the end of the work table and dropped them with a heavy *thunk*. Turning, he offered a chagrined smile. "Sorry. My space looks like a garage. We can go back downstairs if you don't like it here. Or go out."

Oh, no. He must have taken her silence for distaste.

"No way. I love it. I can't identify half the items here, but you're able to fix them. Remarkable." Her gaze wandered to the bench again, spotting Nigel's Rolex. She went to it and ran her fingers over the gold band.

Jacob came up behind her, wrapping his arms around her waist and resting his chin on her shoulder. She set the watch aside, placing her hands on his and leaning back.

"Can I ask you something?" Since her talk with Will, she had a ton of questions.

His chest rumbled with light, quiet laughter. "Why do you even ask? Your imagination scares me too much to let it run wild. What do you want to know?"

Her pulse quickened, nervous her prying would upset him. He kept his emotions locked and buried. The only time he released his anger was with Blake. The rest of the time Jacob gave off a vibe of toughness and solitude. Learning he was the family's caretaker was unexpected. She wanted to know more.

"That day at Belle Isle, you told me you lived with your brother and father to help each other. I assumed the house was your father's. Will says it's yours…"

Jacob sighed and grabbed the closest chair and sat, pulling her onto his lap. "Ah, now I understand the serious faces earlier. Will is *such* a gossip. It's no big deal or secret. My dad needed help. I had it to give." Jacob shrugged. "My mom loved this house. So much of her memory's here. To lose the house would be to lose a piece of her."

Compassion threatened to overwhelm Greta; she had to blink back tears. His selflessness and strength, in the midst of his heartbreak, was incredible. Her admiration grew and, for the second time that night, she was at a loss for words.

She let her kiss express what she was unable to voice.

Jacob accepted her lips and deepened the embrace, though before losing herself to his touch, she leaned back. Resting her hands on the sides of his face, she peered into his eyes. "Why didn't you tell me? Or about helping your brother?"

"Damn. You two were having one hell of a heart to heart. Did Will also tell you I'm claustrophobic? Or the time when I was twelve and was caught trying to steal a pack of gaming cards?"

Greta exhaled a breath of laughter. "No. Guess you interrupted us before we got into more of your criminal past."

"What a shame," he muttered.

She laughed quietly, asking, "Seriously, why not say anything? Why, when we talked, did you leave out huge chunks of your life?"

Jacob's shoulders sagged, and he ran a palm back and forth over his jawline. The gesture shouted agitation. "Our backgrounds are oceans apart.

Do you honestly think I want to bring up drugs, arrests, and foreclosures to remind you of this?"

"Do you imagine these things don't touch the wealthy? We merely have better means to hide them or get help. My uncle, on my mother's side, has been battling an addiction to prescription drugs for years. I'm sure he's not the only one. Wealth allows us to hide our secrets better. Hearing what Will told me didn't make me respect you or your family less. The opposite. You should be proud of what you've done." She slid her hand resting on his shoulder to his chest. "I admire your heart and the way you care for those you love."

"Listen, I'm happy Will's life is getting back on track, but don't give me more credit than I deserve. He did the hard work. He chose to pull his life from the chaos and destruction. All I did was offer a little financial help when he was ready."

Before she could respond, Jacob caught her lips and muttered against them, "Can we forget the past and focus on the now? Like, how much I've missed you. I'm thinking of selling Rework and asking for a position as a mail clerk at Swift. Maybe I'll get to see more of you."

~ * ~

Greta's throaty laugh mixed with her fragrance of lilacs and woman curled around Jacob, the combination was heady. He wanted more.

For weeks, he'd tried to convince himself he was merely attracted to her beauty and hidden passion. It ran much deeper.

He couldn't remember the last time, if ever, a woman had gotten under his skin this thoroughly. The mixture of intense affection, the promise of love, combined with desire, was new. She'd be his undoing, and he was powerless to stop his growing devotion.

He wasn't ready to voice any of this out loud. Instead, he showed her through touch. He kissed her gently, trying to make her understand he loved more than her body.

Greta deepened the kiss and shifted to straddle him. Tenderness became blistering desire when her slender legs encased his torso. He clasped her lower back, driving her closer. When she rocked against him, his mind went blank with need.

He grasped the hem of her shirt, taking it off. She tugged at his T-shirt. He took the hint and yanked it off, tossing it over his shoulder to land with hers. Returning to her soft skin, he explored her curves and contours, ending at the lacy cups of her bra. He nudged aside the delicate material to capture her nipple between tongue and teeth, savoring the taste and the throaty moan of his name from her breathless lips

"Are you now admiring my heart?" she asked with a heated giggle, that became a moan when he unclasped her bra and ran his tongue along the underside of her breast.

"Yes. I'd like to admire every inch of your body with my mouth."

"I don't know if I'll survive it. I need you too much. Please don't make me beg."

Her blunt words and the longing behind them was all the pleading he required. Jacob stood, slipping an arm under her bottom for support. With his free hand, he reached around Greta and shoved aside the many items on the desk. Setting her on it, he parted her legs and pressed in close. She wrapped her legs around him again, and their lips crashed together with equal urgency.

The layer of clothes between them was too much.

He needed more of her against his overheated flesh. Grasping the waist of Greta's skirt, she lifted enough to allow him to remove it, leaving her in barely-there white lace panties.

Stunning.

Jacob ran a finger along the top beveled edges before slipping inside. He brushed through her tight curls, seeking her center, while also capturing her mouth with his lips. He loved the way her body trembled at his touch but wanted to be buried inside her when she came apart.

He withdrew his hand and stepped back. Greta reached for his zipper. She shoved his jeans down far enough to slide a hand inside. She grasped him, making him grow even harder.

"Greta…" The rest of his word fell away, and speaking became impossible, as was delaying what they both wanted.

Jacob pushed his jeans lower and grasped Greta's thighs, tugging her to the edge of the table. Her legs snagged his waist, pulling him to her.

"Now," she demanded.

He eased inside her, her warmth and tightness gripping him, sweet and intense. The sensation was almost too much. He began to thrust, and a loud groan, soaked in ecstasy, ripped from his throat.

"Ah, Jacob. I've needed this…you." Her moan turned to a cry as her climax ripped through her.

He wouldn't let it be the only one of the night.

She wrapped her legs tighter, driving him in deeper. Watching her writhe in pleasure under him was erotic as the act itself. She was a sensual mixture of sweet and sin.

His aphrodisiac.

Leaning on the desk and resting on her elbows, her feverish gaze perused his body. Jacob shifted to watch their joined bodies. The sight was mesmerizing, taking him to the razor edge of his climax.

His fast-approaching release brought into focus what was missing. Reality crashed into him, and he stumbled back. "Damn, Greta, I'm sorry," he choked.

"What?" She sounded bereft.

"No condom." He'd never forgotten before.

"Oh…"

The scariest was a small part of him didn't care. He couldn't picture a future without her, so it didn't seem like a massive risk to him.

Keywords: To him.

It didn't mean she felt the same. Jacob grabbed his jeans, searching for his wallet. Finding it, he removed the foil package and, once covered, he reached for her.

They joined again roughly, crashing together with urgent and commanding thrusts. He slid his hands under her bottom, shifting her pelvis for more friction. Greta's whimpers became demands, telling him she was close.

Her head fell back and her body stiffened, clenching around him as another climax racked her body. Her tight orgasmic pulses sent him over the edge, violently and soul deep.

Chapter Twenty-Four

They lay entangled on the desk, and Greta waited for her breathing to slow. She slid her hand along Jacob's damp, solid chest, her fingers dusting the soft hairs and stopping at his heart. She loved the heavy thumping of it under her palm.

He looked at her hand and started to pull away. He must've thought she was asking him to move.

She tightened her hold, nails digging in flesh. "Please don't go. Not yet."

Wrapping his arms around her, he lifted her from the table, never breaking their connection. He sat them on the closest chair. "I'm happy to stay like this for the rest of the night. You let me know when you're uncomfortable."

He ran his lips along her neck to the edge of her shoulder, leaning back and watching goosebumps pebbling on her arms. He was growing hard again.

"I swear one of these days I will take you in a bed," he muttered, his focus still on her skin.

"I'm in no hurry. Let's try all the places en route to there."

"You're such the woman for me." His lips slanted over hers.

His words and tender kisses made Greta's heart soar.

Someone's fist pounded on the loft's door, and her heart continued its flight straight into her throat. She jerked, and Jacob's arms tightened protectively around her.

"Go away!" he hollered in the direction of the offending door.

"There are…um…some guys here to see you," Will called.

"What the fuck," Jacob muttered, then asked her, "You want to use the bathroom to wash up?"

She nodded. He disposed of the condom and snagged his jeans, putting them on. "Tell them to go away too," he shouted.

Greta eyed the knob and froze. There wasn't a lock.

Her knees went weak, picturing strange, late-night visitors busting in the room. She wanted to run to the bathroom and hide, but being stuck in there naked if they came inside didn't sound appealing. Scanning the room, she spotted her skirt and blouse, her bra and panties nowhere in sight.

Not good.

"I can assure you they won't go away. They want to talk to you right now." Will's anxiety was palpable.

Fingers of dread crept along her spine. Anyone arriving at this hour and demanding to talk couldn't be good.

Before either could ask who the unwelcome visitors were, heavy footsteps pounded up the stairs. *More than one set!*

Greta scrambled to put on what clothes she found. Jacob hurried to the bedroom door, clad only in his jeans.

He opened the door a crack, using his broad expanse to block anyone from entering. "Who the fuck—"

He choked on the rest of his words, his back going ramrod straight. She was about to ask who was on the other side when a man spoke, shocking Greta to the core.

"Jacob Grimm, I'm Officer O'Brien, and this is Officer Smithson. We need to ask you some questions. I have a warrant to search your home."

"What?! Why?" Jacob stumbled back, sounding confused and stunned. It matched her plummeting heart and racing mind.

The men took it as an invitation to enter. Greta caught sight of their uniforms and dread bloomed in her chest. The two officers were from Petite Bois. She even recognized one of them. They'd gone to high school together. Tim O'Brien.

His gaze landed on her, widening in recognition before he averted his eyes, searching the room. The other officer, a man with a round face and small, mean features, was leering at her in a way that made her skin crawl. She crossed her arms over her braless chest and tried to ignore the man's smirk.

Jacob came between her and the creepy cop, blocking her from view. "What's this about?"

"Mr. Grimm, you are under suspicion for grand larceny," O'Brien stated.

"Grand larceny?" Jacob echoed. "What the hell?"

O'Brien handed Jacob an official-looking form. "Here's the warrant." He pointed to the desk and spoke to the other police officer. "Smithson, gather that for evidence."

She was flooded with horror when the officer grabbed Nigel's Rolex. Her blood ran cold. *This is somehow my fault.*

"Don't touch the watch. It's mine!" Panic and anger battled for dominance within her.

A nasty smirk tugged at Smithson's small mouth. He peered from

Jacob to Greta to the floor littered with items they'd knocked aside during their feverish lovemaking. "Thanks for not shoving the evidence off the table, while you were—"

"Enough," O'Brien cut in.

The other officer's offensive manner wasn't her concern. The allegations leveled at Jacob had her attention. "What evidence? The watch is my stepfather's, and it's not stolen. Jacob is repairing it."

Once again Smithson ignored her and instead goaded Jacob. "Tell me, Mr. Grimm. When you decide to go into a rich man's home, you go for everything, don't you? An expensive watch wasn't enough? You had to take his daughter too, huh?"

What is this guy's problem?

Jacob's mouth dropped then slammed shut into a razor thin line. His hands clenched into fists.

O'Brien quickly stepped between the two men, facing his obnoxious partner. "I said enough Bill."

Hostility clung to Jacob like a wet blanket, and, for ten long seconds, he stood stock-still. Taking a deep breath, he swooped down, snatching a discarded T-shirt. After putting it on, he leaned against the nearest wall, arms crossed, watching the two officers with open resentment.

O'Brien faced Jacob. "We got a call from Mrs. Silverstone reporting her husband's Rolex was stolen. They assert they didn't give nor loan it to you. They have a witness who claims you wore it. This is enough to bring you in and search your home."

Jacob's angry gaze jumped to Greta's. "You didn't tell your family you were taking it?"

"I wanted it to be a surprise." She gaped.

He threw his arms in the air and let them fall, slamming to his sides. "Well, surprise!"

She folded into herself. His sarcasm was justified, and she waited for him to slam insults and accusations on her.

He didn't. He took a deep breath and faced O'Brien. "Now what?"

"We have to take you in." He turned to Greta. "However, if this is a simple mistake, perhaps you should call your parents. Get it straightened out, and soon."

Blake was somehow entangled in this, but her mother had to have made the call. He didn't have friends high enough in Petite Bois's bureaucracy to have police officers called out late on a Friday night, a holiday weekend, no less, for a simple larceny arrest.

What a mess. One easily avoided had she bothered to mention the damn watch to her mom. Heck, told her about Jacob. All of this to avoid an unpleasant conversation with her mother. How stupid.

It ended tonight.

Smithson removed his handcuffs from his belt, and again O'Brien intervened. "Those aren't necessary." His gaze fell on Jacob. "Am I right, Mr. Grimm?"

He gave one sharp nod, locking gazes with Greta. The anger reflected in them chilled her bone deep.

Seconds later, the two officers were escorting Jacob down the stairs and through the hallway, passing by his stunned father and brother. Smithson opened the front door, and it broke Greta's paralysis.

She sprinted after, calling to Jacob, "I'm sorry. I promise to fix this."

He didn't respond or even glance in her direction. Instead, he turned to Will. "Call my lawyer. Have her meet me at the police station."

Without another word, the two officers directed Jacob from his home and into their police car.

Chapter Twenty-Five

Watching the scenery pass by, Jacob figured they were halfway to Petite Bois. He had a million questions whirling around in his head but kept his mouth shut. If he opened it, he'd say something stupid and make his situation worse.

Fucking Blake.

Jacob recalled the weasel's expression when he spotted the watch during lunch with Greta last week. The asshole had orchestrated this mess. Though, how the shit he convinced Greta's parents was beyond him.

The pudgy cop, Smithson, twisted around, wearing an expression full of contempt. Jacob gave an inward groan. Whatever was about to spew from the prick's mouth was going to be ugly.

"Tell me, Mr. Grimm, what was more satisfying? Getting your hands on Mr. Silverstone's Rolex or his stepdaughter?"

"Fuck off, dickweed," Jacob snapped, both angry and bewildered.

What is it with this guy?

"Stop antagonizing." O'Brien sighed, glancing briefly from the road to his partner. "I get you had a thing for Greta in high school, and she was never interested. That doesn't mean you have to start shit."

Color flooded Smithson's jowls, and he whipped back around, staring straight ahead. "Whatever. I was making conversation with the River Rat," he muttered.

That explains a lot. Seriously, does everyone in her freaky city know each other?

O'Brien's gaze didn't veer to either man. "Uh huh, whatever, lay off. Meier is out of your league."

"Maybe not. If she opens her legs for this guy, the uppity bitch's standards must not be too high."

"You fucking asshole," Jacob bellowed, erupting. He banged his open palms on the divider, ignoring the sting and their startled jolts. His rage owned him and poured from him like poison. "Keep talking, and you'll be able to add assault to the warrant. I swear—"

"Enough, Mr. Grimm. Calm down," O'Brien barked. "Don't make

the situation worse by threatening a police officer."

Jacob slammed back into the worn seat, taking deep breaths, trying to cage his venom.

It wasn't working.

"And, Bill, for the last time, shut the hell up," O'Brien said.

The rest of the drive was in an oppressive, angry silence. When they pulled into the station and parked, O'Brien opened Jacob's door. Smithson stayed far back, scurrying to the entrance.

Good thing. The desire to tear the man limb from limb hadn't lessened.

Jacob scoffed bitterly at his murderous desire. Now, there'd be something—getting arrested for a crime he actually committed.

~ * ~

After a call to Jacob's lawyer, Greta and Will scrambled to his car, promising to call Roger when they had more information. The poor man was distraught, unable to decide if he should stay or go with them. In the end, he remained at home, afraid too many people would further confuse the situation.

Greta couldn't stop apologizing, first to Roger then to Will. Blake was without a doubt to blame for this mess. His revenge.

Yet, she held some of the blame. She just wasn't sure how much.

"I'm sorry," she said for the umpteenth time.

"I told you, there's no need to apologize." Will braked at a red light. A feeble smile lifted the corners of his mouth. "I know what you're feeling. Jacob was arrested once because of me."

Greta's self-reproach momentarily quieted, and a morbid sense of curiosity awoke. "Really? When?"

"During my heavy partying days, I'd moved away and lost touch with everyone. I think, deep down, I didn't want them to see what I was becoming. Dropping off the face of the earth didn't sit with Jacob. He kept finding me and trying to convince me to come back home. To get help. Anyway, one time he had the bad luck of arriving at my most recent 'home' shortly before a raid. The police assumed Jacob was another drug dealer or user hanging around. Luckily, everything was sorted, and the charges were dismissed."

Greta groaned and hunched into her seat, covering her face with her hands.

Will patted her back. "Don't worry. We'll fix this too."

She hoped it was possible. Doing her part, she tried to call her mother, yet again. To her surprise, this time she answered her phone.

"Mother," Greta said in a frantic rush. "What's going on? What have you done?"

Her mother's indignation carried through the line. "I would like to ask you the same thing. Today I was informed by a close friend my husband's heirloom watch was stolen by a man we hired to install a chandelier. A man you're apparently dating. In fact, I got a call from another friend, whose husband's a city official, and she tells me you were with the man during the arrest...in a rather compromising position." The last sentence reached a hysterical screech.

In Mother's world, this was a catastrophe. Not the supposed theft, the gossip of her daughter sleeping with a possible criminal. Nothing upset her mother more than negative chatter surrounding her family.

The lingering traces of Greta's timidity died in the face of her mother's trivial concerns. The woman was willing to ruin Jacob's livelihood on shallow evidence and pride. Greta's disappointment in her mother had tears prickling behind her eyes.

"Where are you now? Are you at the police station hoping to put the final nail in Jacob's coffin?" she spat.

"Of course I'm at the station. I need to identify the stolen property. Plus, I'm trying to keep your name out of this mess. I don't want my daughter associated with a lowlife thief and drug dealer."

"Drug dealer! What are you talking about? Never mind. I'm almost there. Don't do anything until we talk more." Greta hung up and turned to Will, dread filling her veins. "Jacob will never forgive me for this mess."

"He can hold a grudge, but I suspect it'll be more at who caused it, than at you." He rubbed a hand along his jaw. "Though, I wouldn't plan on too many cozy dinners with your family and Jacob."

Greta gave a bitter laugh. "No problem. After this disaster, skipping any and all family gatherings is ideal." They drove into the entrance of Petite Bois's small brick police station, and she asked, "Would you mind stopping at the door? I need to get in and find my mother."

"Sure."

She said a quick thanks and rushed across the sidewalk. Once inside, she headed straight to the administration desk.

After explaining who she was to an older police officer with receding gray hair, he escorted Greta through a locked steel door, down a barren hallway, and into a plush office. There she found her mother perched in a comfortable visitor's chair, talking with a city representative Greta recognized.

Her mother's expression morphed from solicitous to furious when her gaze landed on Greta. The representative shot from his chair, offering them the privacy of his office and bid a hasty retreat. The man clearly didn't want to be involved in their feud.

When the door clicked shut, her mother stalked toward Greta, pointing a shaky manicured finger. "You break things off with Blake and start dating trash from Detroit? What's going on? I expect better from you."

Greta snapped, "You know, Mother, the sad thing is, I didn't expect better from you. Still, regrettably, you exceeded my expectations."

Her mother reared back, as if slapped. "What's that supposed to mean?"

"I've been dating Jacob for over a month now, and you want to know why I've never mentioned him?" Greta swallowed the anger clawing up her throat. "Because you'd judge and dismiss him, declaring our relationship didn't meet your standards, but damn, Mother, I never dreamed you'd take it to this extreme."

"Oh, please, Greta." Her mother waved a dismissive hand, returning to her seat. She folded her hands in her lap, managing to appear both cool and condescending. "You didn't tell me because you knew what kind of man you're dating. Deep down you're ashamed."

"No!"

"You should be. He's a lowlife."

Greta gasped, gathering her anger and preparing to throw it at her mother.

"Excuse me," Will growled, causing both women to jump. He stood at the door. Behind him was the rapidly retreating form of the old police officer. "The only thing low around here is you and what you've done." Fury emanated from Will.

Sophia tensed at the insult. "Who are you?"

"I'm Will Grimm. Jacob's brother.

"Oh, I've heard about you." Sophia sniffed, scrunching her nose like she smelled something bad. "You're even worse than your brother." She returned her attention to Greta. "Nice company you keep. A drug addict and his dealer."

"What?" Greta spluttered, wondering if her mother was losing her mind.

"My brother isn't a dealer or a thief. Where are you coming up with this shit?" Will snarled.

Sophia took a deep breath, letting it out through her nose, and answered. Condemnation dripped from her every word as she said, "Police reports. He was arrested during a drug raid. Are you telling me he was there for the fantastic company and ambiance?"

"It was a misunderstanding. Jacob wasn't charged," Will said through clenched teeth.

"That he was able to have the allegations dropped doesn't make him any less of a miscreant. It only tells me he had a decent lawyer." She swung her haughty gaze away from Will and back to Greta. "And don't pretend to be shocked, young lady. You know exactly what you're dating."

Oh no, here comes the rant.

Her mother loved nothing more than feeling like she had the high ground. It put her in lecture mode.

Too bad her standing was as steady as a home on the San Andreas fault line during an earthquake. The arrest she was referring to was probably the one Will mentioned on the drive over, and tonight's arrest was utter nonsense. Nothing more than Blake's vicious revenge.

"This Jacob," her mother snapped, "was wearing Nigel's Rolex the other day. And the police confiscated it from his house. I, nor Nigel, gave it to him. What other proof do you need?"

That's her evidence? Seriously?! It's flimsy as old, moth-eaten chiffon.

Greta wanted to scream. She more or less did. "Jesus, Mother! Jacob was wearing the Rolex because I'd just given the damn thing to him."

Sophia inhaled sharply. "Why in the world would you do such a thing? You know how important the Rolex is to Nigel—"

"Because, Mother," Greta cut in, shaking with exasperation. "I asked Jacob to repair it for Nigel's birthday."

Her mother's blue eyes widened in uncertainty. "Why would a simple mover, a drug dealer, be able to repair anything?"

Greta wanted to shout at her mother to stop calling Jacob a drug dealer. To stop spitting out his name like it was a dirty word. Instead, she was shocked into silence, as her father answered her mother's question.

"Because, Sophia, if you bothered to learn more than Mr. Grimm's police record, you would have known he is the perfect man for fixing Nigel's *precious* watch."

Greta's heart plummeted at the same time her guilt skyrocketed. She'd hoped to fix this before it got to her father.

He stepped fully into the room, eyeing Will and Greta, yet keeping his focus on his ex-wife.

Clearly rattled, Mother faced her ex-husband. "What are you doing here, Charles? This has nothing to do with you."

"In fact, yes, it does. Mr. Grimm is one of my clients, and this type of thing could ruin him. A felony charge would automatically cancel his contract, damaging his business expansion before it even got off the ground."

Her father set a file on the table and gave his ex-wife a hard stare. "If I were you, I would worry more about Mr. Grimm suing you for slander than my presence here."

Greta was speechless. Her father was here to help Jacob?

"This isn't baseless slander." Sophia peered past her ex-husband, probably hoping her so-called proof would walk through the door. "I've read his file and have a witness to the theft. You're the one who's made a mistake, taking on that unsavory man as a client. You should be grateful. I've saved you from further dealings with him."

"My clients are none of your business," Charles replied wearily. "However, this supposed theft is."

"There is no supposed. I have a witness."

"Your witness is wrong. And you have your daughter telling you she loaned the watch to Mr. Grimm."

Sophia opened and closed her mouth, as if the truth was physically strangling her. "She's covering for him," she stammered. "Trying to protect her reprobate lover. I bet it's how he got out of the last arrest too. A guy like him uses women."

Wow. Denial is a powerful thing.

Charles scoffed. "Now you're inventing stories."

Her mother crossed both arms over her chest, manicured nails tapping on slim biceps. "Oh, and I suppose you know the truth. Go ahead, Charles, spin your fairy tale version of that man's life. Let's hear it."

"There's no fairy tale, and yes, I know the whole story. *Unlike you.* An extensive background check is done on every potential client. Mr. Grimm's so-called drug charge was nothing more than a mistake, a formality if you will. Everyone in the house was arrested during the raid. Later, the police sorted the guilty from the innocent. One of my people spoke to an officer from the precinct where the drug charge originated. Jacob's only fault was being at the wrong place at the wrong time."

Mother appeared ready to argue. Father held up a hand. "As for tonight's ludicrous arrest, I also have a witness. This person saw Greta give Jacob the watch, with the request to repair it."

I'm a fool. How did I manage to underestimate my father's kindness and loyalty?

She wasn't surprised her father knew Jacob's history. He vetted all possible clients. No. What amazed her was he genuinely cared. He could've sent a lackey. Instead, he came here himself, in the middle of the night, to make sure a wrong was righted.

Tears of gratitude pooled at the back of her eyes. She'd never admired her father more.

"Now, you have to decide, Sophia, do you want to continue this farce? It'd be such great gossip." He bracketed his hands like reading a news breaking headline. "'Next up-and-coming businessman falsely accused of theft by girlfriend's malicious mother.' Not only will you appear spiteful, but foolish. This will surely keep the gossip mills spinning for months…"

Chapter Twenty-Six

O'Brien unlocked Jacob's cell. "Grimm, you're free to go."

Jacob glanced from the bench, letting his hands dangle between his knees. "Is this a joke?"

"Nope. No joke." O'Brien opened the door. "You can pick up the Rolex and the rest of your stuff before you leave.

"Is this what you guys do for shits and giggles? Arrest people in the middle of the night." He stood, stretching his arms wide. "Toss them in a cell. Let them loose an hour later. My lawyer hasn't even arrived yet."

"This has nothing to do with us. There was a complaint and enough to bring you in. The charges have been dropped. That's it."

"Where's your partner? He didn't want to be the one who let me loose?"

O'Brien didn't take the bait. Figuring it best not to press his luck too much, no matter his pissy mood, Jacob started toward the exit. Before he could slip past, O'Brien held his hand in a "stop" gesture.

"What?" Jacob growled.

"I remember Greta from high school. She was a sweet girl and seems like a lovely woman."

"Your point?"

O'Brien might be a decent guy, but Jacob wasn't in the mood for a heart to heart. He needed to get the hell out of this Godforsaken city.

"Don't judge her too harshly because of her mother's stupidity."

Jacob shouldered past O'Brien. Easy for him to say. He wasn't the one behind bars, thanks to his girlfriend's mother.

~ * ~

Greta caught sight of the police station doors sliding open and Jacob emerge. He pounded down the steps, shoulders hunched and hands curled into fists at his sides.

She was frozen to the pavement as his arctic gaze flickered past her and rested on her parents standing by her side. He turned away from them, from her, ready to walk away forever.

No.

"Jacob, wait!" Greta rushed to him, wrapping her arms tightly around his waist. She couldn't let him leave without a word, without her.

He stiffened but didn't pull away. Then, like balm to her soul, he sighed, and returned her embrace.

"I'm sorry," she choked, burrowing into his chest and finding it difficult to speak through the misery of the past and the relief of the present.

After a slight hesitation, he kissed the top of her head. "It's fine, love. I know this isn't your fault. And you came here to make things right."

Greta leaned back to peer into his eyes. "Did you think I wouldn't follow you?"

He shrugged and gave a weary smile. His lack of faith hurt more than his recent and brief icy demeanor.

"There was no way I was leaving without you, though I have to admit, the person most helpful was my father."

"Charles?" Jacob's eyebrows rose. "I figured he'd come here to tell me, in person, that he shredded my contract. He looks pissed."

"His anger is directed at my mother, not you. I guess someone working here saw my name on the arresting papers and called my father. He arrived shortly after me, storming in and demanding your release. Said he had proof you didn't steal the Rolex. Then proceeded to give Mother a tongue-lashing."

"What proof did he have?"

"Do you remember Anna Kincade, Blake's office assistant?"

Jacob nodded.

"Remember, she was with us when I gave you the watch?"

His forehead creased before smoothing. "Oh, yes. I forgot Anna hadn't left when you gave me the watch. How did she pass this along to your father? How did she even know about the arrest?"

"She was with my father when his friend from the station called. Anna was willing to come in as a witness."

A glint of mischief flashed in Jacob's eyes. "Wow. They were working late, especially for a holiday."

Huh. He has a point.

Greta smiled. "Maybe I need to lecture my father concerning romances in the workplace."

"Maybe," Jacob agreed. "Anyway. I'm surprised."

"Why?"

"This was the perfect excuse to get rid of me. I'd gotten the impression your father didn't care for me. More specifically, me dating you."

Maybe she should have told him more of what her father said when he learned she'd been seeing Jacob. His problem wasn't with who she was dating but more with his daughter keeping a certain standard of professionalism at the workplace. Like not kissing clients in her office.

"Even if it were true, which it's not, he wouldn't have let the false charge stand," Greta replied indignantly. "Besides, he likes you."

"Oh yeah, what gives you that idea?"

"If he didn't like you, he wouldn't have come here. He'd have sent someone low on the totem pole."

"Or he wanted to make certain everything was resolved, cutting off the possibility of bad publicity. I mean, I *am* affiliated with his company and dating his daughter. Maybe those are enough to bring him here." Jacob stepped back, letting his arms fall to his side. "Either way, I should thank him."

He made his way to her father. She didn't follow but was close enough to hear their conversation. Her father brushed aside Jacob's gratitude and even apologized for Blake's scheming, telling Jacob, come Monday, Blake was fired.

She was torn. Furious with her ex's vindictive ways and regretful tonight was probably going to ruin a longtime friendship between her father and Blake's parents.

What a mess.

The two men made plans for a business lunch later in the week, ending the conversation with a friendly handshake. Then Father hugged her goodbye and said they'd talk more in the morning. Afterward, he left in his Lexus.

Greta looped an arm around Jacob, needing the reassurance of his warmth and his strong arms around her. "You were furious. When you left the station, it poured from you. I was certain you were done with me."

At such a late hour, most of the parking lot was empty. Will was leaning against his car, a few spaces from her mother's Audi, and waved them over. Her mother ignored everyone and continued to talk on her cellphone.

They walked toward Will.

"I was upset, but not at you," Jacob said. "At least not entirely. What you saw was dread mixed with anger. I thought you were leaving with your family, and it hurt. A lot. I was wound tight and figured it best to leave. I didn't want to upset you further."

After everything he dealt with tonight, because of *her*, and his concern was with *her* emotions?

Under his rough exterior was a true prince.

What had been tiptoeing around her slammed in at full force, wrapping and burrowing into her heart. She loved Jacob, completely and soul deep.

"How did I get so lucky?" she mused.

He gave a sardonic snort. "It seems to me the only luck following me is the bad kind. I mean, how many people get arrested multiple times for crimes they didn't commit?"

She laughed and slid a hand into his back pocket, not caring who was watching. "I have to confess. It's one of the things I love about you—"

He peered at her, a smile tugging at the corner of his mouth. "You love that I get arrested? You're a strange woman."

She matched his grin, enjoying his teasing. "Well no. I love your compassion and that you can forgive."

"Damn. You make me sound like a loyal puppy." His lips pressed into a serious line, but the glint in his eyes told her he was amused. "Please don't tell my new jail cronies. It could hurt my rep on the cell block."

She laughed. "Your secret's safe with me." Greta stood on tiptoes and kissed him, deep and tender, trying to repair the damage between them.

Lost in the sensation of his lips and body against hers, she'd forgotten they were in a police parking lot. That was until Jacob stiffened and took a sudden step back.

An impenetrable wall sprung between them. The tension and resentment radiating off him was palpable. Greta spun around, wanting to discover the source.

Her mother.

Mother raised her chin, managing to look both uncomfortable and patronizing. "I would like to apologize for the misunderstanding."

Jacob didn't respond to the apology. Instead, he thrust a hand into his front pocket, withdrawing Nigel's Rolex. "Here. Take the damn thing. I don't want you to have me arrested again. Good luck getting it fixed."

His tone said the opposite. It sounded more like he hoped it ended up like the white rabbit's watch when the Mad Hatter got ahold of it in *Alice in Wonderland.*

Her mother straightened her shoulders, as if fortifying herself against his scorn. "Charles was correct. I should have contacted Greta instead of the police after learning the person accused of stealing from my home was also rumored to be dating my daughter. However, I assumed she didn't know and you were using her to get closer to our wealth. I made a mistake, I apologize."

"Your mistake could've cost me my career," he replied tightly.

"In my defense, had I known you were dating my daughter, this never would have happened." Her gaze bounced from Jacob and fixed on Greta.

Oh. No.

"Today was the first I learned you are dating the guy who delivered our furniture. I honestly didn't believe it. You've never mentioned him, and, quite frankly, you two make an unlikely pair. Although no matter how questionable, I would have reacted differently had I known he was dating you. Not some laborer I'd hired, who'd been inside my house and later was wearing my husband's expensive watch."

Greta swallowed, avoiding Jacob's gaze. "No wonder I failed to mention us. Look at what happened today." The argument was weak. She was trying to cover for her lousy decisions.

Mother shook her head. "That's unfair. I knew nothing of Jacob, except what a trusted friend told me. And a damaging police report. I'm not going to lie and say I approve of this relationship, but, I repeat, this whole situation could have been avoided had I known before today you two were dating."

Greta's heart clenched. She'd messed up.

She'd only wanted to avoid a confrontation with her overly opinionated mother. Instead, she hurt the man she loved.

"All is well that ends well," her mother continued breezily, as though it were a trivial matter and done with, she turned away. "Come home with me. I'll send someone to get your car from his house tomorrow."

Greta began to suspect her mother's real motive. Regret didn't bring her to speak with Jacob. Her true intent was to cause a rift.

No wonder the apology rang false. *It was.*

No way was she leaving with her mother. "I'm going back to my apartment."

Greta cut a glance to Will, then Jacob. He offered only anger and silence.

"At the University, why?" Her mother crossed her arms over her chest, causing her dainty Hermes purse to fall from her slim shoulder. "Aren't you interning at your father's?"

Like she cares.

Greta shrugged, though, in reality, she was nervous. "I'll speak to Father tomorrow. I should have enough hours to receive credit for my internship."

Her mother's lips pulled into a thin line of dissatisfaction. She seemed to understand she wasn't winning this argument. "Fine. Would you like me to take you to your car?"

Greta glanced at the Grimm brothers. "Ah, no. I was hoping Will would give me a ride back to get it."

Will nodded. Jacob stared back with cold eyes. A vice tightened around her heart. He was going to refuse, overrule Will.

Before he could, Will said, "Yeah, I'll give you a ride back to the house."

Greta could've kissed him.

She glanced at Jacob, and her heart deflated. His jaw clenched tight enough she feared his teeth might crack; everything screamed he didn't want her to go with them. He wanted her gone.

Not the most encouraging response. Didn't matter. She was going to fix this. "Thank you, Will," she said quietly.

Without a word, Jacob walked to Will's old Ford Focus.

Greta trailed after Will and Jacob. She longed to hold Jacob, but the anger that radiated off him in waves gave her pause. Her fragile, scared heart wouldn't be able to handle a brutal rejection.

The ride to Jacob's place was awful. The tension in the car was thicker than cement, and it leaked into her veins, running straight for her heart.

The couple of times she tried talking to Jacob, he grunted single syllable responses, keeping his gaze trained on the horizon. By the time they arrived at his place, Greta wanted to scream, cry, and stop time.

She wanted to fix things but would take this awful limbo if the other option was to face reality without him.

He didn't appear to have the same compulsion. When Will shut off the engine, Jacob whipped open his door, asking if she left anything in the house, not bothering to glance in her direction.

"No." Her voice warbled.

Without saying the exact words, he'd told her to leave. To gather her belongings and exit his life.

He stopped in front of her car, staring past her. "Let's go."

What?

Greta staggered, almost tripping. "Let's? You mean us, together?"

He nodded, a sharp one up, one down.

She'd imagined a brush-off, or perhaps angry accusations. Never did these imaginings include Jacob driving her to Lansing. She'd have him all to herself for the three-hour drive. The cement slowly hardening around her heart melted, morphing into hope.

"I want to make sure you arrive safely," he replied in a monotone, cooling some of her optimism.

Will, who'd been moving toward the house, stopped. "Need me to follow? Give you a ride back?"

Shut up, Will!

She didn't want Jacob to have a way back.

He shook his head. "No, Jamie lives nearby. I'll crash there."

Such a simple remark, yet a million emotions were attached to it.

Hope. Maybe Jacob wasn't only worried about her safety, and a small part of him wanted to work things out. *Dread.* Would this be the last time she'd have with him? *Jealousy.* She'd never met, nor had Jacob mentioned a Jamie. She couldn't tell if this friend was male or female. If he planned to work off his resentment in the arms of another woman, it would kill Greta.

The uncertainty drove her crazy. She shoved it aside, determined to fix the disaster before they ever arrived at her apartment. This time there was no way she'd let him sit in silence, stewing in his anger and thinking how life would be better without her.

"Would you mind driving?" she asked Jacob. "I'm a little nearsighted and don't have my glasses. Driving is difficult at night."

He gave another quick, angry nod. She handed him her keys and told him the address to her place. They got in, neither saying a word as Jacob started the car and set her GPS.

Backing down his driveway and onto the street, she studied the rigid set of his shoulders and the white-knuckle grip on the steering wheel. Her need to hide was fierce.

Her fear of losing him was stronger than her aversion to quarreling. She tried again. "Never in a million years did I see this coming."

Jacob gave a bitter laugh. "Yeah, not how I imagined meeting your mother. In handcuffs because she had me arrested. Though, I guess I should be honored to at least have met her."

That was unfair. "You know, today was the first day I'd met your family."

Jacob crooked his neck, pinning her with disappointed eyes. "They knew we were dating. Your mother had no idea I even existed. Were you also worried you'd come off as unprofessional with her? In all these weeks, you haven't even mentioned me in one conversation?" Each of his questions was more accusatory than the last, and his voice heated in irritation. "Listen, I know we're new, and you wanted things simple, but are we *that* casual?"

Greta hesitated, unsure how to answer. There was nothing casual about her love for him, but what if he didn't feel the same? After tonight, she wouldn't blame him. The last thing he'd want was an unreciprocated confession of love.

Or worse, what if he thought she was saying it merely to cool his anger? Now wasn't the right time. Heck, maybe it was. She didn't know.

His palm slammed on the steering wheel, shattering her contemplations. "Fuck. Never mind. Your silence is answer enough. I should have known from the beginning I'd be nothing more than your dirty secret. Someone to pass the time with, until your prince arrives."

"No. Jacob." She spoke in a rush, words falling from her, messy and in haste. She needed to make him understand. "I'm not close with my parents, especially my mother. I didn't tell her because she wouldn't have approved. You saw how she was this evening. She would've criticized us, paraded every one of her friends' sons playing matchmaker, and done who knows what else to cause problems. To split us. It's much easier to keep my personal life private."

They stopped at a red light, and Jacob twisted in his seat giving her the full impact of his emotions, hitting her with a backdraft of fury and disappointment. "That's your excuse? It's easier?" he yelled.

His gaze roamed over her as if searching for something. The light reflected off his hardened features flickered from red to green, and he turned back to the road, cutting her deeper. "Shit. You're a grown woman. Aren't you a little old to worry what Mommy thinks?"

His anger fused her mouth shut. She wasn't afraid of him, but his fury was like another passenger in the car, taking up Jacob's shouts long after he stopped talking.

She couldn't compete with both.

However, when the miles passed and he didn't speak, the silence was worse than his angry words. She wanted to argue, to make him understand. Though, she kept making the situation worse.

In the end, he broke the oppressive silence, sounding utterly defeated. "I'm sorry. I shouldn't have yelled. I'm overreacting. From the start, you told me you wanted nothing serious. I shouldn't have expected you to want more because I do."

"Jacob, I—"

He held up a hand. "Please, Greta, I'm begging you. No more. My head's killing me. I can't think straight. I don't want to say something I'll regret."

She didn't want him to either. She twisted to face her window, to the night landscape. Perfect. The black nothingness suited her mood and hid the silent tears rolling down her cheeks.

Chapter Twenty-Seven

Jacob looked at Greta. She'd fallen into a restless sleep. The silence was worse than her weak excuses. It gave him too much time in his head to replay the disastrous night and its aftermath.

Damn. All this time together, and she'd never even mentioned him to her family. Was he her filthy secret, or so insignificant he wasn't worth mentioning?

The answer didn't matter. It was time to end things. She'd returned to Lansing, ending whatever they had together. It wasn't like they were in a relationship. Tonight she made his one-sided illusion crystal clear.

He understood his place in her life. He was a diversion until Mr. High Society came along. He was a man to fuck and have a little fun with during summer break. Not the one to meet Mother and Father.

Jacob wanted to curse, to slam his fists against something hard. Anything to release the anger and disappointment boiling inside him and growing.

He couldn't spill his bitterness onto her. She'd made her intentions clear from the beginning. He was the asshole who went and fell in love.

Maybe he could go back to the man he'd been before Greta. When his heart beat for no one, and his only desire was to make Rework a success.

Life might have been flat, but at least there was never a vise around his heart, slowly twisting his soul and leaking out his happiness. He rubbed his chest then gripped the steering wheel, scoffing. Nothing was going to ease the pain.

He pulled in front of her place, putting the car in park and glancing at the three-story brick building. The apartment had one main entrance, and every unit had a spacious balcony. The place had a cozy, sheltered vibe, not how he pictured campus housing. What the hell did he know? Closest he ever got to college was a couple miscellaneous courses at the local JC.

Turning, he touched Greta's shoulder to wake her and found her eyes open and watching him. "This your place?"

She straightened and stretched. "Yup, this is it. What'd you expect?

A white sorority house with drunken people on the lawn?" She offered a weak smile.

He tried to ignore the sadness in her eyes. It made him wish for more. "Yeah, I kind of did. All those college movies gave me high expectations." His teasing fell flat.

"Sorry to disappoint. I'm a fifteen-minute walk, five-minute drive to the University. I prefer living in an apartment off campus than the craziness of college living."

After a couple ticks of silence, Jacob grasped the door handle, opening it. Greta did the same. There was no sense dragging this out.

He needed to get her inside and leave before he lost his nerve and pleaded for her to feel things she didn't. "It's late. Let me walk you to your door."

She came around and planted her feet in front of him. "Stay. Please."

"No."

Damn. Who knew one word could hurt like a bullet to his heart.

She placed a hand on his chest, almost shattering him. "We need to talk. We need to fix things."

The pleading in her voice and the moisture gathering in her eyes confused him. "What's to work out? I get it. We aren't serious and never will be. I'm not worth the inconvenience or arguments it'll cause with your family. Besides, you're back here. Our summer fling is finished. There's no need to talk. We're done."

Forget dropping her off at the door. He should have called Jamie and told Greta to go inside. Neither of them looking back.

She owned his heart; if he stayed even another ten minutes, he'd hand her every piece of himself. He'd be left with nothing but an empty shell of a man.

He didn't move.

"You're not a fling. Jacob, you mean everything to me." She grabbed the sides of his face, making him meet her gaze. "I love you."

He stared at her, not sure he'd heard correctly. She repeated it, her words hitting his heart like a defibrillator.

"Really?" he stammered. It wasn't smooth or manly, but shit, his brain needed to catch up with his emotions. Going from misery to elation in a matter of seconds was difficult to process.

"Yes." Her tone was a mixture of frustration and unhappiness. "I know what I said, what we said. I couldn't help falling. I love you." Her hands slid from his face, and she stared at them. "Do with it what you will. I just wanted you to know, no matter what you decide. I'd like you to come inside with me. Will you forgive what happened? Are you interested in trying the long-distance thing?"

Any and all thoughts of leaving scattered. Slipping his arms around her, he kissed away most of their sorrow, answering the most important thing. "I love you too."

"Really?"

"Yes." He chuckled, wrapping his arms around her. "I love you, Greta, with everything I have. It scares the hell out of me, but you have me. Heart and soul."

"God, yes. All of you. Please, come inside and stay. At least tonight."

Jacob wanted to scoop her into his arms and run full tilt inside. He couldn't. Not yet. He needed to make something clear. "You understand I can't offer you the lifestyle you're used to, nor the approval of your family. Tonight could be a preview of things to come. Are you sure this is what you want?"

"Let go of this lifestyle you believe I need. I want happiness and passion in my life. I have it with you. Also, you're wrong. What happened today was a bizarre misunderstanding, a mere glitch in our relationship. We love each other, and everything else will fall into place."

She ran a hand up his neck and into his hair, tugging gently and pinning him with eyes overflowing with hope and yearning. He almost believed her words. Nodding, he buried his doubts and let her lead him to her apartment.

Reaching the main door, she twisted around and rested against him. "Let's forget tonight, and no worrying about the future. We'll enjoy the now," she whispered, offering a gentle kiss.

His response wasn't tender. He slammed his mouth to hers, wanting to forget his concerns. If she was willing, he was more than happy to use each other's touch and bodies to silence their worries.

Greta eagerly accepted his roughness, matching it. She ran her hands through his hair and down to the back pockets of his jeans, palming his ass and tugging him closer. He was already hard, and the contact, along with her soft moans, inflamed him to desperate levels.

He didn't get the chance to do more than slide a hand under the hem of her silky blouse before a blonde woman barreled out the doorway, almost plowing into them. She stopped short, missing them by mere inches.

The man coming behind her wasn't as agile and collided with the woman, who, in turn, slammed into Jacob. He toppled into Greta, and she yelped as they started to fall.

They were a confusion of chaos and limbs, heading straight for the pavement. Hands grabbed Jacob's shoulders, roughly steadying him and allowing him to right his feet and keep Greta from landing on her ass.

Once he was sure she was okay, Jacob thanked the guy.

The man's smile was full of chagrin as he offered his hand. "Sorry. I didn't see you two until I was on top of you both. I'm Miguel. You okay, Greta?"

She nodded as Jacob accepted the man's outstretched hand, examining him. His grin was wide and friendly, at odds with his hulking frame, shaved head, and scarred eyebrow.

"No problem." Jacob shrugged. "No harm, no foul."

From behind, the women squealed. Both men turned and found the women embracing.

Greta pulled back, hands on hips. "What the heck were you doing, Susan? You almost killed us."

"Sorry. I bet Miguel I could beat him down the stairs. I won," Susan gloated then waggled her brows at Greta. "What were you and mystery man doing? From what I saw, something way more exciting than our race."

Color climbed up Greta's cheeks. Her eyes sparkled with amusement. She was stunning.

"Jacob meet Susan Herbst and her fiancé Miguel Torres. They live across the hall from me." She pointed. "Meet my boyfriend, Jacob Grimm."

Man, he liked the title and the delight in her voice when she said it.

"Rumor was you dumped that arrogant ass." Susan surveyed Jacob, gaze running over him. "Traded up."

"I like you already." He chuckled.

Susan had the whole girl-next-door thing going on, open pleasant face with wavy strawberry-blonde hair and a warm smile. Jacob suspected it hid a devilish personality.

Miguel leaned against the glass entrance door and sighed with good humor. "Don't let it go to your head. Susan likes tall men. It's the only reason she agreed to marry me."

"You are a pretty picture, and getting to wear heels is a bonus. Anyway." Susan focused back on Jacob. "I'm not basing my opinion solely off height and good looks. I mean, you do have a slightly cruel aspect about you. Maybe it's the eyes. However, you don't have the self-important posture like Blake, which gives you high points in my book."

"Thanks...I think," Jacob replied dryly. He smirked. Eyeing Greta. "More fans of Blake, huh?"

"Yeah. We went on a couple of double dates. I wouldn't call them fun times."

Susan snorted. "That's putting it mildly."

Miguel scoffed. "The guy's an asshole." He shot an apologetic glance at Greta. "No offense."

"We *are* going to make excellent friends." Jacob smiled. "You know the saying; my enemy's enemy is my friend…and all that."

"Well, new friend, we're heading to Long Island for a late-night snack, or an early breakfast, depending on what you want. Join us?" Miguel asked.

The mention of food made Jacob's stomach sit up and beg. The same must have been true for Greta because her belly let out a fierce growl. "I'd say my girlfriend's stomach answered for us." He glanced at her. Besides her fitful nap on the way over, they'd been awake almost twenty-four hours. "Or do you need to sleep?"

"No, food and alcohol are needed more."

Susan put an arm around Greta, and they headed toward the parking lot. "Long night?" Susan asked.

"Met her mother," Jacob called, as he and Miguel followed the women, who were a couple of paces ahead.

Mentioning her mother brought back a flicker of worry, and it tried to deflate his good mood. He stomped his doubts into submission.

Turning to Miguel, he said, "It was an experience."

Miguel patted Jacob on the back. "Yeah, meeting the parents sucks."

Jacob gave a sardonic laugh. "Man, you have no idea."

Chapter Twenty-Eight

"Wow. You win. Yours's even worse than the first-time meeting Susan's parents. And that was a freaking disaster." Miguel exhaled, leaning back into the booth and tapping his fork against his now-empty plate.

"It was bad," Susan scoffed. "Sure, Jacob was in handcuffs, but I was certain my dad was going to end the night in them. For killing you."

"This I have to hear." Jacob's laughter carried across the almost-deserted diner.

Their waiter, a middle-aged man with a receding hairline, glanced up from his novel and gave them a distracted smile before returning to his book. He didn't seem to mind the slow pace or the raucous laughter coming from their table. Besides their booth, there were two men at the front counter and a couple sitting on the other side of the eatery.

"Agreed. Let's hear the story." Greta took a sip of her Mimosa.

Her hand resting innocently on her lap then skated to his thigh and grasped his knee. She trailed her fingers along the inside of his leg, moving up.

He cut her a side-eyed glance. She smiled back saucily.

Shit. How many of those Mimosas has she had?

His blood was racing south, making it difficult to focus on anything but the hot trail of her fingers. He curled his hand around hers, stopping her wandering ways and tried to focus on Miguel's story.

"Let's skip it. I don't want Greta thinking less of me," he said.

"Oh, please. She doesn't think anything of you, so how could she think less?" Susan joked.

Both women laughed and clinked their glasses with gusto.

Jacob eyed the scattering of empty flutes. Yup, he was getting to see a tipsy Greta. This side of her was all Cheshire cat smiles and wandering hands.

He wasn't complaining. Hell. No.

"Ouch! You ladies are brutal." Miguel grasped his chest, hand to heart, faking outrage. "But I'll talk. Only because I know I'll get sympathy from my man Jacob, right?"

Jacob thumped the other man's fist from across the table, in solidarity, while also trying to hold back Greta's wandering hand. The last thing he needed was a raging hard-on. It'd make standing to leave a tad awkward.

"Okay. Susan and I met in an Art History class. The professor was a complete windbag. However, the in-class assignments were fun and," he faced his fiancée, giving her a playful leer, "it gave me plenty of time to talk up the sexy woman sitting next to me."

She shoved him playfully and took over the story. "He was into me, big time. I played it cool. Anyway, one day he came to class wearing a Lakeside Riptide shirt. They're a local college band I happen to love. Getting tickets to their shows is next to impossible. I mentioned this to Miguel, and the next lecture he has two tickets."

"Man, you don't even want to know what I paid for those scalped tickets," Miguel cut back in. "Robbery. Anyway, when Susan agreed to go with me, it was worth every penny." That earned him a loud kiss on the cheek from his fiancée. "We agreed I'd pick her up at her parents' house. Summer break started the weekend of the concert, and she was already home."

Susan rolled her eyes. "He arrived late and honked the horn, instead of coming to the door and introducing himself to my parents."

"Aw man," Jacob interrupted, shaking his head. "Now I'm not sure I can be sympathetic. Really? The first time at her parents' house?"

"Screw you, man," Miguel said defensively, without ire. "I called Susan ahead of time because I got caught in traffic and was running late. She should've been waiting outside. She didn't want to miss any of the concert either."

"Oh, believe me, Jacob is not one to judge," Greta interjected, a slight slur to her words. "Speaking of the first time at a parents' home and screwing—"

"Hey, hey, this is Miguel and Susan's story," Jacob said hastily, scooting Greta's drink away and signaling the waiter for water.

Miguel's scarred brow shot up. "Oh no, I'd rather hear this."

"Well," started Greta.

Shit. Exactly how much alcohol has she consumed?

"No. No more Greta and Jacob stories tonight." Jacob covered Greta's mouth, and the other couple laughed.

The waiter stopped at their table. Jacob asked to switch their drinks for waters.

"Fine," Susan smirked. "I'll get it from Greta later."

"As long as I'm not around," Jacob muttered.

"Okay, fine. I'll rescue your tipsy girlfriend from telling too many secrets," Miguel chuckled.

"Thanks. And I'm sure when she's sober, she'll thank you too."

Miguel snorted, taking a sip of his drink. "Anyway, after honking, who should appear? My lovely date and her pissed-off mother. Mother stalks to my car and says, 'No boy honks for my daughter! Come to the door and introduce yourself.'"

Jacob laughed. "Damn, she told you. Were you a good boy and got out?"

"No. Luckily, by this time, Susan had come around and was getting into the passenger seat, telling her mom we needed to leave pronto. I muttered some half-assed apology and hauled ass, the burn of her mother's disapproving glare following me all the way to the concert."

"That's not too bad."

"Oh, it gets worse," insisted Susan, giggling.

"Yup," Miguel agreed. "The concert was great. We had a fantastic time. It ran late, and we arrived at her house sometime after two. No big deal, right? Anyway, I was enjoying our goodbye kiss until the hairs on the back of my neck stood straight up. I was certain Death was standing behind me. Twisting around, I came face to face with a massive, irate man. I thought he was the freakin' Grim Reaper. I nearly pissed myself. Turns out it was Susan's father."

"Aww hell, close enough," Jacob sympathized.

"True that. Dad Reaper booms something along the lines of, 'you bring my daughter back in the middle of the night smelling of drink and marijuana. Then molest her on my front porch, for the whole neighborhood to see!'"

"Damn. What did you do?"

"I mumbled something about the weed not being mine and the concert running late. He didn't say a word, only continued to stare at me like he was mapping the best place to bury my body. Susan saved my ass by shouting a quick good night and pulling her father into the house." Miguel sighed. "Needless to say, it took a while for them to warm to me."

"Now they're okay with you marrying their daughter?" Jacob asked with amusement. Miguel and Susan nodded.

"I'm surprised. Your first meet was almost worse than mine. Hell, at least I had the police to protect me from her parents. Plus, Charles doesn't hate me. He might even like me. Whereas, if I were you, I wouldn't go anywhere alone with your future father-in-law. He might still be picking a spot to toss your dead body."

"No way. We get along great now. And, whatever, dude, your woman's mother tried to send you to prison. Probably hoping you'd become some man's bitch and leave her daughter alone." Humor danced in

Miguel's eyes.

"Aww, too soon. And so wrong." Jacob shuddered. "With that happy image, I'm going to need something stronger than water and coffee." He grabbed Greta's Mimosa and downed it in one gulp.

Chapter Twenty-Nine

"Helluva of a long day." Jacob yawned, sleep pulling heavy on his limbs. He rubbed the stubble on his cheeks, watching the morning sun climb over the horizon.

"Sure was." Greta unlocked and opened the door to her apartment, letting him go first. Once inside, she encircled his waist and rested against his back. "A good one too. Well, except for the trip to Petite Bois Police Station."

He twisted around, wanting her body flush against him. "At least we ended here. I like the idea of waking with you in my arms."

"Same. I much prefer you here with me than in your friend Jamie's arms."

Jacob laughed, loud and deep, dislodging the last residue of misery, even if he was finding it difficult to breathe. *Him and Jamie*. Jacob laughed harder, picturing him suggesting a cuddle with his friend.

Greta eyed him, hands on her hips and a confused smile tugging at the corners of her lips. He inhaled deeply, struggling for composure.

When he could talk again, Jacob explained, "Jamie's a guy, a very *big* guy. Not a chance we'd share a bed. He'd probably want to spoon me, and I like to do the spooning." He shook his head and took Greta's hand, kissing her palm, another chuckle escaping. "He and I would never have worked out."

"Smartass." Greta giggled, entwining her fingers with his, leading him to the bedroom. "Now, the plan is to sleep through our hangovers. With any luck, by the time we wake, the alcohol will be gone from our systems."

Seeing the comfortable bed, a wave of sleepiness nearly drowned him. "That, my dear, is a perfect plan. I don't even have the energy to undress. Mind if I sleep in my clothes?" He fell face first onto the comforter, already half asleep.

"Don't worry, handsome, I'll take care of you," Greta murmured in a low voice, sounding far away as he teetered between wakefulness and sleep.

He rolled to his back, forcing his eyes open, wanting to know why she wasn't next to him. His breath caught. The need to sleep evaporated. Greta was naked and beautiful.

She was a dream come true, a goddess.

He shifted onto his elbows, running his gaze languidly up her body. His pulse thumped in time with his growing lust. "Do you know how beautiful you are?"

"The only thing I know is I need you. I crave the reassurance of your touch. Your body." She kneeled on the bed, crawling to stretch across him.

His body demanded the same; her caresses let his battered heart know they were okay. At least for the moment.

He buried his face into her neck, inhaling the scent of orange juice, Prosecco, and something unique, heady, and all Greta. He smoothed a hand from the dip at her waist to the sides of her breasts. She shifted, giving access. He brushed his thumbs against her peaking nipples. Her soft moan and the sensation of her delicate skin against his calloused hands was heaven.

Greta arched into his touch, dancing her lips along his. He moved, trying to deepen the kiss. She forced him flat on his back. She removed his clothes leisurely, full of seduction and spice.

She trailed her fingers along his exposed skin. Goosebumps rose. Her touch was electric warmth; his body was the conduit begging for the voltage.

"Please, Greta." He wasn't sure if he was begging for her to hurry or slow down.

She slid off his pants and boxer briefs. She hovered above him, her expression full of heat. He damn near melted into the mattress. Never breaking eye contact, she wrapped a hand around his erection, licking her lips.

Holy hell, this woman is going to make my heart stop.

His eyes slid shut, and he thrust into her tight fist. She reduced him to a state where reasoning evaporated, where only sensation mattered.

"Greta, uh…" He couldn't form a thought, let alone words.

Her hot breath brushed against his ear. "I want to taste you. I want, no need, all of you. Your taste on my tongue, your sweat on my body, and, before we leave this bed, you buried deep inside me. For now, let me taste you." She glided down his body, stopping where they both wanted, taking him deep with her full, lush lips.

He fisted her hair, trying to be gentle, probably failing.

Is it possible to drown in erotic gratification?

Too soon, his climax rushed through his veins, fierce and throbbing. He tried to warn her, to push her away, she refused and took him deeper. He catapulted over the edge, shouting her name and shuddering as waves of pleasure raced through him.

"Damn, woman. You're a goddess," he said when the spasms racking his body subsided and he was able to speak again. "Forget Aphrodite. You are my Peitho."

"Hmm?" She shimmied up and cuddled against the length of his body.

"Peitho. The Greek goddess of persuasion and seduction," he whispered, watching the early morning light play across her tantalizing features. "Seriously, I can't move. You've short-circuited me."

She laughed into his neck, sending shivers along his spine.

Rolling her onto her back, he trailed kisses and soft bites on her stomach, relishing her taste. By the time he reached the junction of her thighs, he was hard again.

Her body and passions were made to fit perfectly with his, and he couldn't get enough of her.

"I thought you were too weak to move." She gasped when he traced the tip of his tongue along her inner thigh.

"Guess I'm getting my second wind. And I remember you saying something about wanting me buried deep inside you…"

Chapter Thirty

The sun's warm rays cut through the thin curtains of Greta's bedroom window, warming her back. She rolled onto her side and peeked through half-opened eyes, taking in the blue sky against the vibrant greens from the maple tree. The day was going to be beautiful.

Her gaze shifted from the window to Jacob's sleeping form. The vivid colors outside paled in comparison to the sight of him in her bed. He lay on his back, with the blanket low, revealing his torso and the start of his "happy trail." One arm rested on his flat stomach, the other thrown over his head. His full lips were slightly open as he breathed through his nose. She loved how his handsome features relaxed in rest, making him appear innocent and not so world-weary.

She loved watching him at rest. Her absolute favorite was when he first woke. His gorgeous blue eyes would open, full of sleep and focus on her. The sweetest smile would spread across his face, and he'd reach for her, usually followed by unhurried lovemaking.

Snuggling into him, she threw a leg across his body and burrowed into that wonderful area between clavicle and neck. He smelled of warm mornings, erotic dreams, and cedarwood.

His eyes didn't open, but the arm resting above his head moved to her waist, and his calloused palm traveled up and down her side. Even this simple, lazy touch warmed her.

After the horrible evening at the police station, followed by greeting the sun with Susan and Miguel, Jacob had stayed. The days became weeks. During that time, they'd explored each other's bodies and desires, allowing her to discover unimaginable levels of pleasure.

While the sexual exploration was freeing and fun, what shocked her most was how good they got along. She treasured the simple, quiet times as much as the bedroom play.

With incredible ease, they'd settled into a wonderfully domestic life. She'd found a slice of paradise with the most unlikely man.

How will I survive when he leaves?

His once a week drives to Detroit, grabbing necessary tools or dropping off repaired items to clients, was no longer working. He was falling behind. Plus, he'd signed a lease agreement on a building for Rework and needed to start readying the place for the grand opening.

Tomorrow he was leaving for Detroit and not returning. A gray cloud of misery tried to slither into her morning happiness. She scooted on top of him, for a full body embrace, trying to block the gloom.

He took her weight, wrapping his arms around her, kissing her cheek. "Good morning," he croaked sleepily.

Her heart ached. Once Jacob left, it would be three, possibly four weeks until he could make it back to Lansing. Back to her. A trip to his place was impossible for her. With only two semesters until graduation, her class load was terrible. There was no foreseeable downtime in her near future. The whole situation was dreadful.

Sighing, she whispered into his neck, "I have to go."

He groaned something unintelligible. She didn't need words to know he didn't want her leaving. The way he was caressing her bottom, in the most tantalizing way, and his erection pressing against her belly said plenty.

Surrounded in his warm sleepy arms was paradise, but her class was in less than twenty minutes. "I cannot be late again. Professor Luathed will kill me." Morning classes and Jacob weren't a good combination. "Remember, today's my long day. I won't be back until right before the party starts."

"Be late. Besides, what was your teacher thinking, an accounting class at the crack of dawn?" Jacob's knee nudged between her legs, spreading them.

"How can you already be, um, ready? Your eyes just opened."

"Because you're lying on top of me, smelling like sunshine and ecstasy." He nibbled along her throat to her lips, making her forget why she had to leave. "Come on. You can be late one more time. Who knows when I'll have you alone and naked again."

His argument was valid. Miguel was heartbroken that Jacob was leaving. He'd insisted on a going-away party.

The night before Jacob left.

She had a full day of classes and wouldn't have any time alone with him, before having to go to Susan and Miguel's place.

Jacob's roaming hands had her forgetting about why she needed to leave. One cupped her breast, and the other slid between her legs.

She opened for him. "You are such a bad influence," she breathed, unable to stop her hips from moving in time with his expert touch.

"How can it be bad, if it feels this good?" he crooned wickedly.

Nirvana was his mouth and fingers, and early morning accounting classes were forgotten. All she understood was carnal need and their relentless pursuit of pleasure.

Chapter Thirty-One

Greta walked from the bedroom. "Have you seen my scarlet sweater?"

Jacob froze, midway from grabbing his wallet off the kitchen counter. She was in a pair of black jeans that hugged her curves and an even sexier satiny cream bra. It showcased her breasts in the most enticing way.

"This party better be spectacular." He shook his head, recalling her question. "Your sweater might be on the ironing board."

"Yes, right. It had fallen on the closet floor and needed ironing." She headed back to the bedroom.

"I had many plans for your body tonight, and none of them involved groups of people."

She returned seconds later, pulling the sweater over her head. "No groups, huh?"

"There are certain things I'm not willing to share." He moved behind her, running his hands along her sides, his lips playing at the nape of her neck.

She rubbed her bottom to his front, rocking against his rapidly growing hard-on. Lust exploded through his veins, and he twisted her around, capturing her lips as the front door swung open.

Susan strolled in. "Could you two not have at each other, for at least one evening? It's bad enough Miguel and I have to hear you two through the paper-thin walls. Now you're going to fool around instead of getting your butts to the party?"

Greta's cheeks reddened, and she disentangled her legs from around him. He kept his hands on her waist, not letting her put too much distance between them.

"We weren't going to miss it. Just arrive fashionably late," Jacob goaded. "Do you plan on staying to watch? Is listening no longer enough for you?"

"Maybe I will," Susan deadpanned. "Watching the two of you would definitely be hot."

Okay. She won.

Jacob shook his head and let go of Greta. "You're even more of a perv than me."

Susan's smile sparkled as if she'd received the best compliment ever. "You better believe it. Now, come on, put on your sweater, Greta, and let's go. It's party time."

Jacob shook his head. "We'd better listen. Right now, I'd feel safer in a room full of people than alone with her."

Susan laughed, shoving Jacob. "Come on, Prince Charming, you don't want to be late for your own ball."

~ * ~

"Admit it. You're having fun." Susan handed Greta what was sure to be some delicious alcoholic concoction.

After shelving the liquor and putting several juices back in the fridge, Susan came around and sat on the stool next to Greta's.

"I never said this wouldn't be fun." Greta took a sip of her drink and moaned, relishing the sharp bite of vodka mixed with citrusy heaven. "You know, it's impossible not to have a good time when you're around. Plus," she waved a hand around, encompassing the room, "this crowd is amazing."

She scanned the apartment. The layout was similar to hers, and not a tiny place. Still, the number of people Susan and Miguel managed to fit into their place was mindboggling. It looked like everyone from the apartment complex, and most of Greta's classes were here.

Her gaze fell on one particular neighbor, whose name should've been left off the invite list. "Sorry to be ungrateful, but you could've left a few people off the guest list?"

Susan followed the direction of Greta's gaze, both of them eyeing the blonde in the tight, short fuchsia pink dress. Susan blew out a breath. "She lives two doors down. You two have almost every class together. It'd be rude not to invite her."

"Oh, please. Macy likes me as much as I like her. She isn't here for me. She's man fishing. Rumor is she slept with Professor Yandotte for a passing grade. She probably came here hoping to clean her pallet with a man from her decade. The vapid and narcissistic hussy."

"Damn, woman, put the claws away." Susan snickered.

"The woman is shameless and immoral. And," Greta huffed, "the tramp has been eye-screwing Jacob all night. Poor man's going to need to shower in bleach to wash off her filth."

Susan was swallowing a sip of her drink, and she simultaneously started choking and laughing. Greta rubbed Susan's back until she had her coughing under control.

Taking a more delicate sip, Susan said, "I wouldn't worry too much about Macy. Jacob doesn't see anyone but you."

"You think?" Greta hated the doubt in her voice, the way old insecurities unexpectedly reared up.

Blake had a wandering eye, not Jacob. He didn't even seem to notice the many flirty glances in his direction. He looked past them, seeking her and, after finding her, he'd give her one of his heart-stopping smiles.

The one that simultaneously melted her heart and heated her body.

"Uh, yeah," Susan replied drolly. "When he watches you, he kinda reminds me of a man who's dying of thirst and you're the cool, clean river. He has it bad for you."

"I hope you're right because I don't merely love Jacob. I swear, the man consumes me. The love I had for Blake was only a wisp of smoke compared to what I feel for Jacob."

"Honey, it's mutual. However, you may want to let others know, and right now's your chance."

"What do you mean?" Greta tried to find Jacob.

"Your man just stepped to the balcony, and Piranha Macy followed."

Greta caught a flash of fuchsia slipping through the balcony door. She handed her drink to Susan and stood. "If a body falls. I swear, it was an accident."

"Don't worry," Susan called after her, laughter mixing with her words. "I'm here for you. You know I'll always help you bury the bodies."

~ * ~

Jacob leaned against the metal railing, thinking back on the last couple of months and smiled. He'd never lived with a girlfriend and was shocked to find domestic life suited him. At least with Greta it did. Waking each morning and spending idle hours together, talking, making love, even vegging on the couch was heaven.

Getting to know her college friends was also a bonus. After the disasters back home, getting along with people close to her was nice. The distance from Petite Bois made their upbringing and social circles irrelevant. The idea of a future together didn't seem unbelievable.

If only they could stay in their bubble.

Unfortunately, life was getting in the way. Keeping up with work orders from in and around Detroit was becoming impossible. Some tools were too large to transport, yet he needed them. The drive back and forth was killing him. There was also Rework's grand opening. The building was ready. He needed to start ordering and moving in equipment. Again, something impossible to do three hours away.

It came to one, simple fact. He hated leaving Greta's side, but couldn't put off going home any longer.

170

His chest pulled tight, missing her and wishing they were alone, instead of at a party separated by a house full of people.

The balcony door slid open. Jacob turned, hoping Greta had somehow heard his silent plea. He was disappointed to find an unknown woman. Covering his regret, he offered a friendly nod and focused back on the night sky, hoping she'd go away. He wasn't in the mood to make small talk with a stranger.

The woman sidled next to him, propping a hip on the railing and facing him. "I'm Macy. I live next door to Susan and Miguel."

Guess it doesn't matter what I want tonight.

He gave an inward sigh, trying to curb his pity-party. "Hi. I'm Jacob."

"Oh, I know who you are." She placed a hand on his upper arm, stroking it. "I was hoping to get a moment alone with you."

"Why?" he snapped, not liking her over familiarity.

Her hand fell from him, her smile faltered. However, she didn't move away. "I was told you're amazing at repairing antiques. I'd like to hire you."

Trying to figure her out, Jacob studied the woman. Her statement was work-related. The way she kept eyeing him wasn't.

What does she think my services provide? "What do ya need?"

"My mother has a record player from her childhood. She cherishes the old thing. The stick-thing you set on the record is broken. Is this something you might be able to fix?"

It'd be easy enough, and her request held no flirty undertones. Maybe she was one of those overly touchy women. Her reason for finding him sounded legit.

He worked to arrange his cool expression into a friendlier one. "I could fix it." Jacob pulled his wallet from his pocket. After fishing around, he handed her a business card. "I have to warn you. I'm swamped right now. There's a waiting list."

She ran a thumb along his wrist while taking the card. "I don't mind waiting for you."

He jerked back.

Time to go inside.

He didn't want to deal with her mixed signals. Before he could put some distance between them, the patio door opened, and Greta stepped through, her glare falling on Macy.

She took a quick step back.

Jacob didn't blame her. There was murder in Greta's eyes.

She stormed across the patio and kissed him hot enough to set his blood on fire. He forgot about Macy and her confusing behavior.

Hell, he forgot his own name.

"I couldn't find you," she breathed against his mouth.

"Damn woman, I'm going to wander away more often if this is what you do when you find me."

"I'm staking my claim."

He peered around the deserted balcony then back at her. "I'm not complaining, mark me any way you want, but you know, we're the only ones here."

"Yeah, now we are. Macy," Greta spit out the name like it tasted bad, "was here. She hightailed it back inside since she doesn't have you alone anymore. What did the tramp want with you?"

Jacob swallowed a smile, not wanting Greta's ire to turn on him, but her jealousy was cute. "My card. Someone must've told Macy what I do for a living. She wants to hire me to repair her mother's record player."

"Please. Men are blind," Greta grumbled. "She wants you to work on something all right. Her."

Jacob ran a hand down her back. "You're the only woman I want to work on."

"Good. I do love your capable hands. And mouth." She brushed her lips across his.

He backed her against the iron railing, pressing the length of his body against hers, reveling in her soft curves. "Have I told you today I love you?"

"Love? You sure it's not lust," she teased, wrapping her arms tightly around him.

"There's a lot of that, but love's the overruling emotion."

"Let's go home. I need you to show me your love and lust," she whispered against his mouth.

Chapter Thirty-Two

Excitement bubbled over as the miles passed under Greta's car, bringing her closer to Jacob. Her stress and loneliness melted away, shifting to anticipation.

Their time apart had been longer than predicted. A heavy workload and the upcoming grand opening of Rework kept Jacob from visiting. Her demanding semester schedule held Greta in Lansing.

The taxing workload did nothing to stave off loneliness. Waking each morning without his body wrapped around hers was a level of misery she hadn't anticipated.

She had three weeks off until her final semester began, and the plan was to spend every one of those days with Jacob. The only gray clouds in her blue skies were the upcoming family holiday obligations. Those deflated some of her joyful buoyancy.

Her father wasn't who made her head throb with uncertainty. During these last couple of months, he and Jacob forged a friendship built on mutual respect. No, her worries rested with Mother and Nigel.

The times she'd spoken with her mother, their conversations were tense and peppered with disparaging remarks aimed at Jacob. Mother's position was clear. He wasn't the man for her daughter, more like an unfortunate, passing phase. She even tried to set Greta up with one of her haughty friend's sons.

The scheming hadn't surprised Greta. She was used to it and let it fall away like a handful of sand at a beach. The fallout made her shudder. It ignited an explosive fight between her and Jacob.

It had been their only real argument during those weeks he stayed at her apartment. It had been a bad one. Remembering his anger and hurt was still upsetting. She desperately hoped to avoid repeating it during this visit.

The whole thing played in her mind like a terrible movie she couldn't stop watching on repeat. The day had started innocuous enough. She was studying at the kitchen table, and Jacob was dozing on the couch; an old telephone manual from the late 1800s spread open on his chest. When her cell vibrated with a call, she'd been going through class notes and didn't bother checking caller ID before answering.

That had been her first mistake.

Mother jumped right in with her antics, going on and on about one of her friend's perfect sons, who would be home for the holidays. Greta politely told her mother she had enough plans for the short visit and ended the call.

Though, before she even set the phone back on the table, Jacob was off the couch and full of ire. "Why don't you tell her to piss off? You have a boyfriend."

"Jacob, she's my mother! Could you have a little respect?"

"I'm your boyfriend. Where's mine? Why are you afraid to tell her you have no interest in finding a new one?"

His questions were a rapid fire of accusations, confusing and annoying her. Why couldn't he see fighting with Mother wasn't worth the effort?

"Because it's easier to brush aside her schemes. Anything else will start her on a litany of lectures and debates, fueling her crusade."

"That so? Does your mother even know I'm here? I've been here since the arrest? Or am I still your dirty secret?"

"Would you stop? You weren't then and aren't now," she said with exasperation, her own anger starting to bubble to the surface. "Why do you not believe me? Why do you always assume my intentions are deceitful?"

He rose from the couch and stomped to the kitchen table, keeping it between them. "Because you say one thing with me and act another with others," he shouted. "Greta, I'm fine with who I am. Don't expect me to change for them. If you can't acknowledge our relationship, or accept me around your family, we'll never last."

Jacob stormed from the living room to the bedroom, slamming the door behind him. He had a point. She should have said she was with Jacob and wasn't interested and ended the call. However, he was overreacting. He'd acted like she'd accepted the date.

She left him to cool off, not knowing what else to do.

Later, when she'd begun to drown in the oppressive silence of her solitude, Greta tiptoed into the bedroom, fearing he'd want to continue the fight. However, when she stood at the side of the bed, he'd brought her to him and apologized for shouting.

They ignored the fight. Instead, made love, in a subdued and generous way. With their bodies, they asked the other for forgiveness.

The next day, and every day since, the quarrel was ignored; however, the subject was far from resolved. Rather, they left it to fester out of sight, waiting to rear its ugly corrosive head.

Greta sighed, flipping on the car's blinker and pulling onto Jacob's street. That argument was why she was dreading, but also hopeful for New Year's Day. Her mother requested Greta bring Jacob to the annual party at the Petite Bois country club. She'd agreed, with the utmost trepidation, because, while she hoped the invite meant Mother and Nigel finally accepted Jacob, Greta worried the actual outcome would be a day full of stress and open hostility.

Ice crunched under her tires when she slowed and pulled into Jacob's driveway. Knowing he was near had tranquility melting into her skin and blood. She let her worries scatter from her mind, like the snowflakes dancing around her car.

Studying Jacob's house, her heart sank. There were no cars in the driveway, and the house was dark and lifeless.

Did she have the wrong arrival time?

Locking her Audi, she wrapped her coat closer to her body as the icy wind tried to whip it open. She scurried up the sidewalk, head bowed, trying to avoid the snow biting at her skin. At the porch, she sprinted to the door. Before her gloved hand even knocked, it swung open.

A pair of powerful arms shot out and grabbed her around the waist, bringing her inside. Fear clogged her throat, then Jacob's scent of cedar and man engulfed her, and her panic turned to lust.

His lips were on hers with a soul-searing kiss, leaving no doubt he'd missed her. She gripped his shoulders, holding him tight. "I worried you weren't home. The house looks deserted," Greta said after they'd come up for air.

She needed distance before she did something inappropriate. Like, say, ripping off Jacob's clothes and taking him on the hallway floor.

"My truck's in the garage, and I got my dad and brother tickets for the Pistons." He leaned in and ran his lips along her neck. Delicious shivers sailed across her spine. "I wanted you all to myself tonight."

"Perfect." Her hands glided down his body, and her fingers curled around the waist of his jeans, pulling him flush against her. "God, Jacob, I've missed you." She kissed him again.

She sounded and was acting desperate. She didn't care. She was.

Groaning, he stepped away. "You able to hold back until after dinner?" His mouth spoke of food. His eyes flashed a different kind of hunger.

Moving away from him and his intoxicating scent, she inhaled deeply. The house did smell amazing. "Whatever's cooking smells delicious." Her wicked side was in full control, and she gripped him through his jeans. "I can hold off for a bit if you can."

He ground out, "if you keep doing that, I'll have you for dinner." Taking her hand and sliding his fingers through hers, he led her toward the kitchen.

Once through the archway, he pointed to a bottle of sauvignon blanc resting on the table. "Dinner's almost done. Want a glass of wine while we wait?"

Greta nodded, unable to speak. Love swam through her veins, coming to rest behind her eyes, making her blink back tears of affection.

He'd remembered her favorite wine but hadn't stopped there. Jacob had transformed his kitchen into a romantic dream, one that'd make any woman's heart flutter and beg for his love. Small tea candles lined the counters, and two large pillar candles in simple silver sconces sat in the table's center, bathing the room in soft dreamy light.

He reached for the bottle of wine, and she tracked his sinuous movements. Her gaze landed on an overflowing vase of flowers next to the glasses. She squinted in disbelief.

Lilacs.

How had he managed to find her favorite spring flower in the middle of winter?

She took a deep breath, getting a lungful of herbs and culinary heaven. It helped calm the overwrought emotions threatening to spill from her eyes. "Oh my, if whatever you're cooking taste like it smells, Will might have competition as the best Grimm cook."

Jacob stopped twisting the corkscrew, eyes gleaming with humor. "I'd like to get that in writing."

He returned to the cork and, seconds later, there was the quiet pop of it. Jacob leaned in, pressing against her, grabbing two glasses. His nearness sent tingles of want pulsating south. She yearned to wrap herself around him, to have him naked and buried deep inside her.

She settled for placing a light kiss on the pulse of his neck.

He took a small step back, licking his bottom lip as he poured, making her crave a taste of his mouth over the wine. Handing her a glass, he took a deep swallow from the other then granted her unspoken wish. He kissed her deep and hard, giving her a high no alcohol could ever provide.

He tasted of wine and lust, a potent combination that made her throb for him. She drew him closer, and, from the way he deepened the kiss, dinner was no longer his overruling hunger.

Yes.

His tongue explored her mouth, and she scooted onto the table, wrapping her legs around him. An overheated whimper of need escaped when their lower bodies made contact. He slid his hands under her sweater, taking it off.

He kissed her through the thin, lacy bra. The one she bought specifically for tonight.

"Where do you find your bras and panties? They aren't made from silk and thread, but sex and sensuality." He trailed kisses from one breast to the other before unhooking the front clasp.

Starved of his touch, she lit like a pile of gasoline-soaked kindling. He rubbed his jean-clad erection against her, his hands and mouth exploring her breasts. It had her squirming against him begging for release.

He pulled away. She reached for him, not able to bear the separation.

"Don't worry, gorgeous. I'm not going anywhere." He picked up his glass, letting the sweet wine fall gently across her chest. Her back bowed at the unexpected pleasure of liquid cooling her overheated skin.

He bent and leisurely licked and sucked the drops from her breasts.

She discovered the true meaning of hedonism.

"Jesus, Greta, if I could bottle the taste of you and wine, I'd be a millionaire," Jacob murmured between caresses, sucks, and nips.

He continued his exquisite torture of licking and feasting, while managing to remove her clothes. The man was talented.

There was the quiet scrape of a chair across the wooden floor. Opening her eyes, he sat in front of her open legs. "This is the wine I want," he growled hungrily.

His voice promised paradise, and his mouth delivered. All it took was a couple of mind-blowing strokes of his tongue, and her whole body came apart.

She panted his name and tried to press her legs together. The blissful sensations were almost too much to bear. Jacob held her in place and didn't stop his sensual torture until every last spasm had passed through her body and she was begging for mercy.

He stood, watching her with hooded eyes. "I swear, Greta, you're the best meal I've had on this table."

She lay, naked and exposed. He was fully dressed. She should be embarrassed, instead was incredibly turned on.

"Come here and finish your meal." She hooked a leg around his waist, bringing him back.

"As you wish." He grabbed his shirt and tugged it off, tossing it on a chair. He made fast work of his jeans and boxer briefs, promptly returning between her legs. In one rapid movement, he pulled her to the edge of the table and thrust, burying himself deep inside her.

He swore, stilling.

Guessing his hesitation, she said, "It's okay. Remember, I told you I was getting on the pill? We're safe. It's been over a month."

He released a loud breath. "Greta. The feel of you--there aren't words to describe it."

She understood. The skin to skin contact, everywhere, gave an extra level of closeness with him.

Stretching over her, he blew out the two big candles on the table. He shifted back, his gaze meeting hers, and, never breaking eye contact, he placed her legs on his shoulders. Moved back, he hesitated, then slammed back into her.

Oh. My. God.

"Damn, Greta, I've missed you. Missed this," he grated through clench teeth.

Watching him lose control was intoxicating.

She dug her nails into his straining biceps, knowing this, along with her moans and pleas, spurred him on. His rough rhythm was a heady mixture of pleasure and pain. Her second orgasm built and coiled around her.

Never slowing, he shifted her legs. The added friction had her climax slamming through her. His followed seconds later. His body locked, and his guttural growls filled the otherwise silent house.

Afterward, she lay sprawled on the table, boneless. Jacob propped his elbows on each side of her, smoothing back her damp hair with his fingertips. "Damn. I've missed you."

She opened her mouth to agree, but a slight burnt smell caught her attention. "Um, Jacob, are you sure dinner isn't finished?"

"Oh shit." He dashed to the oven. Shutting it off, he squatted and peered inside. He twisted around, smiling apologetically. "Dinner might be a tad dry."

"Oh well." She laughed, scooting off the table. "At least the appetizer was amazing."

Chapter Thirty-Three

Greta sighed, snuggling into Jacob. Contentment encircled her like a cashmere blanket. His gaze shifted from the TV to her, and he smiled sleepily. His arm draped across her shoulders while his fingers stroked lazy lines up and down her arm, lulling her closer to sleep.

She glanced at her watch and was surprised to find it only a little past ten. Still, it had been a marathon day. She'd caught him rubbing his eyes and yawning often. She understood. Her whole body was fatigued, and her eyes itched to remain closed each time she blinked.

Christmas had started early and ended late, with lots of merriment in between. She'd awoken well before the sun had made its way over the horizon to begin its diamond dance with the snow. She'd been too excited to give Jacob his gift to sleep late.

She'd commissioned an artist from college to make a metal sign to hang in his new building. Greta drew the design on her computer, and the welder's work was spectacular. The hardest part was getting his gift from Lansing to Detroit. The sign was three feet wide by six feet in length. She'd had to rent a truck and asked Miguel, along with two of his friends, to bring it to Jacob's house. Will helped her hide it in the garage, and since then she'd been bursting to show Jacob.

Luckily, she hadn't had to wait too long on Christmas morning. She'd awoken to find him already awake, not a trace of sleepiness on his handsome face. He'd confessed to being up for at least an hour, too excited to sleep. Turning, he clicked on the nightstand's dim lamp then retrieved a small wrapped rectangle box from the drawer. He handed it to her, and with shaky hands, she tore at the wrapping, popping open the lid.

Her breath caught. Inside, twinkling against black velvet, was one of the prettiest necklaces she'd ever seen. It had two platinum chains. The shorter one had a lightning bolt pendant, with a diamond in the center. Dangling from the longer one was a gorgeous sphere-shaped stone. It swirled with blues and blacks, along with a couple of rivulets of crimson.

She sat, letting the sheet fall to her waist, and Jacob placed the delicate piece of jewelry on her neck. While he fastened the clasp, he told her the stone was called a Pietersite. It was supposed to shield her from the harmful effects of technology. He said this gave him comfort since her job required her to spend lots of hours in front of a computer, but what had brought him into the shop when he'd spotted the necklace was the memory it had evoked.

It had reminded him of the first time they'd met. The lightning bolt, along with the chaotic blues in the stone, embodied the storm raging that day, and the red spike shooting through the amulet signified their intense desire.

He shifted, sitting in front of her, running an index finger along the chain to where it fell between her breasts, then went lower. Within minutes, the necklace lay forgotten.

By the time they finished what Jacob started, Roger and Will could be heard moving around downstairs, and Greta's excitement at giving Jacob his gift returned. She dragged him to the garage, hoping he loved his present.

Roger and Will removed the boxes and blanket hiding the sign, and Jacob's face lit up and made her heart sing. He'd given her a bear hug, swinging her in a circle and pronouncing her the best girlfriend ever.

He wanted to leave immediately and hang it at Rework. Only when Will reminded him they had somewhere around thirty relatives arriving in a couple of hours did Jacob relent.

"How was your visit?" Jacob's voice jolted Greta into the present.

"Huh?" Between her meandering thoughts and the Christmas movie on the TV, she couldn't follow his question.

"Your mother's? You came back when everyone was arriving. I never asked how your visit went."

"Oh, fine. Cindy said she looks forward to seeing you on New Year's. Mother and Nigel asked after you."

Jacob gave a derisive snort. "I bet they did."

She smacked him lightly on the shoulder. His sarcasm was justified. Whenever her parents had spoken of Jacob, animosity dripped from every word. In the end, she was glad the visit had been a solo one, although the thought of the New Year's Day party made her stomach tighten in knots.

One day. They could survive one day with her parents.

Best to switch topics. "I like your cousin Tina. She's from your mom's side, right?"

The credits of the movie began scrolling across the TV. Jacob reached for the remote, but Will snatched it first. Jacob shrugged in defeat, turning back to Greta. "Yeah, she is. And I like her, but Jason's annoying."

Greta's lips twitched, trying to hold in a smile. Tina and her brother were in their late to early twenties, and both nice. Though Jason came off a little *too* interested in her. Jacob had noticed, and, a couple of times, Greta worried he might grab his cousin by the collar and drag him off to a dark alley, never to be found again.

"Now that Tina has transferred to Mercy College, hopefully, she'll come around more. You'll have to invite her to your summer barbeque." Greta tactfully didn't mention Jason.

Instead of answering, he rose from the couch and took her hand. "Tired?"

It worried her when disagreements arose they both tended to change the subject. She supposed it beat arguing over every tiny thing.

Jacob helped her up, for she was more than ready to have him all to herself. They wished Roger and Will a Merry Christmas. Hand and hand, they walked to Jacob's room.

Chapter Thirty-Four

Greta eyed her reflection in the full-length mirror, her heart tumbling every time she caught sight of the steep plunge in the back. It dipped to the small curve of her spine, almost showing her backside. "I'm not sure I can pull this off."

"Oh, yes, you can. You're smoking hot." Susan was propped on the edge of the bathroom tub.

Jacob had somehow managed to get four tickets at one of Detroit's hottest nightclubs, Oriole Terrace, on New Year's Eve. They invited Susan and Miguel, and the two had arrived at Jacob's place in the early afternoon, with Susan announcing she was giving Greta a "sex goddess" makeover.

For some reason, she'd agreed. The woman staring back at her from the mirror reminded Greta of her wild side, the one she kept hidden and only let run free when intimate with Jacob. She wasn't sure if she was ready to show her to the general population.

Running her hand along the short hem of the dress Susan had brought with her, Greta tried tugging it lower. She'd be surprised if there were six inches of gold sequin material covering her thighs and bottom.

"What's wrong with the dress I selected?" She asked Susan this earlier but figured it couldn't hurt to try again.

"Don't get me wrong. Your original dress was beautiful, in a refined sort of way. It's better suited for one of your high society parties. We're going to a trendy nightclub." Susan eyed Greta from her 4-inch ankle strap heels to the artful knotted hairdo. "Besides, Jacob will love this, and when he discovers those sexy thigh-high lace stockings, he's going to be putty in your hands."

Greta opened her mouth to protest, but Miguel hollered from the living room. "Come on, ladies! I'd like to be there before the ball drops."

"Okay, okay, don't get your balls in a bunch, Miguel," Susan shouted, then said to Greta, "too late to change now. Come on, gorgeous."

Taking a deep breath, Greta grabbed her evening purse. "Fine, let's go."

~ * ~

"Finally. You ladies are ready. I was afraid we were going to turn into pumpkins before ever arriving at the ball..." The rest died on Jacob's tongue as Greta emerged from the hallway.

"Pumpkin huh? Are you my chariot or my prince charming?" Greta tugged at the hem of a tantalizingly short dress. Her legs were about a mile long.

"Hell if I know." Jacob tore his gaze from her beautiful limbs, feasting on the rest of her. "I'll tell you this, if the women in those fairy tales looked like you two, I might have paid more attention. Maybe remember the stories."

Jacob thumped fists with Miguel and stood, moving in a trance to Greta. She was always the epitome of elegant beauty. Tonight the blast of blatant sexuality had him dreaming of sweat-soaked flesh and savage orgasms.

The tight, shimmery dress hugged her upper thighs and had him yearning to run his hands along the material to the silk of her stockings. He circled her, running his fingertips along her waist. When he saw the back of her dress, his heart stopped. The shimmering material dipped low, almost to the curve of her firm sexy ass.

"Told you, Greta," Susan crooned, somewhere off to his left. "You're scorching. You've left your man speechless and hot around the collar."

All true.

Though, for reasons he didn't understand, Greta's posture was stiff. He faced her again. She wouldn't meet his gaze. "What's the matter?"

"Do I look okay?" she whispered, staring at his chest.

He was astonished. How could she even doubt her sensuality? Hell, she'd be sexy in a potato sack. Not that he'd suggest her changing out of the dress and into one. "You're always beautiful. I've just never seen you like this. It's different."

"Different? In a bad way?"

He traced his fingers along her glittery sides. "Honey, you're always stunning. Tonight, you're a different kind of beautiful, more sexual than elegant. Both suit you."

A smile played at the corners of her sexy lips, and she finally met his gaze. "Flattery will get you everywhere, my dear."

"This isn't flattery. It's the truth. You. Are. Stunning."

A small caveman part of him wanted to shut her away, where he was the only man able to ogle her. The dress showcased her sensuality. It'd attract the attention of almost every male in the damn club.

Luckily, before his jealousy made him say something stupid, a car horn blared from outside.

"That's our taxi. Let's go," Miguel said. "The night waits for no one."

~ * ~

Entering through the brass and stained-glass doors of Oriole Terrace, Greta was dazzled. She expected chrome and sleek edges. Instead, they'd gone back in time. Jacob told them on the drive over the building had been a popular theater in the 1940s but had closed during the '67 riots. However, he hadn't mentioned the new owners had maintained the original style and décor when they reopened about fifteen years back.

Making their way across the lobby, Jacob wrapped an arm around her waist, and she did the same. It allowed her to gawk at the ornate plasterwork without worry of losing him or falling. The detail, colors, and artwork were astounding. It must have taken ages to repair this remarkable piece of history.

Her gaze bounced from the polished wooden bar and its array of drinks lining the shelves behind it to three enormous projection screens. One showed the ball in New York. The other two displayed "the D" dropping in Campus Martius.

Jacob led her through a set of open arches she guessed had held the doors leading to the main floor of the theatre. Where seats once rested in neat rows awaiting patrons was now an enormous polished wood dance floor. Gyrating bodies flooded the area, and all Greta could see of the stage was the upper half. It had been remodeled to its previous French Renaissance glory, which was slightly at odds with the modern music pulsating from the speakers of the live band.

Jacob pointed at a wide, curving set of stairs leading to the upper balcony, indicating they should go there. She nodded, not even attempting to compete with the loud music.

Once upstairs, she discovered another smaller dance area, along with a bar and seating along the balcony's edge. Greta peered at the party revelers on the main floor, letting the magic of the evening sink into her. She didn't want to forget this night.

A complicated guitar riff sliced through the air, and she glanced at the stage. Squinting, Greta eyed the group. They were familiar. The lead singer stepped forward to adjust her mic, the overhead lights shining on the woman's deep purple locks.

"Is that your friend Tanner's band on stage?"

"Sure is. After playing here, he's going to have to make some difficult choices." Jacob raised both hands, palms up, as if weighing Tanner's decisions. "CPA or rock star?"

So true. Greta had learned from Susan the Oriole Terrace was the "it" place for up-and-coming bands. The sort of venue groups played when they were on the precipice of fame.

The two of them had wondered how Jacob managed to get reservations. Now she had an idea.

"I cannot believe I've never been here before." She ran a hand along the intricate iron balcony railing.

"Yeah, well, Petite Bois natives like to keep to their city, eyeing Detroit with disdain," he teased.

She gave him a light elbow to the ribs, though she wasn't annoyed. Her spirits were too high. And he had a point.

"When I was a teenager, this place was one of my favorite places to hang."

Greta loved when he told her pieces of his past, and she leaned in closer to hear him, asking, "Don't you have to be twenty-one?"

"Yup. I was friends with a girl in one of the bands who played here regularly. She used to sneak me in. I became part of the scenery, helping the staff and the bands. Since I wasn't causing any trouble, no one gave me grief about hanging around."

The first chord of a new song rang out. It was rowdy, with a fast beat. Jacob's warm breath tickled her neck. "Anyway, that was a while go. I haven't been here in years."

"Why? Did your rock star girlfriend move to another venue and you weren't able to follow?" Greta hoped her jealousy wasn't showing. His teenage years had long since passed and old girlfriends shouldn't matter.

"The band's popularity grew, and they began touring, and, since I was no roadie or groupie, I didn't follow." He sounded amused, and it didn't escape her notice he neither confirmed nor denied the past girlfriend. "Anyway, after my mom died, I didn't have time for such things."

His words broke her heart, reminding her how much life had suddenly and irrevocably changed for him. In the blink of an eye, he went from a carefree teenager to a boy forced to be a man, as he tried to hold a family together that was rapidly disintegrating into chaos.

She placed a tender hand on his cheek. "I'm sorry for what you've lost, Jacob." She was speaking of his mother and the following difficult years.

The band switched to a slower song, and he kissed her, wrapping his arms around her waist. "That's life. Not always fair, but mostly good. Especially now, with you in my arms and knowing you're coming home with me. Right now, it's damn easy to believe in happily ever afters."

His words caressed her heart, and she clutched them protectively in her soul. Closing her eyes, she leaned against him, placing her head against his chest and listening to the steady rhythm of his heart. The sound was more beautiful than the music.

When the song ended, Jacob asked, "What do you say we go to the main floor? We'll probably find Susan and Miguel there."

Greta nodded, taking his hand, allowing him to lead her back down the stairs.

It took them a while to find their friends. The nightclub was packed, and Jacob kept distracting her with his enticing body, urging her to dance with him instead of searching for their friends. Though, eventually, and, by happenstance, they ended up next to them on the dance floor.

"Okay, people, we have less than five minutes left," called Maggie. "You have two options for ringing in the new one. Option one, spend it with us dancing from one year to the next. Option two, head over to the lobby or balcony bar, grab yourself a glass of champagne and watch the ball drop. Choice is yours."

It seemed like the clock had sped forward and the hands were racing each other into the new year. Greta didn't care. She'd happily meet it with Jacob in her arms.

The band played a song she recognized and loved. Without a word, he brought her closer. They didn't need to discuss their preference, both knew what they wanted. To end and begin the year in each other's arms.

ThreePence flawlessly switched from a modern slow song to *Auld Lang Syne,* and Jacob leaned in, pressing his lips to hers. The kiss was both sweet and hot, filling Greta with a mixture of passion and love.

Moments later, thunderous cheers filled the building and another year slipped away, like the last pebbles of sand in an hourglass.

"Happy New Year," Jacob whispered, running his smooth-shaven face along her cheek.

She kissed him again, and a slender arm wrapped around her waist, right above Jacob's. She turned to the smiling faces of Susan and Miguel. She engulfed them in a hug.

"Happy New Year," the couple shouted in excited, slightly slurred voices. Miguel managed to snag four champagne flutes from a passing waitress.

"May the upcoming year be as perfect as tonight," Susan toasted.

"Let it be," they shouted in gaiety and high spirits.

Chapter Thirty-Five

"What the hell's that?" Jacob muttered.

"The alarm." Greta rolled over, squinting in pain as the morning sunrays stabbed through her eyes and into her brain. She fumbled for her phone on the nightstand and silenced its bleeping alarm. Letting it fall, she faced Jacob and removed the pillow he'd put on his face. "Sorry, sleepyhead, we have to get moving or risk being late."

He peeked one eye open, glowering. "Late's good."

Jacob's grumpy mood, mixed with her headache, wasn't much encouragement to face the new year. Coupled with the fact they were expected at Mother and Nigel's in a couple of hours for brunch made her want to use Jacob's confiscated pillow to smother herself.

Resisting the urge, she grabbed an undershirt Jacob had tossed on a nearby chair. After sliding it on, she stepped to the window, wishing his room didn't face east. She pulled the shades and breathed a sigh of relief. The cool dimness was heaven on her drained senses.

"Believe me. I want to fall back asleep. However, arriving late will only upset Mother and Nigel." Jacob had kicked back the blankets, and she eyed his naked form. The sight improved her mood. "Besides, I cannot wait to see you in your new three-piece suit. I love the charcoal vest."

"I look like an asshole in it," he muttered, sitting and twisting to drop his feet to the side of the bed. He peered over his shoulder and cocked an eyebrow, all sex and sarcasm. "I have an idea. I'll wear a waitstaff uniform instead? Then you won't have people constantly asking why a guy like me is at their country club."

"Wow. You're cranky this morning." She wanted to be annoyed but was distracted by his back. He leaned forward and was rummaging in the nightstand drawer. His muscles were downright delectable, shifting and bunching as he moved.

Leaving the window, she knelt on the bed and leaned forward to kiss the back of his neck, running her fingernails down his back. "No one's going to question you today. You'll be the most handsome man at the party. I, for one, am thrilled you'll be my date."

Jacob exhaled, setting the pill bottle he'd taken from the drawer. "Sorry. I'm being a dick. Feeling hungover and edgy. Starting the new year with your parents doesn't fill me with joy. No offense." He turned and grinned, standing in his naked glory. "I'll be on my best behavior. Promise. I'll get in the shower. Maybe it'll make me human again."

She gripped his waist before he could get away. He stilled, and she ran her palms to his front, caressing his stomach, inching lower. Goosebumps broke out on his arms, and his head fell back.

"I know something else that might help more than a shower..."

"What about being late?" His tone suggested a tardy arrival suited him fine.

"You're too appealing, rumpled and bed ready. We'll blame our delay on the snowy roads."

He turned, and she planted a kiss on his tight abs.

"You're right," he rasped. "I feel much better already."

~ * ~

Cindy eyed them as they stepped inside the massive foyer. Next to her was a woman Jacob assumed was the Silverstone's housekeeper.

Before the door even latched, Cindy started in on them. "About time you got here." She was blunt, unlike her sister. "I thought you two were bailing on us."

Greta handed her coat to the maid, wishing her a happy New Year. Jacob did the same, feeling like a schmuck. He could hang his own damn jacket.

"Sorry. Traffic was terrible," Greta told Cindy.

He wondered if anyone else noticed the pink creeping into Greta's cheeks.

"I'll show them to the dining room, Mrs. Whitehill." Cindy smirked. "Huh, funny. When I drove here, the roads were almost empty."

"I guess traffic was busier later on, when we left," Greta replied flatly.

"I'm willing to bet the traffic wasn't the one getting busy," Cindy snickered.

Jacob couldn't hold back a low chuckle. Yes, she definitely wasn't restrained like her older sibling.

Greta hissed, "Cindy! You are crass."

The other woman shrugged, not the least bit repentant. "And you're in trouble. You know how much Nigel and Mother hate tardiness," she said in a singsong whisper.

"Trouble," Jacob scoffed. "Are we about to be scolded by Mommy and Daddy?

Neither responded; their expressions said all he needed to know.

Following the women, he shifted his neck, trying to dislodge the annoyance crawling under his skin.

Shit. It is going to be a long day.

They made a left, and Cindy opened a set of heavy carved wooden doors, stepping into a formal dining room Napoleon would've loved. It screamed opulence and pretentiousness. The burgundy walls were decorated with a thick, walnut crown and chair molding. Jacob's gaze fell on the floor-to-ceiling windows covering most of the far wall. They offered a nice view of the vast front lawn. Too bad bulky gold and brown velvet curtains blocked most of it.

A chair scraped, bringing his attention to the enormous dining table. Under a set of crystal chandeliers probably worth more than his house, sat Nigel and Sophia, their demeanor both regal and annoyed.

Jacob remembered from his only other time in the Silverstone house they had a smaller six-person table in the kitchen. So, why were the five of them having lunch in this enormous room?

Nigel rose from his seat, eyeing Jacob with distaste, giving him his answer. Greta's parents wanted to remind him he was out of his league. That he didn't belong.

He shot a quick glance at Greta.

Back here, in her parents' home, surrounded by the over-the-top wealth, did she see him the same way? As some vulgar gatecrasher.

Nigel extended his hand, offering a perfunctory handshake. "Are you aware the country club requires formal wear?"

Seriously? It's ten in the morning.

The way his gaze was boring into the open collar of Jacob's white button-down, he figured some of his ink was exposed. He didn't give a shit. In fact, part of him enjoyed giving Nigel a reason for his loathing.

The uptight, snobbish asshole.

Plus, no matter how much Greta loved the suit, it was more a straitjacket to him. He'd left the vest, bowtie, and coat in the truck.

"Are you aware we're not at the country club?" Jacob replied back just as snidely, though it wouldn't have surprised him if Nigel slept in a suit. "I left it in my truck. I'll put it on before we leave."

"I wanted to make sure," Nigel huffed. "I am assuming this is your first visit to a country club."

"You know what they say about assuming...makes an ass--"

"Excuse us for our late arrival," Greta cut-in. "How are you both?"

Jacob swallowed his anger. Why was Nigel able to talk shit to him but he had to keep his mouth shut?

"We're fine," Sophia answered, rising. "Although, I was starting to worry. This is unlike you. To be late, making us worry and wait." She offered her cheek to Greta and a limp hand to Jacob.

The dig was for him. Sophia believed he was a bad influence, corrupting her perfect daughter.

Greta wanted to believe they invited him to their home and precious country club because they finally accepted him. He knew the truth. Today's charade was to prove how much he didn't belong. Guess he should be thankful Sophia hadn't invited another "more suitable" guy to lunch with them.

Jacob took a deep breath, pinching the area between his eyes with a thumb and index finger. *It's one day.*

He held Greta's chair and studied her expression. She was used to her parents' crap. She nodded thanks in his direction while apologizing to her parents, asking if she and Jacob should skip lunch and get ready for the party.

"We will manage." Nigel gave a long-suffering sigh. "If you don't mind rushing a bit."

Rushing?

They had hours, and Greta was dressed and ready. It'd take him all of five minutes to put on the rest of his suit. Though, he suspected the next couple of hours were going to feel like years, no, decades.

He was tempted to tell them he'd be happy to go back home with Greta. It bothered him the way she faded and diminished in their presence.

Not for the first time, he wondered if her parents would win their little game. Too much time around them, Greta's love for him was bound to diminish. They'd chip away at the things she loved about him until nothing was left but dissatisfaction and resentment.

Hell, they hadn't been in the Silverstone house for more than a half hour, and Greta was already kowtowing to her parents, and he was nearly boiling with resentment. Jacob wasn't sure he could handle a whole day of this passive-aggressive bullshit, let alone a lifetime of it.

After taking their seats, he leaned toward Greta and, hoping to lighten the mood, whispered, "I feel like I'm fifteen again. Are we going to get grounded?"

Greta smothered a laugh, her eyes glittering with merriment. It reduced some of his anger, allowing him to believe they were in this together.

"Knowing them, they'd probably try," she mouthed back.

"You better hope not because, under pressure, I might crack and tell them why we're late. And who started it."

Greta's jaw dropped in mock horror. "You wouldn't dare."

Chapter Thirty-Six

"You didn't have to aggravate them." Greta slammed the door of Jacob's truck, irritation ringing in her voice.

"And they didn't have to act like assholes," he retorted with equal bitterness.

So much for their united front.

Lunch had been a total disaster, chock full of tension and stilted conversation. At first, he thought the two of them were united. A team. He'd been wrong. The whole experience was as pleasant as a root canal.

"Come on, Jacob," Greta nearly shouted. "They're still my parents."

"I'm your boyfriend, though I'm starting to wonder if it means anything to you." He twisted the key forcefully in the ignition, and the truck roared to life. Putting it into drive, he whipped it around the circular driveway and onto the street.

"What are you talking about?"

"They talked down to me the entire time, yet you ignored the digs and even fucking censored me." He took a deep breath, trying to wrestle in his anger. "Doesn't it bother you? They view me as your colossal, and hopefully short-term, mistake."

"They don't know you. Give them time. Though, if you keep acting like today, goading them, things will never change. You were determined to make things worse," Greta replied tersely.

Fury raced through his veins and out of his mouth. "*I* made it worse? At one point your parents were giving me etiquette pointers like I was some stray dog that was going to run inside their precious country club and piss on the rug!"

He braked hard at a stop sign and twisted to face Greta, wanting to exorcize all his resentments. She held up a shaky hand. He took in her slumped shoulders and the tears gathering along the rims of her eyes, and some of his temper faded.

She took a tremulous breath and closed her eyes. When she opened them again, she grasped his hand. "I'm sorry they were discourteous. I think they're embarrassed. The whole watch debacle bothers them, and they're overcompensating, acting stiffer than usual."

Jacob scoffed, turning back to the road and sliding his hand from hers, placing it on the steering wheel. "I was the one removed from my house in handcuffs."

She wrapped slim fingers around his wrist. "I know, and I'm sorry. They hate being wrong and looking like fools. They're acting out."

He shot her a side-eyed incredulous scowl. "Again, I was the one in handcuffs."

"They're being ridiculous, I know," she hastily added, patting his leg.

After a pause, Jacob sighed. "That isn't their problem. For one, too much time has passed." He stopped at a red light, tapping on the steering wheel for a couple of seconds. "I'm not from a powerful family. I'm not Blake."

"Thank God," Greta muttered, making him smile.

"They want you with a man whose last name is on the Mayflower registry, with a trail of money and power connecting generation to generation."

"No. Maybe. But who cares. It's not like Nigel's background is stellar."

"What do you mean?" Curiosity overtook some of his anger.

"Nigel's family isn't old money. In fact, his mother met her wealthy husband working at a nightclub. Rumor has it, *a gentlemen's club*. The man isn't even Nigel's biological father. He's never met him."

"Huh, interesting." The light turned green, and Jacob hit the accelerator. "You could have told me this before today's lunch."

"Yeah, right. It would have made everything better. The thinly veiled insults weren't enough? You wanted more fuel?" she replied sarcastically but, from his peripheral vision, he caught the smile tugging at the corners of her mouth.

"Hell yes. What a gem, to know the man's a pompous, posturing fraud."

Switching lanes on her side, he glanced at Greta. She looked miserable. He was acting like her parents, vindictive and petty. Remorse tugged at him.

He entwined their fingers. "I'm sorry. I could've been a little less dickish. For your sake, I'll try harder to get along with them."

"Thank you." She leaned in and kissed his cheek, appreciation evident in her voice. She pointed. "See the brick sign up ahead? That's the entrance to the country club."

He followed the sign. "This is close, practically walking distance."

He skipped the valet and found a parking spot near the front entrance.

"Not with all this snow. And not me in these heels." She pointed to a pair of, in his humble opinion, sexy-as-hell red heels.

His gaze traveled along her legs, remembering the equally attractive dress she wore under the ankle-length classy wool coat.

After the fun morning activities, they had to rush. Greta used his bathroom, and he'd gotten ready in the one on the main floor. When she finished and he saw her on the stairs, he almost fucking swooned.

The scarlet, off-the-shoulder dress hugged her breasts, waist, and ass like a lover, flowing down her legs and pooling around those sexy sky-high heels. She'd called it a mermaid gown. He called it foreplay.

Greta squeezed his hand, pulling his gaze back to her eyes. "Anyway, I'm sorry too. I should have said something, cut them off. They're exasperating. I never know what to say or do."

Yes, she should have done something, but he didn't want to argue anymore. He placed a gentle kiss on her lips. "Let's get in there and get this over with. Then we can get back home."

"I love you, Jacob. You know this, right?"

He nodded. Her words were meant to reassure. It hadn't worked. He'd caught the bleak expression that had flickered across her face, speaking of defeat and lost causes.

He went around to open her door, trying to shove aside the disquiet settling into his bones. Helping her, he placed an arm on her lower back. She cuddled into him, and he tried to convince himself they were solid.

Chapter Thirty-Seven

"You're right. This isn't too bad," Jacob told Greta as they left a small group of acquaintances she knew from the area.

"I told you most of the people here are perfectly pleasant."

Greta hoped he couldn't detect the undercurrent of worry in her voice. After the dreadful lunch and tense drive, she had been positive the rest of the day would be disastrous.

So far, her fears were unwarranted. Her friends and acquaintances had been welcoming. Some even remembered Jacob from Jane Glengarry's infamous party. They joked around with him, thanking him for the added excitement. The interactions with Mother and Nigel were less enthusiastic, polite and distant. That worked for Greta.

"You've got to be kidding me." Jacob was watching someone across the ballroom, a broad smile making his features even more striking.

"What?"

"I know him. What a small world." He pointed to a tall, familiar man off to their left. Lucas.

"There's someone I want you to meet." Jacob took her hand and headed toward Lucas and Elizabeth.

Lucas's eyes widened upon spotting Jacob. Both men broke into gorgeous grins, catching the attention of many of the surrounding ladies. Greta couldn't blame them. The two men exuded too much male sexiness, practically sucking the oxygen from the room.

"What are you doing here?" Lucas took Jacob's hand and did that guy thing, half handshake, half hug, before introducing Elizabeth. Turning to Greta, he asked, "And, how do *you* know Jacob?"

Jacob's brows pulled together, his gaze darting between her and his friend. "How do *you* know Greta?"

His adorable look of confusion made her giggle.

"Elizabeth introduced us back at, oh, Jane Glengarry's party," Greta nudged him playfully, "before you arrived to spice things up."

Understanding filled Lucas's eyes. "Was that you? The one throwing punches? I was inside the house when it happened but heard about it and saw the guy. He was hurting."

Jacob shrugged. "I'd swung by to get Greta. It's not my fault her stupid ex was having a hard time accepting she's with me now. And what it means to keep his hands to himself."

"Anyway, how do you two know each other?" Greta wanted to move away from the topic of Blake and Jacob's notorious night.

"He and Will met years back when they were taking classes at Henry Ford College. We became friends as well." Jacob chuckled. "I swear, I'm becoming part of the Petite Bois disease."

Elizabeth tilted her head, her gaze bouncing between Jacob and Greta, clearly waiting for one of them to explain.

Greta took over. "He says it's odd how tightknit our city is, how we all know each other. Now it's happening to him."

"It is a maddening disease." Elizabeth laughed lightly.

"Oh, speaking of knowing people," Lucas said to Jacob. "You remember Tim Jenkins?"

"How could I forget Jenkins? The guy was hilarious."

"He's here, running the catering service." Lucas asked her and Elizabeth, "Do you mind if we say hi to an old friend?"

"Not at all." Elizabeth took Greta's arm. "We'll do the same, and peruse the wine selection."

The women waved to their men and cut across the banquet room toward the bar. After finding two empty seats, Greta ordered a chardonnay and Elizabeth a cabernet. As they chatted and sipped wine, Trisha Unhoflinch glided over, wearing her usual, one-step-away-from-slutty high-end couture, and a shark-like smirk.

"Hello, ladies. I haven't seen either of you here in ages," she said in a saccharin-sweet voice. "Where have you two been hiding?"

Greta's bubbly mood burst. Trisha was a walking disaster, only happy when causing others pain.

Is she after my blood or Elizabeth's?

Schooling her features, Greta tried for a pleasant smile. "Hello, Trisha. I'm home for the holidays. I live in Lansing until I finish my masters."

Elizabeth started to speak, but Trisha cut her off. "You must have left your university sometime or another..."

It was stupid, a mistake, yet she asked, "Why is that?"

"I'm willing to wager my closet full of Jimmy Choos you didn't meet Jacob on campus."

Greta's heart plummeted. Yup, she shouldn't have gone down the rabbit's hole.

Gripping the side of her stool, she dug her nails into the thick cushion, instead of slapping Trisha. "You know Jacob?" Greta was pleased at how indifferent she sounded.

"Yes. We, um dated." Trisha was evidently trying for coy. She came off smug. "I guess you could call it that."

Bitch

Elizabeth discreetly excused herself. Greta nodded a vague goodbye, and Trisha ignored her completely, too busy playing with her new prey.

"Guess he's still trying to make his way into our crowd." She surveyed the room, giving a loaded sigh.

Following Trisha's line of sight, Greta found Jacob across the room, talking with his two friends. She looked back at the woman she was growing to dislike even more than she had in high school. The way Trisha was watching Jacob made Greta's stomach curdle.

Her cruel eyes focused on Greta. "Oh well, he can try…and at least you can have your fun with him in the meantime. Heaven knows, I did. The man is spectacular in bed."

Greta sucked in a breath as if sucker-punched. Sure, Trisha had hinted at intimacy with Jacob. Stating in black and white, hurt. Greta would've loved to shoot back with a cutting remark, but she couldn't breathe, let alone speak.

Was this the woman Will had mentioned, the "rich bitch"? Trisha, without a doubt, fit the definition. What Greta couldn't fathom was why Jacob would go on a single date with such a vile woman, let alone sleep with her.

She hated herself because a small part wondered if there was some truth to Trisha's cruel words. Had they used each other? Her for a new thrill and Jacob to meet new clients?

No. Don't be stupid.

Since she'd met him, he'd never once sought her family or friends. The opposite, in fact.

A large hand rested on her back, making Greta jump and guilt crash down on her. Without having to check, she knew it was Jacob. Would he sense her recent, fleeting traitorous thoughts?

He stood at her side and let his hand rest on her waist. A deep frown marred his handsome face. "Hello, Trisha. How are you?"

"I'm good. A little lonely." Trisha had the audacity to run her finger along his arm.

Jacob's lips pressed into a thin line, and he stared back, wordless. Trisha didn't seem to mind the tense silence. "I have to admit I'm shocked you're here. Have you changed your mind? Decided we are useful to you?"

"Trisha, you've never been useful to anyone. I'm here for Greta.

She asked me to come, so here I am."

Jacob's response was cruel, and Trisha flinched before smoothing her features. Greta didn't have an ounce of pity. It was impossible to have sympathy for a viper.

"Now, if you'll excuse us." Jacob didn't bother to wait for a response. He gave Trisha his back and guided Greta from the ballroom to a deserted hallway.

It doesn't matter. Let it go.

She found she couldn't.

"Did you sleep with her?" she hissed, her tone dripping with contempt.

"I didn't realize I was supposed to give a list of the women I've been with," Jacob snarled.

She stopped and yanked her hand from his hold. "If the list is too long, could you at least mention the ones who want to humiliate me in public?"

"Oh, come on. I wasn't hiding my past from you. I was with Trisha a while ago, before we met. It didn't work out. Why would I mention her?"

He was right, but the encounter left her raw with too many emotions; surprise, guilt, jealousy, and humiliation were warring for dominance. "Why her?"

"Why Blake?" Jacob growled, running an agitated hand through his hair. "Do I question your choices? Or ask for a dossier of your past?"

"Oh, please." Greta glared at him. "You know Blake is my only past. I haven't been busy, like you. Why would you ever date someone like her?"

Jacob's features became stone. "She was offering it. At the time, it seemed like a good idea. What reason did she give you? I was after something, right? Clients, money, what?"

"It doesn't matter what she said." Greta broke eye contact. Guilt at her fleeting suspicion had her trying to shift topics. "I thought sex meant more to you. Was I wrong?"

"Like hell it doesn't matter what she said." He took a small, hard step forward, almost bearing down on her. "Don't play games with me. Sex and my morals aren't what have you upset. Come on, be honest. Tell me what's really bothering you."

She was acting like a jealous harpy and needed to stop interrogating him. Too bad, irritation overrode reasonableness. "How did you two even meet?"

"You know how someone like me would meet someone like her," he sneered. "Her father's a client of mine. I was delivering one of his antiques."

"Damn, Jacob, sounds familiar." Her mind shouted to stop talking. Her heart bled unwarranted betrayal.

"Damn, Greta, that hurts." He shoved his hands in his pockets; his broad shoulders drooped. "What? Did you buy Trisha's theory? The one where I troll for wealthy women to what, seduce them to further some cause of mine?"

Greta's anger popped like an overinflated balloon. Fitting, since it had the same amount of substance. She was hurting Jacob and, for what reason? Because he'd been intimate with a woman she despised?

Big deal.

He disliked Blake and had ample reason, yet Jacob didn't behave like a petulant brat.

She reached for him. He moved away but then leaned in close, his eyes flashing with anger.

"When it came to Trisha, I should've listened to my gut. It screamed we were a bad match. She loved taking her mongrel guy around to her snobby friends. Trying to shock them, I guess. At the same time, she acted like I should be in awe, privileged to be allowed around such wealth and splendor. As if I gave a shit," he spat. "I didn't need her money or attitude. I dumped her. I guess it still stings her pride. Fuck--" Jacob looked away. When he spoke again, he sounded defeated. "I had my doubts with you too. Maybe I should have listened to them."

His words shredded her heart and made her blood freeze.

Had she let her jealousy shred his love for her?

Closing the space between them, Greta wrapped her arms around his chest and tucked into him. It was like hugging a statue, cold and unforgiving.

"I'm sorry. I was wrong. I can't stand Trisha, and I let her comments get to me. I don't believe a word she said, I swear. It is more picturing her with you--well, it made me want to claw at her face. I wasn't thinking straight. Will you forgive me?"

~ * ~

Forgiving simple jealousy was easy. Greta's lack of trust was what tore at his heart like a dull, rusty knife. Jacob had caught a flicker of guilt in her eyes; Greta believed Trisha's spiteful lies. That was hard to forgive. Even harder to forget.

Problem was, he didn't know what to do.

At a loss, he closed his arms around her. "You know Trisha doesn't care about me. She only wants to start trouble."

"I see the way her gaze eats you up. She wants more than trouble."

"Whatever. I could care less what she thinks or feels," Jacob growled. "The past is the past. We are each other's present."

Greta pulled back, and the regret in her eyes killed him, but it wouldn't change what was disintegrating between them.

"You're right. I overreacted. Please forgive me?" she asked again.

He couldn't answer honestly, so he kissed her. It tasted more of desperation than forgiveness.

Greta either didn't notice or didn't care. She cupped the back of his neck, bringing him closer. A disapproving cough echoed down the hall, and she spun, stepping from his hold. Her absence felt permanent.

Nigel stood right outside the dining hall. "Our old neighbors, the Turners, are asking after you. They were also hoping to meet Jacob. Would you both mind coming back in?" He went back inside, without waiting for an answer.

Greta looked at Jacob. "Ready?"

To leave? Yes. Meet friends of Sophia and Nigel? No.

He gave a tight-lipped smile and motioned for her to follow Nigel. She took his hand, and they went back inside.

Chapter Thirty-Eight

Everything grated on Jacob's nerves. The tinkling laughter sounded like jackals. The low warble of the string quartet skittered along his eardrums. Following Nigel back inside the ballroom had been a mistake. The argument with Greta was too raw. Jacob needed time to decompress, find his civility.

Nigel stopped in front of a crotchety, wizened couple, and Jacob understood what the introduction was about—reinforcing his outsider status. The two seniors studied him with thin, pinched lips and disapproving eyes. He hadn't even opened his mouth, and he already failed their test.

Great. First, I'm doused with distrust, and now it'll be disgust. Fuck.

Greta let go of Jacob's hand and gave the couple each a brief hug before introducing him. "Mr. and Mrs. Turner, this is my boyfriend, Jacob Grimm." She sounded meek and mollifying, like she was apologizing.

Mrs. Turner nodded, not offering her hand. Instead she clutched her purse, as if afraid he was going to snatch it and run.

Her husband took Jacob's offered hand and even managed not to wipe it on his trousers afterward. Then he spoke and ruined the moment. "Yes, we've heard of you," Turner rasped, full of false jocularity. "The Silverstones are helping you, right? Making you a respectable businessman."

"Excuse me?" Jacob sputtered, confused and stunned at the man's blatant assholery.

"No. Sophie's ex-husband is helping him, not us," Nigel cut in.

"Yes, how fortunate for him." Turner's blue rheumy eyes peered from Greta to Jacob.

Greta appeared shocked but, of course, remained silent.

Her acceptance gutted him.

"Okay. Fuck it. I'm done." Jacob raised his hands in surrender. "I'd like to say it has been a pleasure, but since we're being upfront, I'll be honest; the only pleasure I've had in this short conversation is right now, leaving this shit-ass party."

"I never, such coarse talk—" the old man sputtered, pointing a crooked finger at Jacob. "Now, you have the nerve to come here and dirty the place with your language. Guess I shouldn't be surprised with the likes of you."

Greta gasped, and *still*, she remained silent.

Jacob glanced at the index finger inches from his chest and had to resist the urge to knock it away. "You know nothing of me or my kind, you pretentious asshole. Maybe it's difficult to see way up there on your high horse, but my successes are from hard work, not favors or connections."

He glared at Nigel, knowing damn well the Turners' opinion of him was helped along by Greta's stepfather. "Can you say the same, Nigel?"

The other man's face reddened. Jacob didn't wait for a reply. He needed to get away from this place and these people. He gave them his back then headed toward the exit.

~ * ~

Greta's heart pounded in time to her rapid footfalls. She rushed from the ballroom, down the carpeted lobby, and through the main double doors. Once on the sidewalk, she frantically scanned the parking lot.

Jacob was halfway to his truck.

He's leaving!

Hurt, anger, and indignation ripped through her.

"Wait!" She rushed in his direction, trying not to slip on ice, and stopped less than a foot away from him. "Where are you going?"

He stopped and twisted around, throwing his hands in the air. "I don't know. Away. I need to get away."

Dismay propelled her forward, and she clutched his arm. "From here or from me?"

He yanked his hand back, making her heel slide into a piece of cracked concrete. She stumbled.

Jacob caught her but let go, like her touch burned. His next words hurt more than a fall to the pavement. "I need to get away from everyone. From this God-forsaken place. And yes, Greta, even you."

"Why? What did I do?"

"That's the problem. You did nothing. As usual. You never say a word. Tell me, why? Embarrassed of me, or are you afraid they're speaking the truth? Or is it I'm not worth the effort?" He leaned in closer, rage pouring off him in waves. "Can you tell me which it is? Because I'm tired of fucking wondering."

"None of them," she sputtered. "Why are you overreacting?"

It wasn't her fault Mr. Turner had been rude. The awful conversation had escalated so fast she'd been shocked into silence. She'd known the Turners were taciturn, though she never dreamed they'd be outright rude.

"Overreacting?" Jacob bellowed. "You hid we were dating from most of your family. Hell, the only reason they learned of me was because of that stupid fucker Blake. Now they know and treat me like shit, and you don't care."

"I do, and I know you're upset with my stupid neighbors, but why do you have to bring up my past mistakes or make today into a major crisis between us." She inhaled, grasping for calm and glanced around the parking lot. She wished he'd lower his voice.

Does the whole city have to know our business?

"This isn't just about your fucking neighbors. It's you and me. Something is very much wrong with us. You're content to have your family and their friends treat me like dirt. Their opinions matter more to you than me."

They didn't. However, when she tried to tell him this, he talked over her.

"They always have, always will. Then there's the fact, after all this time, you still doubt me. I saw you with Trisha. You wondered if her lies were true," he spat each word louder and louder. "Doubt should never have crossed your mind. I've never given you a reason."

A couple getting into their Bentley, three cars over, stopped and stared at her and Jacob.

"Would you lower your voice?" Greta pleaded.

Jacob's gaze flickered to the gawking couple before slamming back into her. Thunderclouds gathered within him, impatient to burst forth with destruction. Panic gripped her heart.

He leaned in, mere inches from her. "Oh, I'm sorry. I forgot the important thing is not to make a scene in front of your country club friends. That's much more important than us, or what it does to us. To me."

"Stop putting words in my mouth. Of course I care, but it doesn't mean I want to share our problems with everyone." Desperation and anger tore at her. Everything was spilling out of control, slipping away.

She wanted to shove him in frustration and, at the same time, tug him closer. To make him understand he was the most important person to her. He was her heart.

In the end, she didn't get a choice.

Jacob took a deep breath like he was going to shout. Instead, he exhaled through his nose and glared at the winter sky. When he returned his gaze, it was cold as the air around them. "I'm done. Go back inside," he said flatly.

Her heart froze, falling from her chest and cracking on the icy pavement. "Done with what? This argument or us?"

"Both. I knew we wouldn't work."

"Because you never expected us to." A single tear escaped, running down her cheek. She wrapped her arms around herself, hugging her shoulders tight. A shiver ran through her body and heart, and neither had to do with the cold. "You had us failing from the beginning."

He offered her no comfort. "I'm not a dreamer, Greta. This is our reality. We're too different. We'd never have lasted. I'll never fit into your life. There is no fairy tale ending for us."

"What do you mean?" Her words were a choked whisper. She reached for him. "You're going to walk away. Leave me here?"

He stepped away from her outstretched arms. Although, he was mere inches from her, it might as well be miles. "Once again, you're worried what everyone will think," he snarled. Her warm and loving boyfriend had been replaced with a cold and heartless man. "Tell them I went home sick. Tell them whatever you want. After today, I don't give a fuck."

He was wrong. Her wounded pride wasn't what worried her, but her heart. If he left, he'd be taking it with him, tearing it from her chest.

Too late. He was already gone.

Without a backward glance, Jacob got in and drove away. She stood frozen, watching his taillights flicker and disappear around the corner.

How could something so right, so perfect, fall apart in an instant?

Greta took small, uneven breaths, focusing on the line of bare trees running along the parking lot. She tried to get air inside her hollow chest. Impossible.

A pair of hands gripped her shoulders, turning her. Greta stared into her sister's worried eyes.

"What's wrong?" she demanded. "Why are you out here? Where's Jacob?"

Greta's façade crumbled, and she fell into Cindy's arms, a sob ripping from her soul. "He's gone."

Chapter Thirty-Nine

"You need to get out of this funk. Either call her or move on," Will said from his end of the couch.

Jacob turned from the TV, tossing a glare at his brother. "What? Something wrong with how I'm watching the show?"

"Yeah, kind of. It's hilarious, and you haven't laughed once. Haven't even cracked a smile."

Seriously? He's giving me shit about how I watch TV? "What are you, the fucking laugh-track police?"

"I rest my case…"

"Whatever. Shut up. Let me watch it in 'my mood.'" He made air quotes for the last words and focused back on the TV, hoping his brother was done.

Nope. He should've known better.

Will scoffed. "Uh huh, like you're paying attention. I bet if I shut off the tube and asked what we were watching, you wouldn't have a clue."

Jacob shrugged. The show had two guys and a lady. They traveled back in time. Maybe. He couldn't recall much.

"Come on, Jacob. Sulking around here isn't accomplishing anything."

"I'm not sulking."

Okay, maybe he was a little sullen. And slow to pack and move everything to his new building. Nor could he muster much excitement with his upcoming grand opening.

Last year around this time, this was his dream. Now he had it, but ever since walking away from Greta, his professional success didn't seem to matter much.

He didn't plan on giving up on Rework. He had bills to pay and employees working for him, but his business was no longer the center of his life.

It hadn't been for a while. He just hadn't noticed. Greta made him understand there was more to life than work and making money.

She'd filled places of his heart he hadn't known were empty. Now she was gone, and those pockets were vacant again. He had no idea what to do about it.

Hell, he couldn't breathe past the heaviness of regret that had taken root in his soul, let alone fill the hollow edges of his lethargy.

Will had gone quiet. Jacob sighed, silently relieved the topic of Greta was over. It hurt even to hear her name, let alone talk about her.

He was wrong. Again.

"If you've made a mistake, call her." Apparently, Will was going to have his say. All of it.

"I didn't make a mistake."

That was the crux. He was half dead without Greta, yet he made the right decision in leaving her. They were doomed from the start. Better to break it off before they'd become even more entwined.

"Are you sure?" Will insisted.

Jacob slammed a hand on the arm of the couch, his simmering annoyance boiling into a full-blown rage. "Fucking A! Yes!" He had enough of his brother's interference. Talking wouldn't change things. "She believes I'm beneath her. I'm not going to be with someone who doesn't respect me."

Will quirked an eyebrow, indicating he wasn't impressed with the outburst. Hell, since New Year's he was probably used to it. "Why are you certain Greta thinks either of those things?"

Wrestling his anger back into submission, Jacob sighed, leaning his head against the back of the couch. "Come on, Will. What are you, my therapist now? You weren't there those many times she let her family, and others, insult me."

"Okay, fine. Others have disrespected you. Has Greta? Did she ever talk down to you? Acted superior?"

Jacob shifted. A twinge of discomfort snaked around him. "No."

"That's what I thought. Had it ever occurred to you, lack of respect has nothing to do with it? You said it yourself. Her mother's a tyrant and her father's headstrong. She dated and stayed with you, regardless of their disapproval, knowing it would cause problems. That wasn't enough? You, what, want her to out-and-out battle with her family? Maybe it's not who she is." Will smiled crookedly. "We can't all be loud-mouth assholes like you."

Jacob pulled at his ear, his restlessness growing. "Hell, maybe you're right. But what you're saying proves my point." He faced Will full-on, crooking one leg on the couch. "We are who we are. People don't change. Maybe she's able to live under their rule and derision. I can't."

"You're right. It's a mistake to believe we can change people. Where you're wrong, is I don't think she's willing to live under her parents' thumb. She just goes about it differently. You confront life head-on, ready for a fight. Maybe she wanted to—"

"Ignore it." Jacob cut in, slicing his hand through the air, slashing Will's argument in half.

"That was both of you," Will said pointedly. "Anyway, I was going to say take a less hostile route. It's not like she ever shied away from you when confronted with their disapproval or ridicule."

Jacob stared at the TV, wishing his brother would drop it. Will might have a point, but two, close to three months had passed. He hadn't contacted her, nor had she him. Now the chasm of regret, bitterness, and failure was too big to cross.

"You're going to do nothing? Just sit here?" For the first time, Will sounded annoyed.

Jacob studied his brother. "Why do you care?"

"I care because I want you to be happy. And you were with her. Now you're miserable. Don't piss it away because you're a stubborn ass."

Jacob was sort of touched at Will's concern. A bigger part of him wanted to strangle his brother. "I'm not being stubborn. Reality is reality. Greta and I aren't a good match. Look at us together. I'm not polished. I don't fit into her grandiose lifestyle."

"Oh, please. Outward appearances?" The scorn in Will's voice was almost funny. "What matters is how it feels. Did you believe, because you found the love of your life, everything would be problem free?"

"Whoa, love of my life? Slow down there, Romeo…"

"Shut the hell up, dickweed." Will laughed. "You loved her, right?"

Jacob nodded.

"Do you still love her?"

He nodded again. "Given time, it'll fade."

He hoped.

Granted, weeks had become months, and each tick of the clock slammed into his heart like a steel-toed boot.

It's just taking more time than expected.

All he had to do was survive the dreary, never-ending hours.

"Why do you love her?" Will persisted.

Jacob scowled at his brother and shrugged. "Are you sure you weren't born with a vagina?"

"Answer the question, douche bag. Do you love her looks, her money? What specifically?"

"Nothing specific." Jacob slammed his hands on his legs, exasperated. "I love her for her. What's your point?"

"That *is* my point, dumbass. It's what makes you two the perfect match. People don't need to come from the same city or have identical upbringings. They only need to love and respect each other for who they are, not what they can offer. That's what you two had. You're just too stupid to understand love and life are messy. You, more than anybody, should know this." Will lifted his shoulders and his hands, palms up, as if in surrender. He dropped them and stood, moving toward the door.

"Where are you going?"

"I don't know." Will rolled his shoulders. "Maybe I'll lift weights or shoot hoops. Something to make sure my testosterone doesn't morph into estrogen."

Jacob snorted. "Good idea."

Will reached the hall, and Jacob cleared his throat, needing to say something. "Thanks. I'm not sure what I'll do with your advice, but thanks."

Will gripped the doorframe. "Welcome. Think about it, okay? Don't fuck up a good thing. Remember, that's my job."

"Stop saying that shit," Jacob called to his brother's retreating back.

Will waved, not bothering to slow or turn around.

Chapter Forty

Winter's brutal grip was finally letting up. The robins had returned, and the tulips were in full bloom. Greta barely noticed. It could have been the dead of winter, the way icy gloom clung to her like an old itchy wool coat.

She should be happy, elated. Her college days were finished. She'd graduated summa cum laude, secured a job at a large reputable web design company, and even found a fabulous apartment. All without any help from her parents.

On paper, her life was perfect. Independence. A great job. An awesome apartment.

The reality; however, was hollow. Life was dreary and tiresome. Her heartache drained her joy.

Jacob might have left months ago, but he still held a firm grip on her heart. She needed to move forward.

Hopefully today's excursion will help.

As she pulled onto Adams Ave, hope and anxiety surged through Greta, making her heart thump and her pulse race in a staccato rhythm. After finding a parking spot right across the street from Rework, she shut off the car and closed her eyes, listening to a man's velvety voice croon on the radio about illusions and love.

Before losing her nerve, Greta started for Rework. She took in its massive front window. It gave an unrestricted view of an office and a showcase area.

Her heart skipped a beat.

The sign she'd given Jacob for Christmas hung high on the exposed brick wall between two massive display cases. A desk with a woman, head down reading something, sat front and center. Pride for his accomplishment bloomed within Greta.

A door at the back swung open, and Jacob strolled out. She sucked in a breath as a myriad of emotions slammed through her. Love. Hurt. Sadness. Hope. Greta sagged against her car, waiting for her heart to stop thrashing against her ribs.

He walked to the blonde woman at the desk, and parts Greta thought dead, awoke. She had an overpowering urge to run into the shop and wrap herself in his strong arms. Hurt and anger temporarily were forgotten, replaced with a longing so intense it stole her breath.

The woman looked up, admiration spilling from the smile spreading across her lips. Indignation slammed into Greta.

The blonde wasn't a stranger.

What the hell is Macy doing there?

Jacob had his back to the window. His body language was impossible to read. However, Macy's was easy enough: greedy longing. She stood and placed a hand on his chest.

Greta's splintered heart shattered.

She turned from the window.

All this time she'd been pining after him like a fool, thinking they'd had something unbreakable. Meanwhile, he'd moved on. Heck, maybe he'd been waiting, biding his time, needing an excuse to leave her without guilt and go after Macy.

Fine. She'd do the same.

Greta opened her car door and slid back inside, out of Jacob's life for good.

~ * ~

Jacob glanced at the front window; the sensation of being watched crawled along his spine. The street was busy, but his gaze targeted a woman getting in a car the same color as Greta's. He shot across the room and outside.

He wasn't fast enough. By time he reached the sidewalk, the Audi was turning the corner, obscuring the driver.

Staring down the street, he rubbed his sternum, trying to ease the spreading ache. Exhaling, he dropped his hand and went back inside.

His mind was playing tricks on him, which was all. He should be used to it. Since they split, Greta was everywhere, both in his dreams and during his waking hours.

But he had to face facts. She was gone. She'd disappeared forever from his life.

After talking with Will, Jacob understood he'd fucked up. They'd both made mistakes, but he was the dumb ass who walked away. The need to fix things between them had become an obsession.

He tried calling her cell and found the number disconnected, making him wonder if she'd done it so he couldn't contact her. He hadn't been willing to quit. One desperate night he drove to Lansing, only to discover her apartment vacant. He tried Susan and Miguel's place. They hadn't been home. He tried calling them. They didn't answer or call back.

That hurt. He considered them friends.

After those fails, he contemplated visiting Swift but decided against it. Greta despised having her personal life mixed with her professional.

In the end, his obsession turned to defeat.

Time to face facts—Greta didn't want to be found. She'd vanished without a trace, and he was left holding her ghost.

His gaze fell on the sign she had given him, and the memory of their Christmas together slammed into him like a linebacker. Hurt just as much.

He traced the metal lettering. At least there was Rework. Clients and his new side business of finding, fixing, and selling antiques at the shop kept him busy. Work was the only time the enormous hole in his heart eased a little.

He glanced at Macy. She'd been in the middle of telling him something before he ran outside.

She was watching him intently.

Always watching.

"What's wrong?" she asked, placing a hand on his bicep.

Always watching. Always touching.

"Nothing. Get back to work." He gave her his back, staring out the window. The glimpse of the woman outside rattled him, and he tired of Macy's constant touches and flirting.

Back when she contacted him, he thought she was a godsend. She'd called hiring him to fix her mother's Crosley turntable. While they talked, Macy mentioned she'd moved to the Metro Detroit area and was applying for office assistant jobs. Desperate for a receptionist, he asked her to send her resume.

Running both a large shop and the front office was difficult and a time suck. He was drowning. He'd hired a guy who specialized in motors to help in the back. However, finding a good office assistant had proven more difficult.

After reading Macy's credentials, he offered her a job. She accepted, and he'd naively believed his work-related problems were solved.

It took less than a week to understand he'd fucked up. Royally. He couldn't fault Macy's work. She was competent as hell. The problem was her personality.

She wanted to be more than his employee and wasn't shy about letting him know. He wouldn't be the least bit surprised to find her naked and lying naked across his workstation. Hell, she'd basically stated she was game if he was.

In his darker moments, he'd almost accepted her offer. Not from any real desire, more from desperation and knowing it would sever what small chance he had with Greta. She'd never take him back if he slept with Macy. Maybe then, he could move on if he was certain he couldn't have Greta.

In the end, he couldn't do it. Deep down he understood it'd take more than screwing a pretty woman to get Greta out of his system. Plus, he was never a man to use women. No matter how much they didn't mind being used.

Turning from the window, Jacob found Macy had returned to her desk. Her posture was stiff, her movements jerky. He exhaled, guilt ebbing at him. Sure, her constant come-ons were a nuisance. Still, he didn't want to be a dick-boss.

"Listen, I'm sorry I barked at you. I'm stressed." Before heading into the back shop, he stopped at her desk. "We okay?"

She smiled. "Yes."

"Do you need anything else before I get back to work?"

"No. I only had the one question regarding Ms. Delft's order."

All was forgiven. Too bad everything in his life wasn't as easily absolved.

Before his palm smacked against the shop door, Macy called after him. "Tony has to leave early. Let me know if you want company later."

Jacob gave a weary sigh, not bothering to answer before pushing through the metal doors of the workshop. He hoped like hell Macy would leave him alone. All he wanted was to lose himself in work. To forget his colossal fuck up that had ravaged his heart and screwed with his mind.

Chapter Forty-One

"Why did I let you talk me into this? *Again*." Greta asked, sitting on her bed and watching Cindy and Susan rummage through her clothes.

Cindy stuck her head from around the closet. "Because you need a girl's night."

"Yeah." Susan kept digging through Greta's opened dresser drawer. "When was the last time you left your apartment? And no, going to work doesn't count."

"Why not?" Greta huffed. Work required her to leave her home *and* talk with people. Something that, lately, took all the energy she had to give. "Let's order in and watch TV." At least with a movie she wouldn't have to plaster on a pleasant smile or try to follow along with the cheery chatter.

"No," Cindy and Susan said simultaneously.

Geez. These two really wanted to go out.

They'd arrived at her door, explaining they'd joined forces and wouldn't leave until she agreed to come with them. How these two found each other was beyond Greta, but she was touched.

They were apparently worried enough to find each other and work together, in hopes of brightening her permanent gloomy mood. She should tell them they were fighting a lost cause.

Instead, she decided to humor them.

I can pretend for one night, right?

"Fine. Where are we going?"

Cindy emerged from the closet with dresses piled high in her arms. She dropped them on the bed and clapped her hands like a sweepstakes winner. "We're going dancing," she squealed.

"No." Greta fell back on her bed, lying flat. What little enthusiasm she had for the night drained away. "The last time I went dancing with you, it didn't end well."

Cindy's perfectly sculpted eyebrows came together. "Was Glengarry's house the last time we partied together? This time I promise not to leave your side. Though…as I recall, the night ended quite satisfactorily for you. Something to do with a motorcycle and a dark park…"

Susan perked up. "This sounds interesting. Sharing is Caring. Do tell."

Greta warmed, not from embarrassment but a deep yearning. She recalled the sensual night vividly. She could almost feel Jacob's hands on her and the ghost of the pleasure he'd given her.

"Some other time." The gaping hole of pain she experienced those first couple of weeks after the breakup had lessened, but it ached enough she avoided talking about him.

The two women eyed her, pity etched on their pretty features. Greta hated those looks. "I admit that night was nice. However, the fallout wasn't great."

She decided no one was meant to be that happy. At least not forever. Such things only happened in fairy tales. In real life, happiness was permitted in small doses and for short periods of time.

Susan sat next to Greta, taking her hand and pulling her up. "Down the line, when you're married to a hot husband and have two point five kids, you'll remember your whirlwind romance with Jacob fondly, without pain or regret."

"Maybe you're right," Greta said without much conviction.

"I guarantee it." Susan's gaze slid to Cindy's, and she winked. "The best way to banish the blues is with strong drinks, loud music, and a hot man."

Cindy plopped on Greta's other side and giggled. The exchange gave Greta pause. She let it go, focusing on the conversation.

"Fine." She pinched the bridge of her nose with her thumb and index finger, anticipating a *long* night. "Sign me up for your twisted fairy tale, Cindyrella."

Greta smiled at her best friend. "Are you sure you're ready for this?"

Susan rubbed her hands together like an evil witch. "Definitely."

The club wasn't far from Greta's place, and they walked to it. Stepping inside, she blinked rapidly, trying to adjust her eyes to the dim interior of the nightclub and almost ran into Susan.

She'd stopped next to a tall bar table with four guys standing around it, her focus falling on a lean man with neatly trimmed blond hair. "Professor Whiteshawl, what are you doing here? Greta, Cindy, this is my science instructor."

The two women waved, and Greta noted absently he was good-looking, in a conventional sort of way. He was maybe ten years older than her and handsome in his pressed trousers and green polo. He was the kind of man she would have been interested in before Jacob.

"Please call me Thomas," he said with a warm smile before pointing to the other three men. "These are my friends, Robert and Harrison. The guy on the end is my cousin Cade. We're celebrating his recent promotion. What brings you ladies here?"

Susan gave a wicked smile. "We're celebrating my friend's promotion to singlehood."

The men eyed Greta with interest, and she wanted to sink into the floor. She glared at her friend.

Susan widened her eyes, trying to appear innocent. Then she winked. The woman was incorrigible.

"Anyway, nice seeing you, Thomas." She grinned, sliding her arm through Greta and Cindy's, ready to move on.

"You too, Susan. Though remember, back in class I'm Professor Whiteshawl." When they turned to leave, he placed a light hand on Greta's wrist. He leaned closer, a slightly embarrassed smile on his lips. "I know this is forward. Would you like to dance?"

She took in the crowd of gyrating bodies, and her first instinct was to decline. Though, how would she ever get over Jacob if she never even tried?

"Sure, that'd be nice." She caught Susan and Cindy's surprise and also a flash of concern. They should be happy she was making an effort.

Whatever.

Thomas grinned and took her hand. They scooted around tightly packed tables and cut through a section of low-slung black leather couches, finally reaching the massive and crowded dance floor. Bodies twisted and gyrated around them, and music pulsed through her. She loved it.

Before long, Greta relaxed and was even glad Cindy and Susan had forced her to go out. They were right; she needed this. It helped Thomas was a good dancer and not too handsy. There was no real spark with him, and maybe that was better. Being with Jacob had been all-consuming. Maybe being with someone less intense was safer for her heart and sanity.

Thomas leaned in, inches from her face. "Want to take a break? Let me buy you a drink."

She stifled the urge to step back. There was nothing scary or predatory in his kind brown eyes. The problem was that he wasn't Jacob. The only man she wanted close.

She was pitiful.

Taking Thomas's hand, she smiled and nodded. Maybe if she pretended, sooner or later she might feel something.

The place was packed, and they had to press, push, and jostle their way through the crowd toward the bar. At one point, they were knocked apart, and she lost sight of him in the crush of bodies.

Cindy was dancing with a tall auburn-haired man, and catching Greta's gaze she smiled, her gaze flickering past her as if searching for someone. Greta circled around, not recognizing anyone. Shrugging, she turned back, and, from the corner of her eye, she spotted Thomas a couple of yards off to her left. He'd escaped the throng of dancing people and was waiting for her by the bar.

She made it to the edge of the dance floor and sighed in relief. Then some inconsiderate jerk slammed into her, and she catapulted forward into a man's broad back. He whipped around and steadied her before she fell on her butt.

Her body was back on solid ground, but everything within her shifted as she stared into a pair of familiar stormy blue eyes.

Chapter Forty-Two

Jacob's dead heart sputtered to life when he registered who was in his arms. Two beats later, Greta was gone, the crowd swallowing her, leaving him to wonder if she was an illusion he'd dreamed in his desperation to see her again.

No. Apparitions don't feel and smell like heaven.

And Cindy had promised Greta would be there tonight.

I owe the woman. Big time.

Jacob scanned the crowd, spotting Greta by the bar with some straight-laced guy. His hand was resting on the small of her back. The urge to rip the man's arm off was fierce.

Cindy hadn't mentioned Greta was coming here with a date. Jacob couldn't help noticing the guy was her perfect match, dressed in pressed khakis and a polo shirt. He glanced at his worn jeans and faded gray shirt. He hadn't even bothered to tuck it in, leaving the top two buttons open and rolling the sleeves, exposing the ink on his arm and collar. Bluntly stated, he was the polar opposite of the other man.

Doesn't matter.

The other guy might look like Greta's match. However, even from across the room Jacob could tell there was no spark in her eyes. She wasn't attracted to him.

Thank God.

The two might appear picture-perfect, but she was Jacob's heart and soul. The tricky part would be convincing her of this.

Lucky for him, he had nothing to lose and everything to gain. And he was willing to do whatever it took to win her back.

~ * ~

Greta clenched her hands together, trying to hide the tremors. She peered past Thomas and saw Jacob snaking through the throngs of people, his gaze boring into her.

His steely stare and determined stride told her he was ready for a confrontation. Trepidation shivered down her spine.

She understood *what* was happening just not the *why*. What could he possibly have to say after all this time? And why bother? He'd moved on. What did he care if she did the same?

Stopping in front of her and ignoring Thomas, Jacob said, "I need to talk to you."

Not a question, a demand. It annoyed her. He'd broken her heart and now wanted to order her around. No. She was done letting her weak heart dictate her life.

"Why? I have nothing to say to you." Her voice was calm and steady. Her heart pounded loud enough to compete with the music's drums.

"Then I'll talk."

"I'm busy right now." Greta stared pointedly over her shoulder at Thomas, who appeared mildly alarmed.

Jacob's face flushed, and a vein throbbed in his neck. He was furious.

Not her problem.

He swallowed, keeping his laser gaze on her. "Five minutes. Please, don't make me beg."

She stared at him, stunned. Jacob didn't beg. For anything. Fight and shout, yes, but not beg.

Forgetting that she'd refused to talk with him, or that she was sitting with Thomas, Greta scooted off her bar stool.

"Listen, buddy, she already told you, she isn't interested in talking to you." Thomas sounded annoyed and anxious.

Greta understood. Jacob only had a couple of inches on the other man, but way more muscle and a definite don't-mess-with-me aura. Thomas probably didn't revel in the chance of getting beat up for a woman he just met. She appreciated his chivalry.

Twisting around, she rested a hand on his. Jacob tensed at the gesture. Too bad, if he didn't like it. He was lucky for the five minutes she was going to give him. "I'm sorry Thomas. I should speak with him."

"Are you sure?" He glanced at Jacob.

"Yes. He'd never hurt me. At least not physically." She walked past Jacob, holding her head high. "Come on. Let's talk outside."

She shouldered through the crowd. The bouncer at the main door opened it as she approached, and Greta stormed through, not bothering to check if Jacob was following. She held tight to her resentment, afraid to meet his eyes. If she did, her anger might dissolve and turn into pitiful hope.

"What? What do you want?" The door clicked shut, abruptly cutting off the music, and her voice echoed down the mostly empty street.

His gaze fixed on hers, ignoring the smattering of people watching them. "I thought we were a mistake. Leaving you was the mistake. I'm sorry."

His candor surprised her, and it thawed some of the ice she built around her heart.

But only a little.

For months, she'd longed to hear him confess such things. Now, she didn't know what to do with his words.

She went with honesty. "You broke my heart."

"I know," he whispered, placing his hand on her arm. The touch was gentle, yet hurt soul deep. "Can you forgive me?"

Every fiber of her being wanted to lean into him and let his embrace comfort and mend her heart's torn seams. Macy's smug smile flashed before Greta.

She twisted away, not wanting him to notice her tear-filled eyes. "Fine. You're forgiven. Now may I go back inside?"

He didn't release his hold on her arm, making it impossible for her to scramble away. "No. Greta, I want more than forgiveness. I want you back."

What poise she managed to hold on to, crumbled. Elation, anger, and hurt fought for dominance within her. "That's not possible," she whispered, not sure he heard.

He did, and grasped both her shoulders, guiding her around to face him. "Why? We've both made mistakes, but we love each other. We can work through this if you still love me. Do you?"

She peered into his eyes. The depth of his pain cut and confused her. She'd witnessed the familiar way Macy had touched him.

What game is he playing?

She decided to ignore his question and stick to their mistakes. That was much easier. "Jacob, I don't deny my sins. I've done you wrong in many ways, but I never would've walked away. It almost killed me when you left and simply moved on like I was nothing more than a blip, a moment in your life."

"You were never not important to me. None of this has been easy or simple. And let's be honest, a blowup between us had been brewing for months. We both chose to ignore it."

"True. But again, in the end, you left. Didn't even try to fix what was breaking between us." Greta's voice broke, and she hated her weakness. She took a fortifying breath, trying not to dissolve into tears. She needed to get her hurt out. "I won't risk my heart with you again. I don't want to chance that kind of misery again. Next time I may lose my mind, along with my heart."

Jacob slid his hands from her shoulders and cupped her face. "There will be no next time. I won't ever walk away again."

Oh God, I want to believe him.

She couldn't. Trust and second chances hurt too much.

"Your pride is more important than our relationship." She withdrew from his grasp, holding her hands to stop him from interrupting. "You completely disregarded my feelings and my heart. You left without a backward glance."

"On New Year's I let my mounting worries and resentment take over and erupt in the worst possible way. It's no excuse. I was an ass. I made a colossal mistake. I lost everything when I lost you. I loved you then. I love you now. I'll love you tomorrow and every day after."

His words were salve to her wounded heart, but they couldn't fix everything.

"How can you say this? One. You didn't lose me, you left. Two. You've moved on," Greta choked, swiping angrily at a tear that managed to escape.

He tilted his head. "Why do you keep saying that?"

"Macy."

His brows pushed together, forming a small line between them. "What about her?"

Jacob was hot-tempered, but she never figured him for a flake. Would he now toss aside Macy? Greta pitied the woman she'd been and even Macy. He'd played them both.

"Weeks back, I had the stupid idea of talking to you. I wanted to know if we had anything worth saving. I went to your shop." Recalling that bitter day, her anger flooded back.

"It was you," he muttered. "Why didn't you come inside?"

"Because," she rammed her palms against Jacob's solid chest, "You and Macy…you both were quite cozy. I didn't want to interrupt."

"I'm so fucking confused. She works for me, runs the office. Nothing more."

Hope, like a spring seedling, took root in her chest. He'd never lied before, yet the image of Macy's intimate hands on Jacob was forever burned into Greta's mind. "From what I witnessed, she's taking care of more than your paperwork."

"Listen," he took her hands in his, "I have no idea what you *thought* you saw. I promise you, I am not dating Macy. I'm not sleeping with her."

"Then why was she hanging on you like a wet blanket?" Greta shouted, trying to pull from his grasp.

It didn't work. He held tight. "You were right. She did want more than a business card. And she isn't shy about letting me know what she wants. But I swear to you nothing is going on between us."

"If you knew, why hire her? Why keep her?"

They were getting way off topic. She didn't care. She wanted answers. The days of holding in questions and anger were over. Confrontation didn't bother Greta anymore.

"I needed an office assistant, and she needed a job. I had no idea she was going to turn into Clarence Thomas." Jacob grinned ruefully.

Greta couldn't help returning the smile, though it was weak. "The analogy doesn't quite work since you're the boss. And," she leaned back, raising both eyebrows and studying him. "Why not fire her after she made her intentions known?"

"I'm swamped. I don't have time to find a new assistant. And sexual harassment aside, she's good at her job."

"Fine. Whatever." Greta waved a hand, dismissing Macy and Jacob's problems with her. "If you wanted me back so desperately, why haven't you contacted me? Weeks have passed, and you've survived fine without me. Now you've seen me tonight, and what, you now *have* to have me back?"

Jacob laughed a harsh bark without any joy. "It killed me to drive away on New Year's. I had my head in my ass and was convinced we were better off apart. By the time I realized my mistake, you'd vanished."

Vanished?

"I tried to call your cell. Your phone was disconnected. I went to your apartment. Someone else was living there. That's why I'm here tonight."

"Oh," Greta breathed. Without meaning to, she had made herself rather difficult to find. "After graduating, I found a job in Detroit and moved. I broke my cell shortly after our breakup. It fell from my purse, and I didn't know until I heard a crunch under my tires. I went with a different company, and I had to get a new number—Wait," she cut herself off when his last words registered. "What do you mean, 'that's why I'm here'?"

"When Miguel and Susan returned from a vacation in Mexico, they call me back. Susan got ahold of your sister, and she promised me you'd be here tonight." Jacob scowled at the club's door. "Though, they hadn't mentioned you coming here with a guy."

"Those interfering troublemakers," Greta muttered. No wonder they'd been adamant about tonight.

"Greta," Jacob grasped her chin gently and didn't speak until her gaze met his. "I wish I could turn back the clock. I can't. All I can do is love you and promise never to leave your side again. I'll do whatever it takes to get back your trust and love."

She tried to shake loose from his hold, overwhelmed. Wanting to believe him yet finding it difficult.

His hand dropped. Not his gaze. That was unwavering and a little desperate. "When I first met you and didn't call, something was off. Like I was missing out. This time my heart was hollow, and I knew who'd taken it. You didn't steal it; you became my heart and soul. Rescue me from this hell. Forgive me. Give us another chance."

His words were a salve to her broken heart, but wasn't enough. He hadn't merely scraped and bruised her, he left her with a gaping wound. Some hurts couldn't heal.

"I want to," she whispered, brushing at her tears, no longer trying to keep them from falling. "I even understand your earlier anger. It was justifiable. The part I have trouble moving past is how you handled it. You have this habit of making snap decisions. You decided we are doomed, and without giving me any choice in the matter, you ended us. You believe your decisions are infallible, and therefore my opinions and emotions don't count."

He reached for her, shaking his head. "No. Not true."

She cut him off. "Yes, it is. You did it when we first met. You decided we were ill-matched and never called. And fine, to be fair, I didn't call you either. However, by New Year's, we were much more, yet you decided on your own our love wasn't strong enough to overcome our problems. Without even giving me a chance to talk with you, to argue with you, you left."

She crossed her arms and rubbed them. Though, her heart was cold and not her skin. "Jacob, life's full of difficulties and frustrations. How do I know you won't do this again, without even talking to me, decide we're doomed?"

"Greta, we've both made mistakes. We buried our problems and let them fester. I won't let that happen again. I know life isn't perfect, but there's no denying we're right for each other. It's simple."

Oh, if only that were true.

Nearly every part of her being screamed for her to take him back, to let him envelop her in his warm embrace. His love.

One tiny wounded whisper made it impossible.

"Except, it's not. At least not for me. I'm scared, Jacob. I've just begun to somewhat heal, feel whole again. I don't ever want to experience pain like that again. I need to protect myself. From you."

Jacob jerked back like she slapped him. A painful silence swelled between them. She hurt him. It couldn't be helped. She had to protect her fragile heart.

When he finally spoke, his question surprised her. "Where are you working? Are you at Swift?"

"No. Detroit Computer Base," she stammered. "Why?"

"Perfect. I'm taking you to lunch."

"Lunch?"

"Yes, lunch. You still eat, right?"

"Uh, yes." His nearness was affecting her, but had she managed to miss an entire conversation? One minute he wanted her back. Now he was asking about food?

Her expression must've been a sight because he burst out laughing. "Agree to have lunch with me. Please."

"What? When? On Monday?"

"Yes, on Monday." He smiled. "And every day after. Until you agree to more or get sick of me."

"If I refuse?"

She wouldn't deny him. She might not be ready to hand him her heart again, might never be, but the lure of seeing him again was impossible to resist.

"I'll show up each day at your work until you agree. Or," he smirked, his expression a beautiful mixture of hopefulness and humor, "you have me arrested as your stalker."

"We can't have you arrested on my account, again." She laughed, and that small flower of hope grew stronger.

Chapter Forty-Three

Greta watched Jacob joke with their waitress while she filled their drinks. His deep chuckle was like lava cake: molten hot, smooth, and delicious. From the way the waitress drank him in, she wouldn't mind a bite.

When he looked away, the waitress snagged Greta's gaze and gave a woman-to-woman smile before mouthing, "lucky."

Greta nodded.

Ever since Jacob arrived at her work, she was carefree and light as if she won the lottery. Though, instead of money, she was given a pile of bliss.

Corny, yes, and she didn't care.

He arrived as promised that Monday after the dance club, and every day since, much to the delight of Greta and her female coworkers. They loved to speculate and pepper her with questions about the handsome suitor who'd showed up one slow day, with a sexy smile and a bouquet of riotous flowers.

She didn't mind the gossip. She was too happy and past caring what others thought.

"How was your mother's birthday party?" Jacob asked, breaking into Greta's musing.

She'd been staring, unseeing, at the black and white checkered floor and glanced up at his question. They were at their favorite lunchtime spot, the famous Lafayette Coney Island in Detroit. Jacob dragged his last huge onion ring through ketchup, playing it off like the answer meant nothing. Had he been anyone else, she might have believed the act.

He was too focused on his food and his shoulders were tense, as if waiting for the executioner's blow.

"The company Nigel hired to coordinate the party was amazing. Though the best was visiting with family I hadn't seen in years." She hesitated, tapping her nails on the Formica table, not sure if she should mention her mother's ongoing relentless crusade. Greta decided to go with complete honesty. "The not-so-great was Mother used the day to play the dating game with every man I wasn't related to. Heck, she even introduced me to a couple of third cousins."

Jacob chuckled, but the humor didn't reach his eyes. "Not only do I have to compete with most of Michigan's upper crust, now there are out-of-state cousins. Great."

She laughed, taking his hand resting on the table, linking their fingers. "No competition. I explained to Mother I have sufficient male attention during my lunch breaks."

The smile that broke across his face was genuine and exquisite. It made Greta question why she wasn't back in his arms. In his bed.

"You told your mother we've been meeting? What did she have to say?"

"Oh, something disparaging. Along the lines of, 'he probably thinks a grand date is visiting a honky-tonk or a place with plastic menus.'"

They looked at the table's laminated menus propped between the salt and pepper shakers and laughed.

"Sorry." He shrugged.

She glanced at her half-empty plate. "You should be. It's your fault I'm addicted to these chili-cheese fries. You never should've let me try them. If I keep eating like this, I'm going to gain a hundred pounds."

He ogled her and leered playfully. "And you'll still be the sexiest woman I've ever laid eyes on." He cleared his throat and picked at his napkin. "However, if you're tired of plastic menus, there's a new French restaurant that recently opened. Will told me the food's excellent, but they're only open in the evening."

This was the first time he mentioned a dinner date and it took her by surprise. She wavered, having no idea why. Jacob owned her heart.

"Don't answer me now," he said quickly, as if fearing her rejection. "I'll try to convince you when I get back."

Melancholy crept into Greta's veins, and the dinner invite fell from her mind. "Where are you going?"

"Mackinac Island. I have a new client. She wants me to repair the insides of a nineteen ten Bechstein grand piano. It obviously can't come to me. I need to go there. See if I'm capable of the repairs, or if I'll need to subcontract the job." He caught the attention of the waitress and motioned for the check. "Anyway, I'm leaving tomorrow morning. I shouldn't be gone more than a couple days."

"Spring is a nice time to visit," Greta replied lamely, not sure what else to say. She didn't want him to go, yet he owed her nothing.

"Well, I'll be working. I won't have much time to enjoy the island." He accepted the bill and thanked the waitress, glancing at his watch. "Are you ready to go?"

She nodded, trying to hide her disappointment. They made their way to the checkout counter.

The news was unexpected. The work trip would be the first time he skipped their lunch date since he suggested it. With his shop, clients came to him instead of the other way around.

However, what bothered her more than she'd like to admit was his indifference toward missing their lunch dates. Sure, his lackadaisical attitude was her fault. She'd asked him to keep it simple, and he had. She couldn't start pouting now.

Greta followed him to his truck, and they drove a couple of blocks to her building. To her utter disappointment, he skipped his signature sinful kisses. The ones that start feather-light then nosedived straight into erotic delight. Instead, he settled for brushing his lips lightly against hers.

Her mouth pulled in a slight frown at the chaste kiss, and his gaze danced over her, amusement sparkling in his eyes. His mirth spurred her on, and she kissed him with all the passion she'd been holding back.

"Hmm…I should play coy more often," he growled against her lips.

"We're going to miss a couple of lunch dates. I don't want you to forget me."

"Amnesia couldn't make me forget you."

Chapter Forty-Four

Seven days had passed.

Seven long days since Jacob left for Mackinac Island.

He was able to fix the piano and had remained on the island to repair it. To make matters worse, cell reception was terrible where he stayed, and they'd talked no more than a handful of times. When they did, he sounded distracted, offering only vague reassurances about his absence.

Finally, two days ago, she received a text from him saying he planned on arriving home on Friday.

Today is Friday. And nothing. No call. No visit. Nothing.

She worried his delay wasn't his workload, but her. Maybe time away had made him realize she wasn't worth the effort.

When he hadn't called her by noon, she phoned his work and was delighted to find Macy replaced. The new office assistant was a young college kid named Erik Boyne. However, her good mood didn't last.

Erik informed her Jacob was back. He'd stopped by the office in the morning, straight from the airport, to give him the Mackinac paperwork. After checking on some new projects, Jacob had gone home. That had been hours ago, and she wondered why he hadn't called her.

The uncertainty was killing her.

Had she been foolish to hold him at arm's length? She didn't even know why she'd done it because, her heart would never be with another man.

The old Greta would've stewed in indecision, fearing a quarrel or hostility. The new Greta grabbed her car keys and, thanks to the location of her new apartment, was at Jacob's house in less than a half hour.

She might face her fears now; it didn't mean the possibility of Jacob's rejection didn't coil in her stomach, making her a bundle of nerves and pent-up anxiety. *No sense prolonging the inevitable.* With shaky hands, Greta opened her car door and walked to the front door.

Heart in her throat, she made her way to the porch and knocked. Seconds later, heavy footfalls made their way in her direction.

Will swung open the door and stopped short. "Hey, Greta. Didn't expect you. How've you been? Heard you moved and got a new job. How's it all going?"

Not good. It didn't matter. She wasn't turning back.

"Is Jacob here?"

"Uh yeah…did he know you were stopping by?"

Dread became a living entity. It crawled from her stomach and wrapped itself vice-like around her heart.

Unable to speak, she shook her head.

After an excruciating pause, Will stepped aside letting her come in. Closing the door, he asked her to wait in the foyer, like a guest, when he went to find Jacob.

This doesn't bode well.

She waited in a cruel silence. After a couple of minutes, Jacob's familiar tread moved toward the door. Her breath caught.

His hair was damp, but he was dressed for a night out. He was incredibly handsome in a pair of black slacks and an ocean blue long-sleeve button-up with the cuffs rolled. The color made his eyes appear electric.

Where was he headed? And with who?

He stopped in front of her. Droplets of water trickled down his neck. She followed its slow trail. She'd love to press her lips against the moisture, taking in his warmth and scent. After a pause, Greta dragged her gaze from his throat to his eyes.

"Where've you been?" Her voice was whip-sharp and full of accusations.

He raised a brow. "Um. Business trip. We did talk when I was there…"

"Yes, but you've been home all day. Why didn't you call me?"

He took her hand and opened the door with the other. "Come on. Let's sit outside."

Her pulse spiked, and butterflies started to fight in her stomach. Why hadn't he answered her question? He'd taken her hand, but no kiss, big or small.

From the door to the swing wasn't more than a few steps, yet it dragged as if it were her final mile.

She had to know. "Was work what kept you away?"

"Yes, of course." Jacob cocked his head to the side. "What else would it be?" He let go of her hand and sat, motioning with his head for her to sit next to him.

She sat on the swing, shifting to face him. "I don't know, Jacob. I'm worried. You were distracted whenever we spoke on the phone. Then you came home and didn't call me. Also, your brother is acting strange. Treating me like a guest…" The butterflies were no longer fighting each other. They'd banded together and were eating through her stomach.

"I'm sorry I worried you. Though, I do love you've confronted me with your doubts."

He kissed her cheek, and the love reflected in his eyes quieted her fears.

"I wasn't brushing you off. The opposite, in fact. I want to show you how serious I am about us." He stood.

She took in his dressy clothes, smiling. "Oh yeah, how so? Were you going to convince me to go to dinner, instead of lunch?"

His low rumbling laughter vanquished the chill from the spring air. "Yes. It's the reason why I went to Mackinac, instead of Tony."

"You wanted their famous fudge, right?" Greta joked, a bit giddy. "Did you bring me any?"

"No, sorry." A small smile played at the corner of his lips, but his eyes were serious.

She studied him. He appeared nervous. He kept fidgeting; rubbing his forehead, putting his hands in his pockets, pulling them out seconds later.

"Are you okay? Is anything wrong?"

"No. It's only, well, I was going to wait until after dinner." Jacob caught her eye and smiled. "This is better." He stood, rubbed his palms on the front of his pants, then lowered to one knee.

"Oh my," she whispered over her now racing heart.

He looked at her from bended knee, devotion in his eyes. Her heart leaped, and joy danced through her soul, tears filling her eyes.

Shoot. I am going to cry.

"Greta, you are my lover and best friend. Before you, I didn't believe in soulmates or fairy tale love. Now I do." Jacob dipped a hand into his shirt pocket.

Between his thumb and pointer finger was the loveliest ring. The beauty of it stole her breath. An exquisite, flawless diamond sat in an octagon setting. The sides of the ring were inscribed with intricate and beautiful etchings.

"I love you. Will you be my Happily Ever After? Will you marry me?" Jacob asked.

Her gaze flickered from his face to the gorgeous ring. Happiness ran through every inch of her body, rendering her speechless.

Her Prince Charming arrived on a motorcycle, covered in tattoos. He was everything she wanted and needed; he was her one true love.

He cleared his throat, breaking her reverie.

Greta catapulted herself from the swing and into his arms, almost knocking him over. "Yes, Jacob, I will marry you."

About the Author

DK Marie loves to indulge in all things hot. Men, writing, reading, and coffee. The order of importance depends on the day.

Like characters in her books, she lives in Michigan, enjoying her happily-ever-after with her husband and kids. When not indulging in all things hot, she loves theater, concerts, and to travel.

DK loves to hear from readers. You can find and connect with her at the links below.

Website: www.dkmarie.com
Twitter: https://twitter.com/dkmarie2216s
Facebook: http://facebook.com/dkanso
Pinterest: https://www.pinterest.de/DKmarie/
Instgram: http://instagram.com/dkmarie2216
Goodreads: https://goodreads.com/user/show/52007413-dk-marie

~ * ~

We hope you enjoyed *Fairy Tale Lies,* book 1 in the *Opposites Attract* contemporary romance series. If you did, please write a review, tell your friends, or check out the other offerings at Champagne Book Group.

Now turn the page for a quick peek into *The Reluctant* Princess a delightful contemporary romance, book 1 in the *Charm City Hearts* series.

The Reluctant Princess
The Charm City Hearts Series, 1
M.C. Vaughan

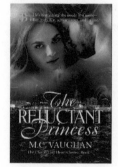

He's everything she needs in a muse—killer body, fun, adventure, and…a dad?

Nothing's more important to twenty-five-year-old goth girl Zara Kissette than making her bones in the art world. When a fire destroys her paintings, she needs two things to fulfill the art gallery's contract for multiple masterpieces—a quick hit of cash for supplies, and a way to rekindle her creativity. Otherwise, she can kiss her career-making gallery spot goodbye. So she reluctantly returns to a lucrative gig as a fantasy princess/face painter, where she meets a hot, divorced dad who could bring a spark to her life…or ruin everything.

Brendan Stewart is doing all he can to keep the world a soft and stable place for his beloved little girl. While his ex breezes in and out of their daughter's life, he's determined be her rock. The last thing he needs is another relationship to balance with the rest of his life. That is, until a gorgeous princess shows up to paint faces at his daughter's birthday party. Zara's open heart and distracting curves tempt him to lower his defenses, despite having been burned before.

Their romance is all cake and bubbles—and lots of steamy sex—until Zara betrays Brendan's trust for her shot at the gallery, and Brendan takes her career into his hands and, well, screws it up. If they can't make peace with each other's mistakes, they risk losing the one person who loves them for who they truly are.

Sample

Brendan Stewart rolled his neck. He was certain this meant surrendering his man card. Didn't matter. A dad's gotta do what a dad's gotta do.

"Okay, Pinterest, let's see what you've got."

He keyed in his daughter's favorite cartoon princess, "Ravenna from *Rising*" and "party ideas," hit return, and boom. His browser loaded with a billion different ways to make his daughter's fifth birthday party epic.

He slogged through the pictures. Elaborate cupcakes, costumes, party favors—all of which appeared to be homemade. What kind of free time must these people have? Even if he didn't have a monster deadline in a month, he'd refuse to spend hours of his free time on stuff like this. His days with Emma were already cut in half.

Nah, he'd buy as much as he could, stock up on the best Party City had to offer, and maybe go overboard on the balloons. Emma loved balloons almost as much as she loved candy.

Now, what the hell would a dozen little girls do during the festivities?

He scratched his neck and yawned.

Kid parties were the worst. There's the party for the kids, but the parents have to hang out because they happen to have kids the same age. Most of the parties Emma'd been invited to this year involved the same conversations—*Are you Emma's older brother? You're her father? You look so young!*

Because he was young. Most of these parents had a good ten years on him.

Maybe he'd hire some entertainment to take the strain off parental small talk. Like a magician maybe? Or a clown? He shivered. No. Definitely not a clown.

He opened another browser tab and searched up children's party entertainers in Baltimore. Hmmm…a face painter could be fun. The third link was for one who dressed like a princess. Bingo. As soon as the site loaded, Brendan widened his eyes. The face painter, Zara, could be Ravenna's twin. Authentic black-and-purple hair, glacier-blue eyes, porcelain skin, and Ravenna's signature scowl. Her austere website could use an overhaul, but never mind the site's design. This girl was *perfect*.

He had to hire her.

After he clicked the 'Contact' button, Brendan typed the details of the party and shot the note off into the ether. Not a bad night's work—he'd ordered the food, decided on the decorations, and had feelers out for the entertainment. Time for a beer.

Eh, who was he kidding? Time to get back to coding. Those queries weren't going to write themselves.

Before he could move from the couch to his workstation, his e-mail alert chimed. Zara had gotten back to him.

Hi there—

Got your note. I'm available. The charge is $200 for 90 minutes and includes a gallery of photos after. If you want to book me, Venmo a

50% deposit to the account below, and Ravenna will be there.
—Z

No hesitation. He paid the deposit and texted the link to her site to Jess.

Adorable! Jess wrote a few minutes later. *I'll kick in half.*

Huh. That was unexpectedly generous of his ex.

Thx, but I've got this.

When is it, again?

Sighing, he texted back. *2 weeks—Sunday, 2/11 @ 1:00 p.m.*

Jess notoriously double and triple-booked herself. But come on. This was her daughter's birthday. Unlike last year, for the sake of Emma, they'd agreed to co-host one party instead of separate events. They'd chosen this date *weeks* ago.

Pulsing dots. They disappeared, and reappeared. Aw, hell. This was no good. Whenever Jess started and stopped texts, she was about to drop a bomb on him.

Oh no! I thought it was the next weekend since that's closest to her actual birthday. I'm away for her party. ⊘ Booked a sponsored blog post for a spa.

He clutched his phone and ground his teeth together. A fucking spa?

Jess, you *have* to come.

It kills me, but I can't. Signed a contract. Her private school's expensive, Brendan. I have to pay for it somehow.

His hurled his phone across the room, and it crashed into wall. Good. He wouldn't have to deal with the follow-up texts she'd shoot his way throughout the night.

Have to pay for it somehow…

What a load of horseshit. They split the cost fifty-fifty. Besides, she pulled down ten grand a month in ad revenues alone. He should know— he'd developed her site. This trip was probably a freebie rendezvous with her selfie-happy boyfriend. Couple of pictures of their feet on the boardwalk, hints she was dating someone new. Lather, rinse, repeat. This kind of nonsense was all Jess seemed to publish since Brendan put the legal clamp down on posts about their daughter.

He stood, shoved the chair away, then paced toward the stairs of his Federal Hill townhouse. He had to burn off some of this irritated energy. Damn, *Jess's me-first* attitude picked at every scab he had about their relationship.

Splitting up and disentangling from the fat cash cow her blog had become had meant sacrificing control over the work he chose to do. He'd given up independent contract work and had settled into a salaried job with benefits. Emma's EpiPens alone were a nightmare without decent insurance. He'd get back to freelancing someday, but for now, he needed a guaranteed flow of money to keep things steady for his daughter.

In his bedroom, he tackled the enormous jumble of laundry he'd meant to put away for the past week. He yanked a Ravenna towel free, almost toppling the whole pile of clean clothes to the floor. As he folded the towel in thirds, and in thirds again, he wished with everything he had that the princess would help Emma have a happy birthday.

~ * ~

The cherry red Mercedes ferried Zara through the streets of Federal Hill, the centuries-old residential neighborhood hugging Baltimore's Inner Harbor. The car purred to a halt in front of the townhouse bearing the address of her gig.

"That," Zara said and jerked her thumb over her shoulder, "is a shit-ton of balloons with my face on it."

Grier cut the engine and peered through her roommate's foggy window. In the front garden, a vast bouquet of silvery orbs strained against their tethers. One more, and they'd probably uproot the black iron address plaque to which they were tied.

"Oh my God." Grier snickered. "It is. You resemble her even more in this new wave of party merchandise. Especially now you've streaked your hair with purple again. It's pretty amazing."

"What's amazing is how lucrative it is to be a dead ringer for Princess Ravenna of Everly."

"At least she's the most gothicky princess. Jewel tones suit you. Think about it—her costume could have been pastel pink."

Zara shivered. "Bite your tongue."

"What I enjoy most about shooting these parties," Grier said as she checked her chirping cell phone, "is your unparalleled acting skill. If I didn't know better, I'd say you actually like kids."

"I don't *not* like kids." Zara flipped the passenger sun visor down and checked her makeup in the mirror. "At worst, I'd say I'm neutral. They're fine when they aren't manic balls of soul-sucking neediness. It's the parents who get to me. I can't deal with the ooey-gooey 'kids are special snowflakes' mentality most of them have."

"Yes. Parents should tolerate their children, not celebrate them."

"That's not quite—"

"Oh." Grier glanced up from her phone. "Andrew texted to ask if I can help him with a wedding next weekend. I need more nuptials to round out my portfolio. Do we have any more kid parties, or is this the last gig before you re-hang up the face paints?"

"Yes, thank the sweet baby Jesus." Zara dabbed a tissue at the overdone eyeliner on her lower lids. "Five done, one to go. Two hellacious weekends, but a girl's gotta make that paper."

"I can't believe your parents wouldn't lend you money." Grier shoved her phone into her coat pocket.

"I didn't ask. They'd use it as an opportunity to highlight how stupid and chancy my career is. Except they'd call it a hobby and enroll me in community college business classes so I can help them run their inn when I retreat home."

"Solid vote of confidence there."

"Right?" Zara reapplied the dark berry stain on her lips. "Can I borrow your Bluetooth speaker thingamajig? I broke mine last weekend."

"Yep." Grier snatched the sleek blue amplifier from the depths of her backseat. "Gimme your phone so I can sync it up."

Zara handed her crackled black device to Grier.

"OMG, Zara, you can't have nice things." Grier poked icons until she found the Bluetooth settings. "What did you do? Use your phone as a hammer?"

"I walked into a spider web. Fear happened. Arms flailed and phones flew."

"One hundred percent correct reaction. So, do you want the normal play list?" Grier scrolled through the music on Zara's phone. "Or a different one?"

She squinted at the screen.

"Wait, why do you have Britney Spears's 'Work Bitch'? I thought you didn't listen to music recorded after 1997."

"It gets me pumped at the studio." Zara clunked open the passenger door. "Come on. I have to hurry and sneak in before the birthday girl arrives."

"I'm judging you so hard right now."

"Yeah, yeah." Zara butterflied her hand at Grier. "I've seen your Top 25. Abba, much?"

"Abba is crazy good. You're not sophisticated enough to appreciate their music."

Zara unfolded herself from the car and dropped the train of her jade gown to the ground. She twisted and tugged her leather breastplate down a few inches. The damned thing had shifted position on the way over and mashed her chest flat.

The costume must have been designed for a B-cup Ravenna, at best. While Zara's cups runneth over. Still, she was grateful for the corset-like piece of armor. It did double-duty, desexualizing her a little, and providing a much-needed shield in the chilly February air. Stiff nipples at a children's party was *not* the look.

"Oh, much better." She sighed once she seated the breastplate where it belonged. "I bet I have bruises."

"What about me? I am such a pack mule whenever we do these parties." Grier wheeled a crate stuffed with Zara's face-painting supplies behind her. The speaker was in her other hand, and a chunky camera hung around her neck.

"I'd offer to help, but princesses don't hump huge crates around." The rear car door creaked when Zara popped it open.

She lifted Ravenna's double-sworded belt from the backseat and buckled it around her hips. Once the belt was in place, she sheathed the gleaming, thin-bladed prop replica swords.

"I would think swords are a bad idea at children's parties." Grier snapped a photo. "For obvious reasons."

"I'm a stickler for authenticity. If Princess Ravenna of Everly carries swords, then so must this humble impersonator."

"I worry you'll chop a kid's arm off if she tries to hug you."

"I wouldn't. Probably." Zara arched an eyebrow. "But I might spank a kid with the flat of the sword."

"Hey, do you have plans after dinner tonight?" Grier trailed Zara as they made their way along the tidy fieldstone path to the front door.

"Yeah." She yawned. "My studio's usable again. I'm hitting Pla-Za tonight to buy canvases and oil paints."

"Oils?"

"Yep. Didn't I tell you? I'm not feeling the watercolors anymore. They seem weak, and if I have learned anything, it's to…" Zara ticked off her fingers, "…one, get business insurance, and two, use more durable materials. I'd fucking sculpt in steel if I could weld."

"If you change your mind, Melinda and I are watching a bunch of movies that pass the Bechdel test."

"Thanks." Zara gathered her skirts before climbing the steps to the glossy red door. "But I need to concentrate on work."

Before she could ring the doorbell, the front door swung inward. A heart-stopping heap of dimpled handsome filled the doorway.

~ * ~